What Readers are Saying ...

"A veiled Victorian lady with a hidden past finds love and self-acceptance on a rail journey through 1854 America in *The Wayfaring Widow*. Casey Cline's writing is sweet, intelligent, and rich with historical detail. The perfect read for fans of road-trip romances!"

—MIMI MATTHEWS, *USA TODAY* BESTSELLING AUTHOR

"*The Wayfaring Widow* by Casey Cline is the perfect weekend read. Set in the 1850s, readers will love touring the various American cities alongside Victoria, Isabella, and their escort Harrison. Victoria is none-too-happy at having the closed-hearted Harrison along, especially since she's struggling to overcome a difficult past. But soon she discovers that Harrison is battling his own troubled past, and the pair slowly learn to see beyond each other's protective exteriors. *The Wayfaring Widow* is a slow-burn romance that will take you on a sweeping journey of love, healing, and second chances."

—HEATHER B. MOORE, *USA TODAY* BESTSELLING AUTHOR

THE WAYFARING WIDOW

BIRD'S-EYE VIEW SERIES

1

CASEY CLINE

Scrivenings
PRESS
Quench your thirst for story.
www.ScriveningsPress.com

Published by Scrivenings Press LLC
15 Lucky Lane
Morrilton, Arkansas 72110
https://ScriveningsPress.com

Printed in the United States of America

Paperback ISBN 978-1-64917-529-8

eBook ISBN 978-1-64917-530-4

Editor: J.L. Burrows

Cover design by Casey Cline

With the exception of Isabella Bird, all characters are fictional, and any resemblance to real people, either factual or historical, is purely coincidental.

To Vince, for your unwavering faith in me, and to Leena and Cora, may you have unwavering faith in yourselves.

UNIT
THE CAPITOL, WASHINGTON
WASHINGTON
SCALE
Miles
MISSOURI
ARKANSAS
IOWA
WISCO
LAK
MEXICO
Arkansas
Red Fork
Canadian R.
Rio Grande del Norte
Nacogdoches
AUSTIN
Houston
Bexar
Goliad
Refugio
Laredo
Matagorda I.
Padre I.
New Madrid
Alexandria
St. Charles
Galveston
Liberty

FRANKLIN

One

September 1854

Victoria Clarke lay on the bottom bunk in the cramped stateroom aboard the RMS *Canada* and waited for her stomach's next revolt. How was this adventure a better fate than being the widowed family member no one wanted?

Though the steamship had survived last night's storm and the previous ten days of the voyage across the Atlantic Ocean from Liverpool, it still dipped and rolled in the lingering winds. Would they make it to Boston today?

Salt and sickness wafted in the air, and Victoria cursed herself for believing she could brave such a journey. Back in England, the possibility of adventure for a twenty-eight-year-old widow had seemed exciting, alluring even, especially with Isabella's convincing stories about America's enticements. Now, in the dark and dank bowels of a tossing ship three thousand miles from home, it seemed downright ridiculous.

Victoria would meet her younger friend in Boston. Though Isabella's father had paid her passage to America, it was difficult to conjure up appreciation for her friend's generosity at present.

The ship pitched again, as did Victoria's stomach, and she scrambled to her washbasin. She hadn't been this sick since the early weeks of her pregnancy. Oh, she would have doted on the child, but apparently, it wasn't meant to be.

Thankfully, the ship's signal whistled—a timely interruption to the melancholy direction her thoughts were headed and a sure sign they were nearing their destination. She, too, must look ahead to the future. After all, she was nearly to America, the "Land of the Free."

When the ship's speed and lurching both slowed, she took the opportunity to set her appearance to rights and tidy the cabin. She combed her raven-black hair into its typical, serviceable chignon and smoothed the wrinkles on her careworn, faded black mourning gown.

Even though the requisite two-year mourning period following Silas's death had passed, Victoria still wore dark colors, not out of any devotion or homage to her late husband, but out of grief at the loss of herself. She picked up the final piece of her ensemble—the black lace veil—and pinned it to her hair under her bonnet so it covered the left side of her face.

Isabella had grown accustomed to Victoria's appearance, but strangers had not. When the two discussed the trip a few months ago, Isabella had promised they could avoid any mention of, or interaction with, men on the trip. Learning to trust men again was thankfully not on the itinerary. Clicking her valise shut, Victoria donned her mantle and gloves to ward off the chill and made her way up to the rain-slicked deck, ready to catch her first glimpse of this foreign land.

With her hands gripped firmly around the slippery railing, Victoria squinted into the black night. The still-heavy mist in the air swallowed any light from the port, but its sounds and smells reached her, as the port workers exchanged shouts with the ship's crew while other vessels, docked at the wharf, creaked and groaned against their mooring lines. The pervading top note of fish, combined with base notes of rotting food and unwashed bodies, threatened to send Victoria back to the washbasin. The native tongues of the other passengers crushed around her—German, French, Spanish, Dutch— mingling in a motley hum accompanied by the rhythmic churning of the steamship's wheels.

The curtain of mist parted, and the wharf—and Boston— finally emerged into view. Hundreds of ships' masts bobbed in front of the shadowed facades of brick and stone buildings, while pinpricks of light winked determinedly through the dark. Anchoring took a veritable eon, and when the gangplank finally banged to the wharf, the passengers became a crush, jostling and pushing against Victoria as they moved *en masse* toward solid ground. *Was such incivility necessary after the days of accord they'd shared aboard the ship?*

A sharp elbow jabbed her ribs.

"Ouch!" But the commotion drowned out her cry of pain. Victoria took a deep breath to force her pounding heart to calm. As she squeezed farther into the multitude, the opportunistic hands of another passenger snagged her valise. *The audacity!*

"Unhand it, please!" Either the would-be thief obeyed her petition, or she successfully wrestled the luggage from his grasp. Regardless, she'd regained control of her baggage. Now, to regain control of her emotions.

Avoiding the shouts and scuffles for the hired carts and

hacks, Victoria found refuge in a relatively quiet corner of the wharf and scanned the crowd of bodies for Isabella. At just under five feet tall, Isabella would be challenging to find in the throng of towering gentlemen and their tall top hats.

Mother Nature resumed a steady rainfall, further adding to the gloom. Cold and wet seeped through Victoria's mantle, gown, and petticoat layers, numbing her toes despite the newness of her sturdy ankle boots. Shivers wracked her body.

A hand gripped her shoulder from behind, and she emitted a small shriek. Whirling around, she met Isabella's bright eyes.

"Victoria!" Isabella enveloped her in a tight embrace with a strength belying her diminutive size. She took Victoria's valise and led the way through the swarm.

"How was your journey? My voyage had calm seas the entire way, so I had to entertain myself. I became quite adept at backgammon—and avoiding my cabin mate. When she wasn't imbibing, she would regale the passengers, especially the men, with her coarse and profane anecdotes. Quite deplorable, really." Isabella gave an insouciant wave. "But such is the price one pays for adventure, right?"

No, adventure had exacted far too high a price already, but perhaps with some sleep, Victoria's outlook would improve. She pressed a wet strand of hair back behind her ear and did her best to follow Isabella's ramblings, while navigating the muddy street. Her feet squelched in the soupy mess, and at one point, she almost lost a boot entirely to its clutches.

"Don't worry, dear," Isabella soothed, now half-dragging Victoria through the slog. "The three of us will be settled at the hotel soon enough, and you can change and rest. You must be exhausted given the delay and middle-of-the-night landing. We've been waiting here at the wharf for hours. They kept assuring us the ship would be arriving any minute."

Victoria uttered a sound of agreement and then focused in on one word in Isabella's monologue. "Three?"

Isabella did not break stride. "Oh yes, you did receive my letter, did you not?" But instead of providing the detail Victoria craved, Isabella went on to say, "Oh, we are almost there. We just need to take a left here. And no need to fear. The driver surely has your trunk loaded by now."

Well accustomed to her friend's easily diverted ways, Victoria steered the conversation back to the number in their party, anxiety rising in her throat. "Isabella, who is the third person? I thought it was to be just the two of us."

"Oh yes, that. My father insisted we have an escort. I reminded him it wasn't required of American women when traveling, but he was adamant." Isabella sighed, then shrugged. "You know how he is. Having been a clergyman for many years, he's extra-sensitive to propriety and safety."

Victoria stifled a cry of impatience. *Why couldn't Isabella just answer the question?* She tried once more. "Isabella, who will be traveling with us?"

"Oh, not to worry. Just an old family friend," Isabella said with another airy wave of her hand. Victoria waited for her to elaborate, but her once-garrulous friend was now infuriatingly tight-lipped.

Victoria's racing heart calmed a bit as she focused on the descriptor "old," picturing a balding, bespectacled man with a penchant for falling asleep on a whim as those of advanced age are wont to do. The man surely bore liver spots and a portly stomach too.

"Here we are!" Isabella held open the door of a waiting carriage, its two horses stamping restlessly to get going. Rain dripped from the brim of the driver's hat. He made to get down to help Victoria in, but she waved him off, took her soggy valise from Isabella, gathered her equally soggy skirts, and climbed into the carriage's black void, eager for the sheltered rest the carriage offered.

She tried to sit, but met with a pair of legs instead of the carriage seat. Startled, she stood, only to bang her head on the roof, then trip over the other occupant's limbs.

"Take care, madam." The bodiless male voice, deep and gruff, was sharp and accusatory.

Victoria could find no words to respond. Instead, she moved to the other side of the carriage, but not without bumping the man with her valise in the process.

The voice let out an, "Oof, perhaps if you removed your veil at nighttime, you would see better."

Finally seated, Victoria flinched at the man's acerbic objections and tried her best to maintain her manners. "Sir. I— I do apologize." She licked her parched lips.

"Oh, come now, Harrison," Isabella chided as she slid in beside Victoria with no trouble at all, much to Victoria's chagrin.

So this, this gentleman—dare he be called such—is Harrison. Victoria shrunk into the corner of her seat.

The carriage lurched forward into the inky night, the clip-clopping of the horses' hooves harmonizing with the raindrops' beat.

"Harrison Wright, meet my dear friend, Mrs. Victoria Clarke." Isabella offered the introductions. "Victoria, this is Mr. Harrison Wright, an old friend of our family."

There was the word "old" again.

The gas streetlamps intermittently illuminated the carriage's dark interior and confirmed what she feared. Piercing eyes sat below a mop of inky hair bordering on disheveled. A rugged, clenched jaw rounded out what she could see of this man who wasn't in his seventies, or even his fifties or sixties. He couldn't be much older than her twenty-eight years.

Oh no. Isabella had meant *old* as in long-established, not old as in advanced in age.

Harrison spoke first. "It's a pleasure, Mrs. Clarke," he said, his tone indicating it was anything but.

"Likewise." She attempted a smile but was capable of only a strained grimace.

Oblivious to the charged air in the carriage, Isabella prattled on. "Harrison so graciously agreed to accompany us. His father is a lawyer. And so is Harrison. They live in New York, you see, but Harrison had some business in Boston earlier this week, and it all worked out so perfectly for him to join in the journey, as we take a more circuitous route back via rail to New York, with sightseeing stops in Boston, Chicago, Detroit, and Niagara Falls, of course."

Nothing about this arrangement sounded perfect, and Victoria's already exhausted body couldn't comprehend the taxing itinerary Isabella had rattled off. Instead, she clung to her valise's handles and kept quiet.

"And, Harrison, I neglected to ask earlier. How is dear, sweet Georgina? Why, she must be nearing four years old already," Isabella said. "Are the spells still occurring?"

"Yes, she'll be four in March. And yes, with regularity." Harrison kept his eyes focused outside the carriage's window.

Isabella sighed sympathetically. "Such a shame, but she's lucky to have you as an older brother to care for her so. I do hope you soon find answers as to the cause."

"We know the cause." His tone implied the line of discussion was over.

Victoria looked from Isabella to Harrison.

He pierced her with a glower, and she quickly averted her eyes, swallowing around a lump forming in her throat. Isabella had broken her promise that just the two of them would journey together. And she had chosen a cold and brusque man as their traveling companion.

Fear iced Victoria's veins—how similar Harrison's mannerisms were to Silas's. How would she survive the next few weeks with the formidable Harrison Wright?

Two

Harrison raked his hand through his hair and checked his watch fob. Almost nine o'clock in the morning and the women still hadn't appeared in the American House's dining room for breakfast. They'd miss the meal altogether when the waiters stopped serving on the hour. But more importantly, Harrison had a bone to pick with Isabella.

He viewed her as another younger sister, so her antics shouldn't surprise him. But this particular lark—*forgetting* to tell him another woman would travel back to New York with them—reigned supreme. His fingers tangled in his hair again before snatching up the newspaper poised at the table's edge.

A pair of women at the corner table smiled in his direction and exchanged whispers. Though he only overheard the word "handsome" from his unintended eavesdropping, he could easily fill in the gaps. He studiously ignored their tittering and attempts to catch his eye—necessary habits from his history—and flicked open the newspaper. It served as a suitable shield from the women's unwanted attention.

A well-timed "Good morning" from Isabella further saved him from the simpering spectators, and he rose out of chivalric habit, folding the newspaper and welcoming the women to the table with a slight bow.

"Victoria, we are in for a treat." Isabella took her seat directly across from Harrison. "See, American gentlemen are extremely deferential and attentive in their manners to ladies," she added with a nod to Harrison. "Holding open doors and giving up their seats on trains—the sort of etiquette often lacking back in England."

A strangled scoff escaped Harrison's mouth, and it took all his so-called manners to quickly mask it as a cough instead.

He glanced Victoria's way. Seated to Isabella's left across the table, Victoria still wore the veil and avoided his gaze. The only evidence she had heard Isabella's remark was a slight nod of her head.

So, they were going to have a repeat of last night then. Victoria had said nothing besides apologizing for practically sitting in his lap in the carriage. She'd trod over him, bumped him with her valise, and would now be perpetually underfoot the entire journey.

He had no doubt she was a widow; the black mourning wear and *Mrs.* appellation were telltale. On the hunt for her next husband, he supposed. Well, it wouldn't be him. If he could avoid the snares of the wolfish women on the other side of the dining room, he could certainly avoid the taciturn widow across from him.

Isabella leaned to the side as a waiter delivered her tea. "We have all day to explore Boston, the *Athens of America*." After declining sugar for her tea, she continued, "Dinner's at one, tea at six, and there's no shortage of entertainment to keep us busy in between—Griffin's Wharf, Faneuil Hall, Bunker's Hill, the Athenaeum."

Harrison inwardly sighed. He would have to travel with the women to all these sights, and on only a few hours' rest. Though sleep had come surprisingly easily to him last night, the noise from the awakening wharf had roused him much too early. The stirrings of one of his head pains already lurked behind his eyes.

Isabella made way for her breakfast plate and gasped, nearly causing Harrison to drop his teacup. "Grapes! Victoria, aren't they marvelous? And we each have an entire bunch to ourselves."

Victoria kept her focus on her plate and uttered a noncommittal, "Hmm."

Isabella gave a little bounce of delight and popped a grape into her mouth. "Mmmm. Simply divine!"

Harrison's willpower—strained though it was—kept his snort of amusement within. He'd forgotten how much Englanders prized the little, round fruit given they were a crop aplenty in America. Isabella jabbered on, unaware of her lack of audience. He cast his eyes Victoria's way, but she appeared unimpressed by the small purple globes on her plate. She deftly slid her food behind her veil without dislodging or soiling it.

Why didn't she just remove it to eat? Was it permanently affixed to her head? She'd insisted on wearing it in the middle of last night, too, though it surely impeded her vision. Ridiculous.

As if sensing his gaze on her, she raised her head, the right side of her face angled in his direction. She met his eyes for the first time, her only visible eye a penetrating, cerulean pool that sent a jolt of something through him.

He'd never felt anything like it before and couldn't quite name it. In his haste to glance away, his eyes drifted to her lips. *Stop, Harrison. You will not become your father.*

"Do you have it too, Harrison?" Isabella asked, her interruption timely.

"I'm afraid you caught me quite off guard, Isabella," he croaked. They likely noticed his distraction, but hopefully didn't discern the reason for it. "Of what are we speaking?"

Isabella glanced pointedly between him and Victoria before continuing. "Why, Americans' restless energy. Their knack for ensuring everything is conducted with extreme rapidity and little repose, like this meal, for instance." She quirked a meaningful eyebrow when the waiter reappeared to clear the plate she hadn't yet emptied. "Do *you* ever enjoy yourself, Harrison?"

"Of course," he huffed.

Isabella arched an eyebrow at his immediate affirmation. She knew him too well.

When *had* he last truly enjoyed himself? Long before he joined his father at the law firm. And long before the accident, after which he assumed the mantle of a positive fraternal example for Georgina in his father's lack. And certainly long before he discovered his father's untoward undertakings. Perhaps when he was six or seven? Had it been more than two decades since he'd found any enjoyment at all? But what choice had he had? None. That's what.

"It's exactly as I thought!" Isabella exclaimed, correctly interpreting his silence. Putting her hand over his, she gave him her usual wide, friendly smile. "Then we shall ensure we all have fun on this adventure of ours."

Utterly impossible. From across the table, Victoria frowned, and he couldn't find a reason to summon a smile at Isabella's edict either.

~

Harrison clicked his hotel door shut and stripped off his stifling frock coat, pinching the painful knot in his forehead that had only grown earlier during their thoroughly tiring tour of Boston.

With the unseasonably warm, late September air as their constant companion, the three had seen every stop in Boston that Isabella had mentioned at breakfast, and more.

Isabella had tried her hardest throughout the day to fulfill her promise of adventure, though he hadn't exactly helped in the matter, the heat and the pounding in his head both compounding as the hours wore on, further souring his mood. But in his defense, Victoria hadn't seemed inclined to cooperate either. She had stayed as far away from him as possible.

Now, lying in his shirtsleeves and trousers in the cool darkness of his room at the American House, at least he'd been released from any duty to play host to the women for the evening. Isabella had a dinner invitation elsewhere, and Victoria had retired early to her room, her claim of fatigue confirmed by the pallidity of her skin and darkening circles under her eyes.

Demanding knocks pounded on his door before he registered fire bells clanging from the street outside. So much for quiet. *How long had the bells been ringing?* He was so accustomed to their frequent disruptions in New York, he had become adept at tuning them out. The peals were already fading, taking with them any reason for alarm. Then why were the knocks on his door growing more insistent?

"Mr. Wright! Are you there?" The muffled female voice outside his door was frantic.

Grumbling under his breath, Harrison rose and crossed the small room to open the door. Victoria's hand was poised to knock again. As usual, she wore her veil, the pupil of her right eye wide. Taking in his state of undress, her pupil expanded farther.

Why hadn't he reached for his coat on the way to the door? He fidgeted under Victoria's gaze and tried to stifle the red heat surely creeping up his exposed throat. What was it about this woman that so befuddled him?

"Yes, Mrs. Clarke?" he asked, annoyance taking the place of his discomfiture.

"Wh-what do those bells mean?" She wrung her ungloved hands and glanced up and down the lengthy hallway.

"Only the fire brigades." He didn't try for a reassuring tone as he continued. "They're quite common in the large cities here."

"F-fire?" She was visibly trembling now.

A few doors in the hallway opened and heads peeked around doorframes, likely people checking on whether the ringing bells required any action on their part. Lamentably, the onlookers could interpret Victoria's presence at his door in his state of dress as a compromising tête-à-tête, and the very last thing he needed was any insinuation he behaved like his father.

Harrison steeled himself with a deep breath and lowered his voice. "Hear how the bells are quieting? The fire's not in or near our building. Return to your room, please, Mrs. Clarke. We are attracting unwanted attention in the hall."

"Yes, yes, of course." Her veil bobbed in acquiescence.

Before he could stop himself, he added, "Allow me to bring a drink of iced water to your room. I'll be there momentarily."

"Iced water?"

Did this woman only speak in questions? "Yes, we Americans abound in iced drinks as well as grapes." So he was trying to be funny now, was he? Less than twenty-four hours in this woman's company and he was already losing his typically tight grip on his emotions.

Still noticeably shaken but calmer, she nodded. "Th-that would be lovely, thank you, Mr. Wright." Then she turned around and returned to her room, her steps as hushed as her voice.

Harrison donned his full ensemble and went in search of the water he had promised her. He could use a glass himself, though it'd do little to curb the pounding in his head. This trip was just one aggravation after another, and its end couldn't come soon enough.

Three

As Victoria waited for Harrison to return with the water, she struggled to quell the overwhelm at her circumstances tightening in her chest. The sleep deprivation from her nights at sea and single, too-short night ashore. The unceasing bustle of the big city. The knowledge that somewhere nearby fire was consuming a building. Harrison's imposing presence. Meeting his blazing amber eyes at breakfast this morning, and then again, a few minutes ago at his door. The indignation burning there was a fresh stab to her already fragile heart.

At least Harrison's eyes weren't the same haunting ice blue of Silas's.

Suppressing a shudder at the memory of her former husband, Victoria opened her valise and retrieved her small apothecary set. Selecting lavender, she dabbed a few drops of the oil on her wrists and behind her earlobes, breathing deeply to allow the herb's aroma to work its calming effect.

Its familiar smell transported her to another time, back to when she watched her father use it and other alternative ministrations on his patients. She had quickly become adept at combining the oils with acupressure techniques to alleviate neighbors' and friends' minor ailments. Her mother had especially relied on Victoria's skill during her frequent nervous spells.

Before the accident with Silas, that is.

A knock on the door startled her back to the present.

Harrison.

Upon opening the door, she found him re-dressed, his ever-tousled dark hair the only part of him pushing propriety now. He appeared about as wrung out as she felt. He had mentioned head pains when making his excuses earlier in the evening. Were they still plaguing him now?

As she took the cool glass he silently proffered her, her ungloved fingers brushed his and he jerked back at the touch. The glass wobbled, and though she caught it with her other hand from an all-out tumble to the ground, a few drops sloshed onto Harrison's hand and the carpet below. Heat flamed across her cheeks.

Unable to meet his gaze, Victoria murmured a thank you.

Harrison wiped his wet hand on his trousers, and an all-out conflagration of mortification broke out within her.

She was about to ask after his head pain, when he gave a curt bow, a "Good night, Mrs. Clarke," and turned toward his room.

She whispered a fleeting good night in response to his retreating back, doubtful the iced water was enough to douse the burn of humiliation within her.

Victoria awoke the next morning to Isabella's cheerful humming. Despite tossing and turning after the encounter with Harrison, she must have fallen into a deep sleep and missed Isabella's return to their shared room.

"Good morning, dear." Isabella bustled about the room, repacking her trunk and valise. "I'm so glad you finally slept well. You were quite out last night."

"Yes, thank you," Victoria responded around a parched throat.

A glance at her nightstand and the now empty water glass Harrison had brought sent another wave of embarrassment at how she had acted last night coursing through her. He must think her so feebleminded, losing control like she did over the fire bells and nearly breaking down his door. Fire still triggered the unwanted memories of her final confrontation with Silas, and in her fatigue last night, the recollection had overpowered her.

But she couldn't very well explain that to Harrison.

"I don't want to rush you, but breakfast service ends in thirty minutes, and I am ravenous." Isabella had finished packing and stood in a deep blue muslin gown, an expectant smile on her face. "You look refreshed this morning. I'm glad to see it. We have another busy day ahead of us, and the railcars in America wait for no man. Or woman. Although, the railroads have not yet taught punctuality to the Canadians, or so I found out in my weeks up north," she finished with a wave of one hand.

"I'll be but a moment," Victoria replied and hastily completed her morning toilette while Isabella chattered on about Canadian railcars.

Victoria changed back into the dress she had arrived in, marveling at the speed and efficacy of the hotel's steam laundry. Yesterday, she had relinquished her two worn dresses to the clerk, who, after making a notation in his record book, took the dresses and returned them washed and dried the same day. And all for a charge of eight shillings each. *Americans and their industry for speed.*

As she was securing her veil in place, she caught Isabella's reflection in the mirror.

"You know I don't mind," Isabella said, appearing at her most solemn state the entire trip thus far.

"I know, my friend," Victoria replied. Trying for light-heartedness, she jested, "But Mr. Wright might very well have a fit of fright."

To Victoria's surprise, Isabella responded in all seriousness. "Harrison's compassion is not to be underestimated. He's been through his own trials. Sure, he might appear gruff, but he's not like Silas."

Unsure how to answer—particularly as thoughts of her former husband resurfaced—Victoria gave Isabella a reassuring smile and nodded. "Well, then. Let us go see how far our tardiness has stretched Mr. Wright's compassion."

Isabella let out a small laugh of delight at her quip, and the two made their way downstairs.

Every time Victoria traversed the American House's halls, its grandeur astounded her anew. It certainly matched America's reputation for monster hotels Isabella had touted. Upon reaching the ground-floor entry hall and its soaring ceiling and black-and-white checkered floor, they joined the hundreds of other guests and retail establishments' visitors milling about.

Gentlemen lounged on settees in the hall reading newspapers or stood grouped together, talking. Piles of luggage abounded, with little regard for lighter items crushed by heavier. Thankfully, their luggage was still in their rooms.

They passed the main counter, behind which the clerks distributed keys to those arriving and collected them—and the two-dollar-a-day charge—from those departing, all the while responding to the brass bells wired to each room that jingled at each guest's whims.

Though the endless bedlam of ringing bells, tramping feet, and chattering voices unnerved Victoria, Isabella glided through the hubbub unfazed.

A left turn took them into the dining room, which was mercifully emptier than normal that morning. Only a few dozen people sat scattered throughout the room's round tables, though it could certainly hold nearly twenty times as many patrons. Victoria expelled a breath of relief.

"There's Harrison," Isabella called, pointing to where Harrison sat at the same table as yesterday morning, flipping through the newspaper. Victoria's stomach clenched at the sight of him, and she tried not to dwell too much as to why, as she took her usual seat at the table. Isabella sat beside her again.

"Victoria, Harrison, you'll never guess where I dined last night," Isabella said. Apparently too eager to wait for a response, she continued, "Longfellow's mansion!"

Isabella's excitement was contagious. Victoria gasped, and she looked up from her plate for the first time. "Why, Isabella, that is incredible. What was it like? What was *he* like?" She even let a small smile expand over her lips. She admired the American's lyrical prose and often retreated into it and other books during particularly lonesome times, which happened with increased regularity lately.

"It's a stately house, with a generous side verandah and large garden out front. Quite impressive, especially given its history as General Washington's former residence. But its current owner was most endearing."

Isabella leaned forward, the grin of one who holds key information spread wide across her lips. "Mr. Longfellow personally greeted us at the door. His merry blue eyes and joviality were instantly welcoming, and while I found him tall, I daresay you would tower over him, Harrison."

Victoria glanced at Harrison. He was listening attentively to Isabella too, although he flicked his gaze momentarily in her direction as if he'd sensed her eyes on him.

Her stomach clenched again, and she refocused on Isabella.

"Oh, the library." Isabella was all but wiggling in her seat. "Victoria, you wouldn't believe the number of books it held. And though old-style paneling adorned its walls, the room revealed Mrs. Longfellow's feminine persuasion too."

"But I've saved the best for last," Isabella added, growing even more animated. "We were all sitting there talking in the library, when the door opened and a little boy of no more than ten—Longfellow's son—bounded into the room, scrambled into his father's lap, and asked Longfellow to whittle a stick for him. Such a darling."

A pang shot through Victoria's chest at the picture of parental domesticity, and her eyes sought her plate again. Would the ache of never knowing if her child was a boy or girl ever subside?

Oblivious to Victoria's inner turmoil, Isabella carried on, "Longfellow even graced us with a reading from his poetry. You could feel the truth, energy, and earnestness of his "Psalm of Life," and I believe it might be my new favorite of his. Here, I wrote down my favorite part," she said, opening a flap of paper she'd pulled from her pocket and reciting its contents in her strong, melodic voice.

> *"Lives of great men all remind us,*
> *We can make our lives sublime,*
> *And, departing, leave behind us*
> *Footprints on the sands of time;*

Footprints, that perhaps another,
Sailing o'er life's solemn main,
A forlorn and shipwrecked brother,
Seeing, shall take heart again.

Let us, then, be up and doing,
With a heart for any fate;
Still ..."

Here, Isabella faltered. "Oh my, I can't seem to decipher my penmanship here. Still ..."

"Achieving, still pursuing, / Learn to labor and to wait." Victoria finished, belatedly realizing Harrison's gravelly baritone had matched her word for word. She glanced to him, and his amber eyes echoed the surprise likely showing in her blue ones—well the one he could see that is.

So, the gruff Harrison has a soft side for poetry?

He shrugged one shoulder as if trying to appear indifferent.

What felt like ages, but was surely mere moments, passed.

"Yes, nicely done." Isabella's interruption broke the invisible communication between them. "Why, I think we can count two more among the ranks of Longfellow enthusiasts."

Isabella held up her half-full goblet of iced water and called for a toast. "To being up and doing, still achieving, still pursuing."

Harrison hesitantly lifted his glass. Though she also had reservations about Isabella's ambitions for this trip, Victoria lifted her glass too. For how could she "take heart again" and expect a future "life sublime" with all that had happened in her past?

Four

When their hired hack clattered to a stop at the railroad depot's entrance later that afternoon, Harrison exited first, then helped Isabella down. Though Victoria now had her gloves on, when her hand settled in his as he reached into the carriage for her, it sparked the same sensation as their ungloved hands meeting last night over the water glass. Instinct told him to immediately pull his hand away again, but propriety won out, and after she'd secured her footing on the cobblestones, he finally released her hand.

She silently slipped past, leaving a cloud of lavender in her wake. She didn't meet his eyes either, like she had at breakfast this morning when they'd finished the Longfellow poem together. He swallowed, stifling the hint of buoyancy rising in his chest at the recollection. It was for the best that she continue to ignore him. He shouldn't let his guard down. A bit of shared poetry shouldn't alter the course of his life now. No, he must remain vigilant.

He led the women into the crowded depot, Isabella appearing as eager as Victoria seemed wary.

"Please have a seat," he said, pointing them to the last two empty seats together in the waiting room. "I'll check our trunks in with the porter."

He wove his way through the throng, pausing a moment to remove his hat and wipe his brow with his handkerchief. It was proving to be another hot day, and his proximity to Victoria had only spiked his body temperature further.

He concluded his business at the porter's counter and had just turned around when Isabella's not-so-quiet, "Well, I'll say," reached him from a few yards away. Bracing himself for trouble, he arrived back to where he'd left the women and found them standing and a man sitting in one of the seats.

"What seems to be amiss here, Isabella?" Harrison asked.

"This man," Isabella began, "took our seats." She punctuated her remarks by bringing her hands to her hips.

Harrison turned to the man and attempted to appeal to his courtesy. "Sir, I'm afraid these two seats are for these ladies." He gestured to Victoria and Isabella for good measure.

"I was here first," the man said in a strong English accent, unconvinced.

"Well, here in America, men give up their seats for ladies," Isabella countered.

Harrison clenched his jaw. Isabella's interjection wasn't exactly helping things.

"I'm an Englishman, not an American, and I mean to keep my seat." The man opened his newspaper, signaling he was finished with the conversation.

Harrison's temper rose to match the near boiling temperature in the stuffy depot. *Who does this man think he is?* At the light hand touching his forearm, he swallowed the angry retort ready on his lips.

"Mr. Wright, it's fine." The busy depot's din nearly drowned out Victoria's quiet petition. She'd retreated deep into her wide-brimmed bonnet, her veil in its usual place. When he looked down at her hand still clasped on his forearm, she yanked it away.

"It's not fine," Isabella huffed, her voice loud enough to draw the attention of others. "But it would be unseemly for us to continue carrying on. Come, we will wait nearer the platform, so we can get the end car. Farther from the boiler should it explode."

Ah, yes, Isabella and her reassuring ways. But Isabella's antics *did* alleviate the worst of his anger, and he regained his equanimity by the time they'd reached the platform.

Their train waited, its engine belching large bursts of steam in impatience to get going. A line of six passenger cars trailed behind the engine, and at the engineer's call of "All aboard," three hundred or more people vied for the best seats inside.

With a bit of clever jostling from Isabella—which appeared to include ramming her valise into no fewer than five people— the three successfully claimed a grouping of four seats facing each other in the last car.

Isabella and Victoria sat next to each other looking toward the train's front, and Harrison sat in the aisle seat facing the women. Hopefully, his positioning would dissuade a lone traveler from claiming the empty window seat, so they could take turns sleeping.

The engineer finally called "Go ahead" and tolled the heavy bell, signaling their departure. Victory coursed through him. However, even with the extra open seat, the space was limited.

With his long legs, the ladies' voluminous skirts, and the rocking train, every so often, his knee brushed against Victoria's. The first few times, he murmured an apology, and Victoria adjusted her position. But they couldn't keep this charade going the entire one-and-a-half day journey, eventually reaching a tacit agreement to ignore future brushes altogether.

After passing the outskirts of Boston, the train picked up speed, the open windows allowing glimpses of the city's retreating spires and rooftops and a refreshing breeze into the car.

Isabella fanned herself. "I do hope it's cooler in Chicago. I've been in the Americas for a few weeks already and so far, no sign of fall's usual temperatures."

"Summer does like to encroach on its successor season here," Harrison replied. "Some years, my younger brother, Alfred, and I would run barefoot on our country estate outside of New York City all the way until mid-October." He hadn't intended to voice aloud the fond memories his mind had called forth. Doing so only allowed the unpleasant memories to surface too.

For the last two years since the accident, the same questions that had plagued him every day rose, unbidden, to his mind. Why had Alfred—the obedient, genial son—been called to his heavenly home that night? And why leave a stubborn, temperamental child—*him*—to live an undeserving full life? And just two days before Alfred's seventeenth birthday.

Out of reflex, Harrison reached up and fingered the two-inch scar above his right eyebrow, one of the two ever-present reminders of that night. The other being his head pains. He took a deep breath to calm his inner turmoil, forcing himself to unclench his jaw.

He raised his head and found Isabella's astute eyes on him.

She proffered a reassuring smile, so she must have at least some idea of what he'd been thinking.

He nodded once in acknowledgement of her empathy.

As if sensing the need to lighten the mood, Isabella carried on. "Why, fall is my favorite time of year. Not only is my birthday contained within its months, but so is Halloween. A tradition, which I fear, hasn't quite the same fervor here as in England."

Isabella then regaled them with stories of the supernatural —ghosts, wraiths, apparitions, and second sight—and her animated gestures and speech provided a welcome reprieve from his thoughts as the train churned up the miles of track. How fitting. Hearing about paranormal happenings was far preferable to dwelling on his past.

Victoria was hot, tired, and hungry—a dreadful combination. After nearly four hours on the train, their first stop in Albany, New York, neared.

The sun had set about an hour earlier, bringing with it only marginally cooler temperatures and a slight abatement of the malodorous smell permeating the packed car during the afternoon's heat.

Victoria's body ached from the conflicting goals of maintaining a comfortable position on the wooden seat and not touching Harrison's knee. Naturally, she'd failed at both, but she no longer cared. Her stomach growled in an irritable reminder the apples and cheese they had brought with them were long ago digested and a wholly unacceptable substitute for a proper dinner.

Having offered to take the night watch against the enterprising hands of any would-be luggage thieves, Harrison was resting now, the brim of his black hat dipping to his nose and hiding his eyes—and his scar—from view.

Victoria first noticed the scar when he'd fingered it earlier.

He had appeared lost in thought then, his features brooding. What had he been thinking? Isabella had quickly begun her tales of the supernatural, almost as if they were a diversion.

With Isabella now immersed in a book and Harrison asleep, Victoria openly assessed him. His nose quirked just left of center. The square of his jaw was slightly softer in rest, and the twin slashes of facial hair tracing from each ear to jawline had darkened in the presence of night and absence of a razor.

Despite his efforts to squeeze his large frame into as small a space as possible, his broad shoulders and long legs spilled out. She'd felt the cords of muscles coiled under the sleeves of his suitcoat at the train depot, as if he was always tense and ready for action. No doubt, his formidableness only added to his handsomeness. And while she couldn't see it now, his scar distinguished him.

Whereas her scar deformed her.

Victoria averted her gaze to stop the swell of self-pity. She needed to move, do something, anything.

"W—water. I'm going to go get some water," she told Isabella as she rose to her feet. "Would you like any?"

Isabella glimpsed up from her book. "No, dear, I'm good. But by all means go get some yourself. You appear quite flushed."

Victoria's cheeks were warm. But that was because of the heat in the car and not the man across from her, right? A feeble excuse.

On legs wobbly from disuse, Victoria stumbled in the swaying train to the water filter in the car's front, gripping seatbacks along the way to balance herself. The water was cold, and again her thoughts jumped back to Harrison and the water he had brought her. *Does everything have to remind me of him?*

The liquid soothed her throat and calmed her thoughts. It

was just what she needed. Refreshed, she made it halfway back to her seat when a baby's wail interrupted her progress. A young woman, who appeared to be alone and long past exhausted, was trying to console the child who couldn't be more than eight months old. She gently bounced the infant and shushed every so often, but the baby was not to be mollified. Others in the car stirred and stared, as if the poor woman could do more to quiet the child.

Victoria's heart and hands reached out to the woman. "May I help? I walked my two squawking nephews many miles when they were this age." She gave the woman a congenial smile and pointed over her shoulder to her seat. "My seat is just over there, a stone's throw away. I won't be far."

Relief flooded the woman's face. "Thank ya, ma'am. That'd be mighty kind of ya," the woman said over the baby's increasingly loud crying. She relinquished the wriggling, wailing bundle to Victoria. "Now, Leah, you be good for the nice lady."

Leah—a little girl. And an upset one at that. Tiny fists swatted surprisingly strong blows in all directions. Golden yellow curls, matching her mother's, sprung out from the crown of her small, round head, while tears left trails in the dirt smudged on her little cheeks.

As Victoria returned to her seat, she tenderly bounced the child, all the while whispering words of motherly comfort she had stowed away to use on her child.

"What a darling," Isabella cooed from her right. "Wherever did you find a baby? Do American trains dispense them with the water?"

Victoria chuckled, gently wiping Leah's grimy face and wrapping her snugly in the frayed blanket. "No, this one came by way of its mother." She glanced over her shoulder, pleased to see the young mother was getting some much-needed sleep.

"Well, you are quite the soothsayer."

"She's probably just stunned into silence at a stranger, is all."

Leah quieted, and Victoria beamed down into the cherubic face. No longer squinched in sorrow, Leah's eyes were two circles of sky-blue blinking wide with wonder at the new face before her. She snaked an arm out of the swaddled blanket and grabbed at Victoria's veil.

"Oh no, little Leah," she said, her rebuke entirely tender. "I need that."

"Do you, now?"

At Harrison's irascible entrance to the conversation, Victoria's stomach dropped. She turned her head and met his stony gaze. His rudeness roused the rancor in her. An ugly emotion.

"Mr. Wright, please forgive me, but I can only handle one petulant child at a time." Leah fussed, likely sensing Victoria's angst, and she offered her finger to Leah's grasping ones, instinctively rocking the child back and forth.

Commendably, Harrison had no outward reaction to her derisive remark other than a slight clenching of his jaw. Growing up, her sharp wit had earned her many a reprimand from her parents. She had learned to school it for the most part, especially after marrying Silas. Disastrous consequences had followed the few times she'd failed to hold her tongue during their marriage.

Isabella's guffaw cut the silence. "Why, Harrison, I think you may have met your equal."

Flustered, Victoria's cheeks warmed again. Why couldn't she gain control over herself before speaking to Harrison? And should she be pleased or insulted Isabella had compared her to him?

Five

ow Isabella could find humor here was beyond Harrison. Her comment rankled him. He and Victoria were nothing alike, their desires entirely opposite. If the looks she'd given the baby were any indication, she wanted to be a wife and mother, while he was determined to avoid matrimony altogether. He had his career to focus on, his investments.

Well, good luck to her next husband with a wit like that. Yes, he shouldn't have remarked on her still wearing the mourning attire and veil. But with all he'd endured the last few days, the comment had slipped from his lips before he could stop it. He'd hardly slept. His whole body ached from the discomfort of the cramped quarters. His last full meal was almost twelve hours ago. And he was indeed a sweaty, wrinkled mess by now.

Waking to find Victoria rapturous over a baby in her arms had been too much for him. He'd seen his mom wear the same expression with his younger siblings, first to Alfred and then, sixteen years later, to Georgina.

"You three are my ultimate joy," his mother had said when he and Alfred had met Georgina shortly after their little sister was born. "My wish for each of you is to have the same joy in your children someday."

Twenty-six at the time, Harrison had already resigned himself to life as a bachelor. Surely the torment his mother had suffered at the hand of his father's duplicity eclipsed any delight she'd had in the children he'd given her. And so Harrison had vowed never to chance causing the same pain to a woman.

While he'd been stewing, Isabella and Victoria carried on without him, alternating between chatting with each other and gushing over the baby. Thoroughly scolded and superfluous, Harrison resumed his recumbent position, pulling his hat back down over his eyes to block out the sight of the women across from him. Though sleep evaded him, he kept up the ruse so he wouldn't have to blunder his way through additional conversation with them.

Harrison's fictitious sleep lasted an agonizingly long time. Unable to either clearly overhear or completely ignore the women's whispered exchanges, his frustration mounted.

Mercifully, the train finally tolled its bell and slowed its momentum. A flurry of activity commenced within the train car as people prepared to disembark at Albany. Harrison sat up, not having slept a wink.

His eyes unwittingly found Victoria, who was returning the child to its mother, smiling at the other woman in the same genuine manner she'd smiled at the child earlier. A smile that lit her demeanor. A smile that was nonexistent in his presence, fading even now as she returned to her seat across from him.

It shouldn't bother him the way it disappeared.

The train's wheel brakes squealed to a stop, and he, Isabella, and Victoria joined the crush of passengers exiting. If luck were on their side, they'd have time to fill their stomachs and stretch their legs.

He squinted in the depot's bright lights after enduring hours aboard the dimly lit car. Ever-industrious, even near ten at night, his home state capital hummed with activity. Along the adjacent Hudson River, sailing sloops and steamers hurried southward down the waterway, headed for New York City. *Home.* All he'd have to do is find a train headed south, and by sunrise, he'd be back, away from this nightmare of a trip. But he'd promised Isabella he would escort them, and, unlike his father, he didn't break his promises.

"Watch your things now," Isabella cautioned as they fought through the throng of bodies in line for refreshments. "It is said everybody loses a portmanteau at Albany."

Further conversation was impossible in such a swarm of bodies, but that suited Harrison just fine. Forty-five minutes later, stomachs full and luggage in hand, they reclaimed their original seats in the back of the last car. Harrison recognized some passengers from before. Others were new to this leg of the journey. Noticeably absent were the mother and baby.

At the conductor's "Go ahead," and with bells pealing, the train accelerated into the darkness beyond Albany's metropolis. A quiet settled over the car, borne of the late hour, and Harrison took an inordinate interest in the stars outside. Anything to avoid looking directly at Victoria across from him.

"It's your turn to rest, Victoria," Isabella said, moving to sit beside him, thereby giving Victoria both seats.

"I'm quite all right—" But Victoria yawned, effectively cutting off her protest.

"I insist, dear. My insomnia's out in full force and won't let me miss any excitement right now."

"Maybe for just a bit, then." Victoria yawned again, and Harrison stifled the impulse to mimic the action.

Victoria folded her mantle into a pillow, then curled on the double bench seat. After only a few minutes, the steady rise and fall of her torso confirmed her slumber. How could she find comfort and rest when he could not?

"You're staring," Isabella said from his right.

"Still astute as ever, Isabella." It was more a comment than a question.

"And you're still gawking."

"I'm only calculating how much height I'd have to lose to fit on the bench," he answered dryly, finally tearing his gaze from Victoria. "I doubt losing the eight inches would be worth it in the long run, though."

"You could lose a bit of your surliness."

Ah, Isabella had artfully steered the conversation to what she really wanted to talk about. "You know how I feel about husband-hunting women." He stretched his legs and crossed them at the ankles, reveling in the room afforded now that Victoria slept. He crossed his arms over his chest too.

Isabella was silent for so long, he finally hazarded a glance her way. She arched a meaningful eyebrow. "As a lawyer, you should know to verify your facts."

"Care to enlighten me, then?"

"It's not my story to tell, Harrison."

"You are so good at storytelling, though." But appealing to her vanity was futile.

"You'll have to perform your own questioning of the witness, counselor."

"My strengths lie in the contractual side of the law," he said, his attempt at playful banter falling short.

"Harrison, she's a person. Not a document to read and nitpick."

"I can read people better when I can see their whole face, both eyes and all that."

Isabella let out an exasperated sigh. "You are incorrigible."

"Now that, we can both agree on." He gave her an unrepentant smirk.

"Victoria wasn't far off with the petulant child remark, you know," Isabella said, elbowing him and letting out a small laugh at the rejoinder.

Harrison couldn't help but give her a full grin in return. Retrospection was casting new light on the wit in Victoria's comment.

"Now that's the Harrison I know and love." Isabella patted his knee, her face a huge smile. "Please let us see more of him this trip, okay?"

Harrison nodded, the only response he could give around the sudden thickness in his throat. If only others could see the good in him like Isabella did.

Especially he himself.

Victoria stirred as the train slowed. She opened her eyes to find both Harrison and Isabella asleep, Harrison sitting nearly upright in his seat and Isabella with her head leaning against the window. Darkness permeated the view outside. Where were they?

The conductor poked his head in and announced, "Thirty-minute stop."

While it didn't exactly answer her question of where, it was apparently all the information she was to be provided. It also awoke Harrison and Isabella.

Isabella stretched, then peered out the window. "Well, we shouldn't dawdle with only half an hour at our disposal." She rose and Victoria did the same, as did Harrison. He held his arm outstretched, indicating she and Isabella should go ahead of him.

Isabella patted his arm on her way to join the herd of passengers disembarking. "Thank you, dear."

Victoria ducked her head, mercifully squeezing past Harrison's large frame in the cramped quarters without touching him. "Thank you," she murmured, earning a small nod in response. He trailed her as she traversed the aisle.

"Oh, my." Isabella stopped short at the exterior doorway.

Victoria halted too, and Harrison's hand braced in the small of her back, likely to keep himself from barreling full-on into her.

"Sorry," he whispered, his breath right above her ear. He immediately withdrew his hand and made space between them, but the contact left its mark. Her skin was still trying to make sense of the searing spot.

"I'm guessing it's too much to expect food at this stop," Isabella sighed, then carried on down the stairs.

Victoria grasped the railing to steady herself, then followed on still-shaky legs. She couldn't eat anything now, even if she tried.

The depot—should it even be deserving of such a term— was little more than a wooden shack encircled by forest. A small clearing was to be their platform, tree stumps their chairs. A lone gas lamp swung erratically in the whistling wind's strong gusts, its mottled ring of light sweeping circles on the grass below. Above, millions of stars pricked the black tapestry of the night sky in a breathtaking reminder of her diminutiveness.

Like a moth to a flame, she sought the light and security it offered.

"I'll join you two in a minute," Isabella called over her shoulder as she headed the opposite direction. "I must ask that gentleman where he procured his walking stick. I promised a friend back home I'd bring him one as a souvenir."

Without a word, Harrison joined Victoria, leaning against the depot's wooden frame and crossing his arms. His silence was louder than any speech. *Does he expect me to apologize?* His actions certainly didn't merit an apology from her.

In her nervousness, she toyed her bonnet strings loose. Before she could re-secure them, however, a hot gust whirled the bonnet up and away. She yelped in alarm, and her fingers flew to her veil. Thankfully, it was still in place, though its pin was precariously loose.

Before she could step outside the light's circle to retrieve it, a gentleman approached her, bonnet in hand. A few inches taller than she, he was smartly dressed with manners as polished as his appearance. His smile was wide and honest; a dimple in his left cheek adding a boyish charm to his demeanor.

"Yours, madam?" he asked with a slight bow and an American accent.

Reassured by his kind and gracious behavior, Victoria took the bonnet from him, her stomach free of the churning usually present in such interactions with men. She even smiled at him, her confidence bolstered behind the bulwark of her veil. "Thank you, kind sir."

He gave another dimpled smile. "Till we meet again," he said, his departing words more promise than question.

"Well, there's one potential new husband for you."

Harrison. She'd all but forgotten he was there. She whirled around. "So that's what you think this trip is for, Mr. Wright?" She quivered with indignation at his presumption.

Harrison stepped away from the structure and into the light. "Yes, for what other purpose could a widow be here in

America?" His eyes flashed in displeasure, and he recrossed his arms over his chest.

What about her did he find so disagreeable? He was the one who had taunted her, mocked her, frightened her. With fists clenched around her bonnet brim, her tongue took over again.

"You judged me from the start," she said, stepping closer to him. "You don't know me. How dare you assume the worst."

She'd stepped too far, however. She'd crossed the invisible line that put her squarely in his domain. His strong, powerful domain. Her head came only to his shoulder, and mere inches away, his expansive chest rose and fell as his shallow breaths of frustration puffed in and out.

At such a close range, she involuntarily took in his scent, a mix of leather and soap with an undertone of masculine salinity that wasn't at all unpleasant. She chided herself over the distraction before raising her gaze to his face. His eyes were hardened amber. His jaw gritted with barely bridled ferocity.

"I encourage you to return to the train, Mrs. Clarke," he ground out, uncrossing his arms and raising his right hand to point to the train over her left shoulder.

She reacted instinctively. The past harms inflicted at the hands of a man, a man who had vowed to love and honor her, rose to the forefront of her mind, and she raised her left hand, ducking right to shield herself.

Her reaction dislodged her veil and sent it fluttering to the ground. The left side of her face, her great secret, was now exposed.

Harrison inhaled sharply.

He'd seen. Seen the deformed trails of puckered skin zigzagging down her left cheek before they met in a point just above the left corner of her upper lip. Of all people, why did he have to witness her deformity?

Victoria froze. What she wouldn't do to have her lavender oil with her now. Her breath came in shallow gasps as she tried to swallow the lump of rising tears in her throat. Too late. They burned out of her eyes, tightly shut against Harrison's unrelenting stare.

Now she was crying in front of this infernal man.

His fingers grasped her left wrist, and even though his touch was gentle, she jumped slightly. He slowly guided her arm away from her face.

The tears were unstoppable now. Her clogged throat prevented any speech whatsoever, but at least she managed to not sob uncontrollably. A small favor.

Harrison released her wrist, and she swallowed once more before opening her eyes. The blur of tears cleared, and his features came into focus. She raised her chin and boldly met his eyes in a silent challenge.

His gaze held more curiosity than the disgust and pity others normally displayed when they happened to see what she concealed under her veil.

A question was also in his eyes, and while she'd stopped crying, she still couldn't find any words to answer.

When he raised his thumb and gently wiped an errant tear still making its way down the irregular furrows of her scar, she didn't flinch. His thumb stilled just above her lip, and she could not breathe again, but this time for a different reason.

Harrison found his voice first. "A childhood accident?" was his whispered inquiry.

"No," she finally managed, also in a whisper. "My late husband ..."

The anger returned in his eyes, but it wasn't directed at her this time.

Six

"Chicago," Isabella's voice rang out from around the corner, and Harrison jumped away from Victoria. Victoria dipped down and retrieved her veil, but Isabella arrived before she could re-secure it and her bonnet.

"He procured the walking stick in Chica—" Isabella trailed off and momentarily halted when she saw Victoria's state. "Oh, well, the cat's been let out of the bag, I see. Harrison, I'm so pleased you could finally make Victoria feel comfortable enough to tell you."

He was a cad, plain and simple. He'd instilled no such confidence in Victoria. Instead, he'd scared the secret out of her, forgetting his promise to Isabella to be more pleasant mere hours earlier.

But something had flared within him when Victoria had smiled at the man who had returned her bonnet. The man had easily gained her trust, drawing out an almost jubilant smile. It'd been more than he could tolerate, and he'd lashed out at her. He suppressed the word surfacing in his mind as the excuse—for that was impossible. Wasn't it?

The call of "All aboard" interrupted any chance he had to explain.

"Come, we must try to secure our same seats," Isabella said, bustling toward the train without a backward glance. Victoria brushed past him, her veil and bonnet re-secured. He trailed behind the two women, his thoughts churning like the train's wheels were about to do.

Isabella's speed had served them well—when he finally boarded, she sat on the double bench seat in the back of the train car. But why was Victoria across from her instead of beside her?

"I believe it's my turn to rest," Isabella said in answer to his unspoken question, settling into the seat. He eyed her, but she didn't appear to be scheming. Likely oblivious to his and Victoria's charged interaction, then.

He sat beside Victoria, and she edged as close to the window as possible. She didn't speak, nor did he. In the absence of a chattering Isabella, only the hushed conversations of the other train passengers and the clattering of the train wheels along the track sounded for some time.

Once he was sure Isabella slept, he finally spoke.

"Mrs. Clarke, I—I didn't know," he said. An insubstantial apology even to his ears.

"Mr. Wright," she said, "that is because I did not wish for you to know." She folded and unfolded her gloved hands and kept her eyes resolutely focused on the black beyond the window. "My appearance tends to repulse others, so I trust it only to those with whom I share a strong accord." She covered the slight crack in her voice's bravado by clearing her throat. It was the most she had ever spoken directly to him.

"I wasn't repulsed—"

"Mr. Wright, please," she interrupted. After a deep breath,

she continued, "False platitudes serve no purpose here. I do not wish to speak more about it."

A further response from him would likely hinder more than help, so he simply said, "Of course."

She shifted even closer to the window. And although only inches separated them on the cramped bench, it might as well have been fathoms.

While the train chugged along, time crawled for Harrison. Twelve more hours aboard, with only a brief stop in Cleveland to interrupt the monotony. Isabella and Victoria peered out the window, exchanging whispered gasps and muted conversation. Harrison checked his pocket watch. Nearly eight in the evening. From his calculations, they had another seven hours or so before Chicago and a proper bed to sleep in.

Harrison had traversed these rails enough times that the scenery no longer captured his interest. Still, the view outside was preferable to accidentally catching Victoria's eye, especially after she'd accused him of finding her repulsive.

The dense forests of New York and Pennsylvania had given way to the rolling hills of Ohio. The train's right-hand companion for hundreds of miles—Lake Erie—stretched to the northern horizon, where its glinting sapphire surface merged with the sky's cloudless light blue.

Something about the flat, grassy prairies westward attracted both the extravagantly dressed elite and the burly, bearded trappers and hunters. The mixed company didn't bother him, but Victoria warily eyed the trappers and hunters and their leather jackets, sheathed Bowie-knives, and double pistols. The only thing truly alarming about them was the racy stories of western life with which they regaled the other passengers. It was the pickpockets, swindlers, and luggage-thieves one really needed to worry about, as every train depot placard from here on out warned.

He angled his neck side-to-side, trying to undo the tension more than twenty-four hours on the train had caused. Another of his head pains niggled behind his eyes, and he hoped to stave off a full-blown attack.

The sun was setting, slowly darkening the landscape. The waving grasses disappeared with the last vestiges of daylight, but then glowed again, brighter and brighter. And red.

Odd, that.

A moment later, a conductor burst through the door at the car's front and cried out. "Close the windows. There's a fire ahead."

Almost as if the train itself were ablaze, the car's once-sleepy occupants rushed to obey the conductor's command, Harrison included. He shot to his feet and slid their window shut. Despite the closed windows, smoke seeped in, stinging Harrison's eyes and scratching his throat.

He joined the orchestra of coughing within the car, as did Victoria and Isabella. Isabella moved to sit beside Victoria, who appeared possessed by the same fear she'd exhibited back at the hotel in Boston.

"We'll stop, won't we?" Victoria choked out between trembles as Isabella rubbed her back. Isabella's eyes were also wide with alarm. Was it from fear of the fire or concern over Victoria?

Someone had to remain calm, though, and apparently it was to be him.

"I don't know," he said before wryly adding, "This is my first prairie fire."

"This is not the time, Harrison," Isabella scolded.

He attempted to be congenial, but his efforts were disregarded. Perhaps a crisis *wasn't* the right time.

Except how could he help? Especially when the train didn't slow and instead plunged, full speed, into the fire's core. Flames licked the glass of the closed windows, igniting shrieks and cries of terror amongst the passengers. The fire devoured the dry grass beyond the tracks, its insatiable appetite crackling with fervor.

Surely, they would roast alive inside the scorching car. Tense seconds passed, the temperature in the car spiking ever higher, until the train must have finally outpaced the conflagration.

Outside the windows, the landscape returned to idyllic country twilight, almost as if the last few terrifying minutes hadn't occurred at all. The clamor within the car died down to an exhausted titter, the passengers uniting in their shared distress.

Harrison's temperature, pulse, and breathing gradually returned to normal too. "Well—it's good that's behind us." He winced internally at the inadequacy of his remark. *That's the best my highly trained, legal mind can come up with?*

"Y—yes." Victoria's response was as shaky as she looked.

"I'll go get us some water," Isabella said, rising to join the throng at the water filter up front, only teetering a bit as she disappeared down the aisle.

It was the first time he and Victoria had been alone since her scar was briefly uncovered. Well, as alone as two people could be in a crowded train car.

Fire appeared to trigger intense fear within her, and her former husband had apparently caused her scar. But was there a connection between the two? And what had happened to her husband?

Her scar didn't have the typical raised blotches resulting

from a burn. It was fingered, jagged. Despite his curiosity—for that's what it was, not repulsion as she had claimed—he would do his best to honor his agreement not to push her on the issue.

But that left the question of what to talk with her about. The awkward silence between them grew weighty. He momentarily caught her eye as she scanned her gaze from the other passengers back to the window. Soot smudged her right cheek, the only spot on her otherwise regained composure.

She was always polished, always proper. Perhaps he wasn't the only one who had found little enjoyment in life lately. A wave of guilt hit him. This trip was likely meant to be an indulgence for her, and here he was, ruining it.

He cleared his raw throat and offered her his handkerchief. "Mrs. Clarke, you have a speck of soot here." He reached his other hand across to motion to her right cheek but caught himself. She'd balk at his hand coming toward her again. Instead, he ended with a bungling gesture to his cheek.

"Thank you, Mr. Wright." She took the handkerchief with only a slight tremor of her hands and removed the spot with one deft wipe, then returned the handkerchief to him. This time, her hand didn't brush his.

He adopted his default dry tone again. "Well, Isabella took my job as water retriever."

She'd apparently registered the humor he'd intended, and she quirked a small smile, a fleeting levity sparking in her right eye.

A return smile spread across his lips. His stomach constricted again with the same, foreign feeling from the American House in Boston. It was equally alarming now as it was then, and he shuttered his smile. For like father, like son.

Seven

"I do not understand. I wrote ahead for a room." Isabella was the only one of the three with enough fortitude left at three in the morning to contend with the hotel clerk.

Victoria struggled to remain awake and upright in the Tremont Hotel's lobby. Would this trip only involve a series of middle-of-the-night arrivals? They'd reached Chicago's two-story brick depot about thirty minutes earlier and, after claiming their trunks and rattling down a few blocks of paver bricks in a hired carriage, had entered the five-story hotel. Elegant inside and out, unfortunately, the hotel's 260 rooms were apparently full.

"Yes, but you arrived asking for two rooms, which we do not have available." If the clerk was trying to show empathy at their predicament, he was failing miserably, and Victoria's spirits plummeted further at his confirmation they wouldn't be staying here tonight. "You could try the inn around the corner," he added, "but I cannot guarantee you'll have any luck."

Isabella's lips pursed in annoyance. "Well, I suppose we must. We can't very well sleep on the street, can we?"

But her question hung in the air unanswered—the clerk had already disappeared.

"No use lingering here," Harrison said, his tone short. "Come, let's go inquire at the inn." He spun around and strode back out into the night.

Isabella looped her arm through Victoria's. "I suppose he has the right to be surly at this hour. Not to worry, dear, we shall make the best of it."

Isabella pulled her in Harrison's wake to a waiting carriage outside. Harrison silently handed her and Isabella in before climbing in and taking the rear-facing seat opposite them.

As the carriage sprang to life, she couldn't help but peek at him. He faced out the window, affording her a view of his profile. Even at such a late hour, he maintained a ramrod posture, with no hint of the brief smile he'd given her on the train. Had she done or said something to cause it to disappear? And for him to all but ignore her since?

Her memory flickered back to his feather-light fingertips on her scarred cheek at the ramshackle depot. How could the touch of such a strong, ominous man be so gentle, almost a caress? And how disappointed she was that he hadn't actually touched her again on the train when he'd given her his handkerchief?

She mentally shook her head to clear these inane thoughts. In her near-sleepless state and heightened anxiety over all the fires America had, she was clearly losing her wits.

For what did she really know about this man? After all, the handkerchief was embroidered with pink flowers and initials that were not Harrison's: C.B. He wouldn't give her another woman's handkerchief, would he? She couldn't make sense of all the thoughts and emotions warring within her.

Thankfully, the carriage jarred to a stop—a welcome diversion. The inn before them, however, was not welcoming. In fact, it appeared more wearied than they did.

"It doesn't even have a name," Isabella said, nodding to where the establishment's name had long worn off the building's brick exterior.

"I can think of a few choice words to call it," Harrison muttered.

Victoria would have laughed at his witticism, but for the reality, they'd have to sleep in this decrepit building.

Inside was no better. It took all of Victoria's restraint to keep from visibly recoiling at the sights and smells assaulting her when she entered after Isabella. The floors crawled with insects, and her boots squished in puddles of tobacco juice— the floor was evidently the chewers' preferred target over the six spittoons scattered throughout the room.

The proprietor, a large-set woman, greeted them with a gap-toothed grin. "Oy, how many rooms will ye be wanting?"

"Two, please," Isabella spoke on behalf of the group.

"Yer in luck," the proprietor said, edging out from behind the counter and jangling the key ring dangling from her belt. "I've got just two left. Follow me." She led them down a dark hallway, the smell from her unwashed body wafting in the dank air.

Victoria nearly covered her mouth and nose with her hand, but didn't want to jeopardize their chances at the last rooms available in Chicago. She breathed through her mouth instead, but that only meant the stench bit her tongue too.

At a woman's shriek from a nearby room, everyone paused but the proprietor. "Aye, that one's got typhus, she does. The fever's makin' her plum mad. Another's got the cholera a few doors down. Nasty business it is."

Victoria exchanged a quick, anxious glance with Isabella,

who had been providing them with an ongoing report of the cholera outbreak plaguing America that summer. Isabella squeezed Victoria's hand as if to reassure her they'd be fine, but she wasn't completely mollified. *Would anything on this trip go well?*

Oblivious to their increasing alarm, the proprietor stopped her limping journey at the end of the hall and gestured to two open doors next to each other. "Here ye are. Home sweet home. Nevil will lug yer trunks up when he wakes to start breakfast." She opened her hand, dirt encrusting every wrinkle and crevice of her palm. "Ye gotta pay now. Dollar a day. Fer each room. No discount for arriving late."

Isabella let out a disgruntled huff from Victoria's right, but thankfully didn't voice any of her thoughts aloud. They likely mirrored Victoria's perception of the scant amenities proffered to the guests at such an exorbitant rate.

The glint in the proprietor's eye revealed she likely knew of their desperation and was taking advantage of it.

Victoria reached for her valise and the coins it held, but Harrison was quicker. He jammed a handful of bills in the proprietor's outstretched hand and then took the two keys she handed him in return. "That should ensure my companions and I have an agreeable stay for the next two nights." He set his jaw, a sign that he was trying to control his anger.

The proprietor leered in Harrison's direction. "I can make your stay more than agreeable, sir." She even gave him a meaningful wink before turning and limping off, counting the bills as she went.

Victoria caught Isabella's amused expression, then lost control of the fit of laughter bubbling up inside her. Isabella did too, the lack of sleep making the absurdity of their circumstances all the more hilarious.

"Why, Harrison, I believe you've caught the keen eye of our proprietor," Isabella said between snickers.

He cast an irritable look their way, which only served to start another round of laughs between the two women.

Certain she was adding to the repartee, Victoria added, "Although is she one your mother would approve?"

Harrison's entire countenance steeled.

Her cheeks heated. She must have made a mistake.

"My mother's dead," he ground out, turning his back to her.

She could find no words to mitigate her blunder.

"Harrison," Isabella assuaged, "she didn't know. Grant her some grace, please." Isabella reached for Harrison's elbow, but he yanked it out of her reach.

"I fear my benevolence is quite tapped out at the moment, Isabella." His response was curt, and with his back still to them, he surveyed the two rooms. "I'll take this one," he said, claiming the dirtier, smaller one for himself. He gave a clipped "Good night, ladies," before clapping his door shut.

With her throat thick with unshed tears, Victoria still couldn't speak.

"Don't fret, my dear," Isabella said, squeezing her into a one-armed embrace from the side. "I fear he gets quite cantankerous when he's tired and hungry, and his mother is still a tender subject for him."

"What happened to her?" she asked, finally finding her voice. She followed Isabella into the room.

"You two are quite the pair." Isabella shook her head as she shut the door. "As I told Harrison when he asked about you, I will not play Western Union between you two. You are both adults. You can talk to each other. If not for your own sakes, then for mine, please."

Isabella lit the bedside lamp, giving them the first full view of their room. Victoria joined Isabella in a horrified gasp. Unsurprisingly, the small room's condition was no better than the rest of the inn, bare of furniture except a mattress on the floor in one corner, a spindly chair in another, and a washbasin beside the lamp on a rickety table next to the door. Though the room had one small window, that made it no less prison-like. To think they were paying for this.

A movement in the corner caught Victoria's eye, and she shuddered. The creature was too quick for her to discern exactly what species it was, but it had fur, of that she was certain. Her misery compounded.

Isabella gestured to the lumpy mattress and sighed. "Well, we must make the best of it. Left or right side?"

With her head still reeling from the past few hours, Victoria mumbled, "right," voluntarily giving herself the side wedged into the corner as penance for her earlier actions.

"I suggest we leave our dresses on," Isabella said as they readied for sleep. "I fear whatever creeping things might be housed in this mattress and the buffalo skin covers."

Victoria shuddered in fresh disgust at the stains blotching the would-be blankets. Facing an equally stained wall with her back to Isabella, she lost the fight to a fresh wave of tears, all too aware Harrison could be mere inches away on the other side of the thin wall.

What was contributing most to her tears at that moment? The hurt etched into Harrison's features from her remark in the hallway, or her exhaustion from the train journey, or the sudden surge of homesickness that struck her in this sickness-infested excuse for an inn? Mercifully, even in such circumstances, sleep came before she could work out the answer.

∼

Victoria awoke the next morning to an empty spot beside her and the sun already halfway to its zenith in the sky outside the room's single grimy window. She'd slept later than she'd meant to.

She took advantage of the relatively clean water Isabella must have refreshed in the washbasin to splash her face. Oh, how indulgent a real bath would be at present. Perhaps at their next stop in Detroit.

Clicking the door shut behind her, she traversed the narrow hallway in the swish of a somewhat fresh black skirt, only to stop after a few paces. She'd forgotten her veil.

She could forego it altogether—an unprecedented occurrence indeed.

No, that'd be too much, even though Harrison had already seen her scar. She scurried back to the room and retrieved her ever-present companion, pinning it in its usual place. She also dabbed a drop of lavender oil on each wrist for good measure.

Day cast the inn—and its inhabitants—in no better light. Victoria passed one open door to a dormitory-style room with four beds, two of which were occupied by women clad only in their chemises, groaning and writhing in evident pain. She averted her gaze to the floor and hurried on.

A child's mournful howl from behind another door joined the commotion, and Victoria picked up her pace. Gooseflesh rose on her arms, and she hugged them to her chest to ward off the panic rising within her.

She collided with a strong, solid form, swallowing a shriek.

It was only Harrison. Practically in his arms at this point, she froze with a different type of fear.

"Mrs. Clarke, are you all right?" he asked, constraint underlying his cordiality. The hurt of last night was likely still raw.

Yet he didn't let go. His hands gripped firmly, but not

painfully, around her upper arms, his knees hollowing into her skirts. He, too, seemed immobilized from some invisible force, his amber eyes searching her face as if it answered the question of why neither moved.

His eyes flicked lower to her lips, and her breath hitched. At last, she mustered her courage and stepped back, though remaining would have been more courageous.

"M—Mr. Wright." She stumbled over her words, trying to find those that would make amends for the ones she'd spoken last night. "I'm genuinely sorry for what I said last night. My attempt to be funny fell far short, and I apologize."

He raked his hands through his hair, sending one onyx lock dipping down onto his forehead.

Victoria itched to reach her fingertips up and brush it back in place. Instead, she took another step back, a flush creeping up her neck. Where were these ridiculous thoughts coming from?

"I'm the one who should be sorry," he said almost abashedly, his eyes anywhere but on her. "I let my emotions get the better of me." He cleared his throat and smiled with a boy-like sheepishness. "Believe me, Isabella's already lectured me this morning."

"Whatever you're saying about me, Harrison, it better be complimentary." Isabella joined the impromptu meeting in the hall, a tray of food in her hands. As much as Victoria loved her friend, Isabella had the most inconvenient timing.

"Always," Harrison replied with an exaggerated bow in Isabella's direction.

"As you can see, Harrison's mood has improved with food," Isabella said, turning to Victoria. "Now let's get you fed, dear." She lifted the tray in her hands. "They've closed the kitchen, but Harrison managed to coax the proprietor into letting us bring you a plate."

"Sounds like quite the sacrifice," Victoria said, cautiously attempting banter.

"Yes, it really was," Harrison drawled, another boyish grin animating his face. He really was too handsome for his own good. It was no wonder the proprietor was enamored with him.

Victoria's stomach growled in the most unladylike manner, and her cheeks flushed again. She was always embarrassing herself.

"Good thing you're too hungry to let the state of the dining room and the appearance of this food prevent you from eating," Isabella said, leading the way down the hall. "Come, you can eat in our room, Victoria. Harrison has some business to attend to in the city, so the two of us will explore without him until dinnertime."

Following Isabella, Victoria glanced over her shoulder at Harrison. He was angled against the wall, his head in his hand, pinching the bridge of his nose and shaking his head. Oh, if only she could read another's thoughts, especially his at present. He was clearly flustered, discomfited. Had she ruffled the ever-stoic Harrison?

Eight

Once Victoria had choked down the marginally palatable breakfast of bitter coffee, stale bread, and an unidentified strip of meat, she left the confines of the dowdy inn with Isabella. With a sunny, slightly less-stifling September day, Chicago truly shone.

Another of America's Great Lakes—Lake Michigan—sparkled to the east, fingering into canals that wound through soaring stone buildings and lofty church spires. The city pulsed with an eager energy she had come to recognize as the Americans' constant quest for progress. Pedestrians hurried this way and that, completing ever-important errands with all haste.

"It says here that over 60,000 people call Chicago home," Isabella said, reading from a pamphlet she'd nipped from the Tremont. Ever since, she'd been rattling off a litany of facts about the city as they ambled along its wooden sidewalks.

Victoria kept her eyes on the planks below their feet, dodging holes and uneven joints to keep from stumbling.

Meanwhile, Isabella, nose still in the pamphlet, glided along and continued her reading. "The lumber trade is quite profitable, apparently, and Chicago is one of the largest exporters of grain in the world."

More interested in the city's sights than statistics, Victoria tuned Isabella out and focused on her surroundings. Stores, some three high in a building, peculiarly displayed their goods in the street instead of inside. Bolts of red flannel, barrels of nails, and suits of oilskin spilled from the shops' open doors, attracting as customers the burly western men that still alarmed her.

A cacophony of rolling wheels and hoofbeats sounded over the dirt-packed street. Carriages, wagons, carts, and men on horseback all paraded by, their movements made all the more miraculous by the fact that they didn't collide. Even a ragged dog trotted through, as if it had its own important business to conduct. In the distance, the trains' whistles exchanged calls with those of the steamboats' in continual conversation.

"That must be one of the hundred trains traveling through Chicago daily," Isabella said, raising her voice over the noise.

After a late lunch of piping hot pockets of meat-filled dough—"knishes" the street peddler's cart declared them— they traveled to the pier and harbor. The sun danced along the lake's rippling surface, for the traffic here was just as bustling as on the streets. The smell of fish permeated the air. How strange it wasn't mixed with salt, as Victoria was used to in her ocean-bound country.

En route back to the inn in the waning light, Isabella stopped abruptly, and Victoria nearly bowled her over.

"Victoria, look!"

Isabella was likely pointing out another of Chicago's must-see phenomena. Victoria craned her neck around Isabella's petite form and followed Isabella's finger to a barrel of knobby walking sticks outside a shop. "Perfect for Mr. Havershire back home," Isabella said, exchanging two metal coins with the proprietor for one wooden rod.

Isabella took great delight in brandishing the stick as a cudgel, and Victoria couldn't discount its efficacy at clearing a path on the crowded sidewalks, trying, albeit unsuccessfully, to hide a smile at Isabella's antics. The last thing she should do was encourage her, right?

They rounded the corner, their inn in sight, but halted when a crowd blocked their way to the inn's entrance. Shouts and hollers emanated from the swarm. The throng fanned out into a circle, in the center of which stood two men in what appeared to be a heated debate. Each man had a second man standing behind him, clutching two shiny pistols, the muzzles pointing toward the ground.

"A duel," Isabella said, supplying the answer before Victoria's brain could. Isabella gripped Victoria's hands in hers. "Oh, and no way to escape to the safety of our inn, even with this walking stick."

The crowd's shouts and hollers rose to a crescendo.

Isabella's anxiety pulsed through their clutched hands, settling low in Victoria's stomach. "I'm guessing that means the seconds didn't reach an agreement, and it'll come to shots," Isabella whispered.

Victoria was too worried to dwell on how Isabella was so knowledgeable about duels. Naturally, she'd traveled halfway around the world only to be struck dead by an errant bullet from two puffed-up peacocks shooting at each other in the name of honor.

The crowd reached an eerie quiet, far scarier than the noise of mere moments before. Time slowed to a crawl.

"Ready." The call came from within the circle.

A steady hand clutched Victoria's other wrist and dragged

her and Isabella through the back of the crowd. "Follow me." At Harrison's low timber, Victoria instinctively curled closer to the protection he and his voice provided.

"One." The same burly voice sliced through the quiet.

Harrison edged them through the throng of spectators.

"Two."

Everything was happening far too fast now.

Victoria's left shoulder slammed into another's, but still she held fast to Isabella's wrist, stumbling to regain her balance. Harrison's grip on her right hand never wavered as he led them along.

"Three."

With a whoosh, the three tumbled through the inn's front door, and Victoria lost her grip on Isabella's wrist as she careened back into one of the inn's brick walls. She squeezed her eyes shut against what would come next.

"Fire."

Two blasts, one a half second behind the other, reverberated in her ears, and she jumped. She couldn't move, couldn't breathe. All the air left her lungs when she was thrust into the wall, but her lungs weren't allowing any back in. Had she been hit?

No, a warm body pressed against hers. That's why she couldn't inhale. She pushed down the panic clawing its way up her throat and cracked open her eyes.

Harrison's left arm was wrapped around and behind her right side, his right hand splayed at her head's height on the brick wall to her back. His body crushed against nearly every inch of hers.

His ragged breaths pushed against her chest until he lifted his weight off her a bit, but not enough as propriety warranted.

Her heart raced. Whether from the danger of the past few minutes or from Harrison's proximity, she wasn't sure.

When she finally raised her eyes to his face, it was creased with concern. His pupils were inky orbs in pools of liquid gold, and they widened ever so slightly as he took in their closeness.

With her next inhale, her nose registered his unique scent —the clean tang of Castile mixed with the primal suppleness of leather. As masculine as the man himself.

"Are you all right, Mrs. Clarke?" His hoarse query rumbled in her chest.

"Y—yes, thank you, Mr. Wright," she said, willing her body to stop acknowledging his nearness. "I do believe we quite owe you our lives."

"Harrison, will I have to call you out now for besmirching my friend's virtue?" *Isabella and her impeccable timing, as always.*

Harrison startled at Isabella's interjection, then snaked his left arm from behind Victoria and pushed both hands against the wall to separate himself fully from her, but not before the telltale red crept behind the white of his shirt collar.

"Just making sure she's recovered."

"I've made a full recovery too, in case you're concerned." But a spark of humor lit Isabella's eyes. With her walking stick in one hand, she reached for Victoria's hand with the other. "We'll catch up with you at dinner, Harrison. We won't be ready in time if we tarry any longer."

Isabella dragged Victoria down the hallway, her legs wobbling with each step. But was she so trembly because she'd just dodged a duel, or because she'd just been wholly wrapped in Harrison's arms?

Victoria paused outside the door to the dining room and took as deep a breath as her dress would allow. After returning to their room, she and Isabella had washed and scrubbed their traveling dresses with hands still shaky from the earlier excitement.

True to the proprietor's word, albeit a bit tardy, Nevil had delivered their trunks while they were out. As if to distract from the weighty thoughts of what they had witnessed during the duel, Isabella mourned at the inn's lack of a steam laundry and marveled at the tiny fish pumped into the washbasin from the water's ultimate source—the lake.

So, with her other two daydresses dripping wet up in the room, Victoria had unearthed a deep, plum-colored evening gown from the bottom of her trunk as her only option of being clothed tonight.

With the dress's dipping neckline, short sleeves, and silky, bold hue, however, it was much more conspicuous than her usual black mourning wear. When had she last shown her neck, much less her shoulders, in public? At least she still had the familiar security of her veil.

What would Harrison think of the new attire? Another jolt of nerves shot through her stomach. The more time she spent with him, the more his care and kindness peeked through from where he tried so hard to keep it hidden. He'd all but risked his life for theirs earlier today, after all. Yet he seemed purposefully to close himself off from others. What internal war was this man fighting? And when had she begun to care so much?

Her stomach dipped at the memory of his body pressed to hers earlier today, at his seeming reluctance to move from their precarious position. In his accidental embrace, she'd been safe, the fright she experienced near men absent. And his gaze, though penetrating, had emboldened her. Under it, she'd been seen, accepted, confident. A line from the Longfellow poem flittered to her mind—*Shall take heart again.* Was this how that happened? Was this how that felt?

"Shall we?" Isabella's light tone interrupted her heady thoughts.

Nodding with more confidence than she felt, she cautiously followed Isabella into the combined kitchen-dining room. Her stomach churned at the unfortunate state of where they were to dine this evening. So much for mustering bravado.

A large fireplace dominated the far side of the room, at which the cook undertook his duties by the literal sweat of his brow. He only just managed to keep the perspiration from dripping into the food pot with periodic wipes of a filthy handkerchief.

Victoria shuddered and diverted her attention to the rest of the dining room. But it was no more agreeable. A handful of greasy, gangly scullery boys darted about, barefoot, collecting the dirty plates and giving them a cursory rinse at a water bucket and a brief wipe of their long-ago-clean aprons.

The waiters at least wore shoes, but they unceremoniously dumped the food in front of the guests while wearing expressions akin to hardened outlaws. Victoria suppressed another shiver and instinctively sought Harrison in the crowded room. When had his presence grown comforting?

He was already seated at the single long communal table in the middle of the room. He, too, had over-dressed for their surroundings in a jet-black tailcoat, tan trousers, and steel-colored vest. A black necktie was knotted into a bow under his chin, and his hair was more tamed than she'd ever seen it before. Though this chiseled, sleek Harrison had its appeal too, she may well prefer the more unkempt and tousled version of him.

As if sensing her eyes on him, his eyes met hers, then dipped to take in her dress, causing the heat to return to her belly and creep up her neck and cheeks. A small upturn on the right side of his lips told her he knew the effect his attention was having on her.

Averting her gaze, she crossed the room and took a seat facing him, next to Isabella.

"Good evening, Mrs. Clarke," he said, his deep voice having just as much effect on her as did his presence, his notice.

"Good evening," she responded, taking great interest in arranging her skirts about her on the hard wooden bench to avoid his gaze.

She peered around at the other guests, though. They were a diverse bunch and, from listening in on the surrounding conversations, they hailed from across the country and the globe.

There were Scottish and Irish from near her home country, French traders from St. Louis, those headed to California and its lure of gold, packmen from Canada, and, of course, the trappers and hunters from the prairie. Never before had she seen such variety in what counted as acceptable dinner attire, nor so many weapons—both knives and pistols—at a meal.

When the waiters placed a meal before her, however, she rather wished she had a knife, for the mutton, fowl, and pork were more sinew than meat and the silverware extended no further than a fork.

"I trust you ladies enjoyed your tour of Chicago. Duel aside?" Harrison asked.

"I fancy Chicago is more worth a visit than any other of the western cities," Isabella crooned. She wisely bypassed the meat altogether and instead picked at the vegetables, yams, corn, and squash.

"And you, Mrs. Clarke? How did you find the city?"

His amenability in directly addressing her was surprising, but not unwelcome. "I daresay it serves as a model of American progress," she responded, her focus still on her plate. "The industry, the energy. It's all very captivating." She tentatively nudged around the contents of her plate with her fork, wary that the grease it was swimming in might splatter her gown.

"I'm in agreement, Mrs. Clarke. But wait until you see New York. I'm only one of more than half a million people that call it home—nearly ten times the population of Chicago. I can't wait to show you." She raised her head then, in time to witness another of his devastating smiles.

Harrison's enthusiasm was contagious. "It sounds extraordinary," she said, now eager for the final stop of their trip.

"Did you enjoy your business today, Harrison?" Isabella supplied before Victoria could dwell much more on Harrison's excitement to show her his home city.

"Enjoyment is often not a word I use to describe my work with the law," he said, a frown returning to his face.

"You don't care for the law?" Victoria asked. Hadn't that been his ambition in life? Apparently, the opposite was true.

"It's heavy on paperwork and pushing others around under a thin veil of purported justice. It has always suited my father's personality more than mine." He punctuated his final words with a hint of bitterness.

She understood what it was like to live a life you didn't enjoy. That you were trapped in. Harrison was apparently living the same sort of unhappy existence she'd experienced for years. Even if she didn't have a chance of escaping hers, hopefully he could evade his.

Sensing now wasn't the time to press for more information about his past, though, she asked, "Is there anything else you would like to do?"

"I'm afraid law is the only skill at which I have any level of proficiency," he said, the lack of hope in his response evident.

"Rubbish," Isabella piped up. "You have your investments."

"Yes, well, those are really more of a diversion than anything else." He leaned back so the waiter could remove his plate.

"And you write poetry," Isabella continued. Another waiter took her and Victoria's plates.

Harrison reddened and cleared his throat.

Is he embarrassed? That he was bashful about such an aptitude was rather endearing, and it made sense. A legal wordsmith would be equally proficient at writing prose.

"Yes, well. That's even more of a diversion. It's not as if I'll be the next Longfellow, at any rate."

"Victoria, he's being modest," Isabella said. "The one about the stubborn colt had me near tears."

"Er—"

The waiters cut off Harrison's response by unceremoniously delivering the next course, and an expression of supreme relief flooded his face.

Isabella inspected the dozen or so steaming orange pastries now before them. "Pumpkin pies?" Her cry was equal parts excitement and disbelief. The savory sweetness of the pies added a small measure of warm contentment to the otherwise disastrous meal, especially when Victoria washed down her bites of pastry with a cup of molasses-sweetened tea.

"Oy, lawyer-man. Give yer sweetheart here a sonnet, then." At the sharp voice to Victoria's left, the bite of pie in her mouth soured.

A man a few feet down the bench from her leered in her direction, his mouth liberally dotted with gold teeth, his right hand dangerously close to his pistol holstered at his waist. She squirmed under his unabashed ogling.

She flicked her eyes in Harrison's direction, trying to gauge his reaction to the man's implication that she was his sweetheart. From his clenched jaw to his reddened cheeks, he seemed both embarrassed and angered by the man's insinuation.

"Sir, I believe you are making my *friend* here rather uncomfortable," Harrison said, his voice terse, but not discourteous. "I ask that you please conduct yourself with more propriety in the presence of ladies."

"Ah, she's yer mistress, then," the man replied with a knowing smirk, his eyes shamelessly roving over her again. "Sounds like yer the one with the improper conduct."

Harrison leaped to his feet and pointed at the man. "You crossed a line, sir. How dare you treat a lady of such character and virtue with disrespect?"

The man sneered in Harrison's direction, gold teeth glinting, and patted his pistol at his waist. "Am I to win two duels today? Do ye want ta know what happin'd to the other feller from earlier?"

Victoria gasped, and a fresh surge of fear iced her spine.

"Harrison!" Isabella's warning cut through the standoff. She stood and leveled her eyes up to his. "It's time for us to take our leave."

Victoria held her breath as Harrison considered Isabella's plea for an interminable amount of time. His eyes flashed with anger. His chest expanded, held, and finally contracted. Now composed, he nodded once. After a curt, "Good evening," he circled the table and guided her and Isabella out the dining-room door ahead of him.

They made it up the stairs before Isabella unleashed her rebuke. "Was that truly necessary, Harrison? Angering a man prone to dueling?"

Harrison didn't break stride as he neared their rooms. "I wouldn't intentionally put our lives at risk, Isabella. My judgment was clouded by a head pain. It won't happen again."

He paused outside his door and turned to sketch a brief bow toward her and Isabella. "I will see you ladies in the morning. Good night."

Even with that brief glance at Harrison's face, however, Victoria could tell there was something more bothering him. And with her newfound aplomb, she knew just what to grab from her room to find out.

Nine

Harrison lay on his mattress, head pounding. With the lantern light low and his forearm propped over his eyes, the throbbing in his head was marginally better, but only just so.

The day had been an abominable disaster. First, there was the argument with his client, Mr. Peterson. The man refused to see reason, and Harrison had left the man's office after hours of heated discourse with the important paperwork unsigned. Harrison's father would be furious at his failure.

Then his heart stuttered when he'd found Isabella and Victoria frozen in fear on the outskirts of a duel. It hammered even faster when he'd ended up nearly smothering Victoria. He'd tried tamping down the memory of her warm body under his, but his efforts proved futile when she'd shown up to dinner in a gown with a cut and color far different from her usual black mourning attire.

It wasn't just her beauty that had struck him—she had also been possessed of a new confidence, of a poise suggesting an underlying nature of her personality she rarely shared, but that his inquisitive mind begged to understand more. He'd even dressed in his best clothes for dinner, as if that would earn her favor.

But the other lewd man's implication that Harrison treated women like his father had sent him over the edge. Thankfully, he'd regained control—with no small thanks to Isabella. Still, it'd triggered the head pain that had been brewing all day, unleashing it in its full vigor.

A soft knock on the door sent another wave of pain through his forehead. Probably someone from the inn's staff. *Please don't let it be the proprietor.*

"I do not wish to be disturbed," he called, wincing at the loudness of his voice.

"Mr. Wright?" The voice was feminine, but not the grating rasp of the proprietor's.

Harrison froze. Why was Victoria coming to his room?

She knocked again, and the door cracked open. He must not have latched it all the way.

"Might I come in?" Thankfully, she kept her voice at a whisper.

"How may I be of service, Mrs. Clarke?" he asked, trying to conceal the note of impatience in his voice. The tolling day had roused his irritability.

Apparently taking his question as assent to enter, she opened the door farther and peeked her head in.

"Oh, you're still abed," she murmured, ducking her head to the ground.

He didn't have the energy to be abashed. "What is it you require?"

"Actually, Mr. Wright, I was hoping to help you," she said, her tone ever clipped and efficient. "With your head pains." Before he could say anything in return, she rushed on. "You see, I am versed in acupressure, which scientific research claims may help relieve the pains ailing you."

"Acupressure? Quite an unusual interest for someone in your position, wouldn't you say?" It was his foul mood, his need to put distance between them again, that made him snip back. He immediately regretted his snide remark, but he was entitled to a bit of peace given his current condition. Plus, she should stay far away from him; if not for his sake, then for hers.

"Well, Mr. Wright, I'm afraid my circumstances prevent me from having typical pursuits."

Thoroughly chided, he simply said, "Come in, then." If he acted unaffected, maybe he'd feel so too.

He kept his eyes averted as her footsteps clicked across the short span from the door to his mattress, and she situated herself on the floor beside his head in a rustle of fabric.

Curiosity got the better of him, and he cut a glance to the side. She wore the deep purple gown from dinner, but, surprisingly, her veil was gone. Even so, she sat just to his left, still presenting the right side of her face to him. She set a small leather valise beside her and opened it to reveal a variety of colored bottles.

"Not to worry, the door is ajar, and Isabella is just outside," she said.

Her assurances of decorum did nothing to assuage his distress, for though she was diminutive beside him, her presence commanded all the air encircling him.

When she craned her neck over her valise, his betraying eyes took in the long wexpanse of alabaster skin from her jawbone to the deep "V" formed by her collarbone. Her pulse thrummed slow and steady in the small pocket below her earlobe.

His pulse, however, ticked up a notch. He'd gone twenty-nine years in this world without becoming distracted by the annual batch of frilled, young women parading around husband shopping, only to lose his senses when this maddening woman, a widow and a scarred one at that, got within two feet of him.

He closed his eyes and turned his attention back to the ceiling, forcing himself to unclench his jaw with each deep inhale and exhale.

And then she touched him.

He should have inferred acupressure would require some sort of physical contact, but the excruciating pain in his head, not to mention her proximity in that dress, prevented logical thought. She pressed her thumbs into the hollow behind each ear, and in his surprise at the touch, he couldn't stop a sharp intake of breath.

Her fingers were adept and sure, and if she noticed his reaction, she made no outward sign of acknowledgment. She worked in silence for a bit, alternating the location of her fingers on his face—near his eyebrows, at the base of his skull, then back to between his eyebrows—holding the pressure for a few minutes each time.

During one longer pause, her bottles clinked, and lavender infused the air.

"This answers the question of why you always smell of lavender."

She froze. He must have spoken those very private thoughts aloud. *Why do I always make a fool of myself in front of her?* He sent up a silent prayer, begging for any red creeping up his neck from his *faux pas* to be quashed.

She was quiet for so long he almost risked peeking his eyes open.

"So, Mr. Wright, you've paid particular attention to how I smell?" She quipped in response. This time he did peek and confirmed that, yes, she was jesting with him. She was actually humoring him.

This was a pleasant, albeit surprising, development. He was at a loss for a response. A small smile quirked the right side of her face. It was glorious. But it made him greedy for a full smile, and perhaps even a small laugh, but surely that was asking too much.

"Harrison," he all but croaked. It was the only thing he could think to say, but it did little to meet his goal of showing he was intelligible.

She paused her actions. "Pardon?"

He cleared his throat. "Please, call me Harrison. Our trip together certainly warrants such familiarity, does it not?" He held his breath, more nervous than he should be about how she would respond.

"All right," she finally answered. "Then you are at liberty to call me Victoria."

She resumed her treatment, and he exhaled, the pain in his head and tension in his shoulders lessening. *Perhaps he might relax for once.*

"Will you tell me about this, Harrison?" She lightly fingered the scar above his right eye, and he tensed again. So much for relaxing.

He liked the way his name rolled off her tongue, zestfully, yet slowly, as if she wasn't in a hurry to finish saying it. But it wasn't fair of her, using his Christian name for the first time when asking such a weighted question.

She moved her hands into his hair, pressing various points on his skull, which only added to his inability to think straight. She bided her time, letting the silence hang.

"There was an accident," he said, unable to stand the silence any longer, even if it meant divulging some of his greatest secrets. "With a carriage. Almost two years ago." He tried to keep the emotion out of his voice.

There, he'd answered her question, fulfilled his duty. They could go back to silence now.

"Sounds utterly frightening," she said, her tone genuine. Then, after a moment's wait, she went on. "Were you alone?"

Of course, she'd desire to know more. Her question took him back to that fateful night. Back to the narrow road outside the city. Back to the pouring rain and pitch-dark. Like the deluge that night, his words now flooded out, no longer contained behind the fortification he'd so carefully built over the last two years.

"Unfortunately, no. My mother, Catherine, was there. She sat next to me on the right side of the carriage. My sister, Georgina, who was a year old, rested in my lap. I wanted to give my mother a break, you see." He gave a wistful, somber smile at his mother's memory. She was a paragon of all that was good and virtuous. If only he had ended up just a bit like her.

"Alfred, my not-so-little brother, was in the carriage too. Though I had ten years on him, he had six inches on me, if you can believe it." Out of the corner of his eye, Victoria's lips formed a solemn smile, but she didn't interrupt his monologue.

Instead, she resumed her ministrations, moving from his hair back to his neck and shoulders.

"Alfred sat across from my mother, sleeping, his long legs veritably folded in half in the cramped carriage. It all happened too suddenly for him to wake—the horses bolting, the carriage sliding in the muck and then overturning on its right side. The doctor said he likely died on impact. And the driver too."

Victoria gasped.

But there was no stopping him now. He couldn't get the

words out fast enough. "If only I could have said the same for my mother. She survived. Initially. For six long days she suffered. Coming in and out of consciousness, crying out Alfred's name, her agitation abated only when the doctor administered increasingly larger doses of laudanum. Until she finally earned her eternal rest. The doctor said she was likely so heartbroken over Alfred's passing that she couldn't go on."

Victoria's hand pressed on his shoulder, steady and reassuring. "I'm so sorry, Harrison," she said, empathy radiating from her words and her touch. "But Georgina survived, correct?"

"Yes, and relatively unscathed, thankfully. She's had fainting spells since the accident, but is otherwise a strong and healthy three-year-old who gives the governess no small measure of difficulty." He couldn't help another forlorn smile at how his younger sister disguised her antics behind her deceptively innocent chestnut curls and beatific face.

"Alfred inherited my mother's fair hair and blue eyes." Unable to keep the acerbity out of his voice, he added, "I, however, am my father's duplicate in both appearance and temperament. And yet, I was the son that survived."

"Certainly you don't mean—" Victoria began.

"I promise you this world would have been a better place had Alfred survived that night instead of me." Harrison didn't even try to keep the bitterness out of his voice now. "Though I don't wish it upon you, if you were to meet my father, you would understand."

"And your father?" She hesitated a moment, and he held his breath, knowing full well what was coming but waiting to see if she'd ask. When she continued, apprehension laced her words. "He survived unharmed?"

Harrison wouldn't lie to her, but he also wouldn't tell her the whole truth. The pain was too raw, the words themselves so disgraceful he couldn't ask Victoria to shoulder them as well.

"No, Richard Wright avoided the entire ordeal altogether. He was back in the city. On so-called business."

As if sensing he was finished with the line of conversation, Victoria didn't pry further. A dark cloud had descended, but Harrison had long ago resigned himself to his fate. That night would tinge every interaction, every relationship he had. Which is why he usually spoke nothing of it.

"I'm truly sorry for all that happened." Victoria's voice startled him out of his maudlin recollections. Her right hand found his left one resting on his chest, and she gave it a small, reassuring squeeze.

The moment was over in an instant, before he had time to truly register the softness of her ungloved hands, the warmth of her skin on his. He wished her hand had lingered longer, but they were already pushing propriety as it was with her in his room. *Is Isabella even outside the door?* If so, she was being awfully quiet by Isabella's standards.

Victoria spoke again, and her tone contained a levity likely intended to bring him out of his foul mood. "Take heart, though. For I have it on good authority that, as a man, your scar is distinguishing." She repacked her valise, signaling she was finished.

Harrison caught her subtle reference to the Longfellow poem and pushed himself into a seated position, facing her. Mere inches separated them, yet her gaze remained intent on her valise.

She added, "Mine, I'm afraid, is disfiguring."

Her self-deprecating was probably all the invitation he'd ever have. He tried to catch her eyes, but they remained averted. Attempting to convey genuine sincerity, he asked, "Victoria, how did you come about your scar?"

Ten seconds passed.

Then fifteen.

He held his breath, certain she would find some way out of answering. And he wouldn't blame her for doing so.

Twenty seconds.

His patience—and his breath—were nearly tapped out. Then, after a ragged inhale, she spoke.

Victoria struggled to regain her composure after Harrison's revelations. Naturally, he would want to know about her past too. And she'd all but encouraged him to do so with her self-slighting remark. Perhaps on some primal level she wanted him to know, but was it because she hoped the awful truth would bring him closer to her, or push him farther away?

Oh, how she wished she had the fortification of her veil right now. He sat so close, the flickering light dancing along the etched contours of his face. His collar was unbuttoned, his shirtsleeves rolled up, and his hair as rumpled as ever after her acupressure treatment.

She glimpsed then what he must have been like as a little boy, using his dark features to charm his way out of mischief and into whatever he wanted. She was just as enamored by them now, especially because they contained an underlying vulnerability that proved downright irresistible.

"My marriage to Silas was one of convenience. For my family, that is." Sounding detached would hopefully keep her tears at bay. "He was my father's acquaintance and a fellow doctor. With my older sister advantageously wed, my father was impatient to have me wed as well. However, I could not find a match. It wasn't as though I was trying hard to find one, but perhaps, in retrospect, I should have put forth more of an effort."

With nothing else for her hands to do in her nervousness, they twisted about each other in her lap. "Silas and I didn't always see eye to eye." Here, she paused to swallow around her thickening throat. "We weren't married long when he first struck me. I can't even remember now what it was over. Something trivial, most likely, as that was the usual course of things."

Harrison stiffened.

"One night, Silas came home angry about something that had happened at work. He reeked of liquor and had an almost full bottle in hand too. I had made him one of his favorite meals and lit a few candles to help lighten his mood. But to no avail. A comment I'd made set him off. He swiped the whole meal off the table, dishes and food and all. I began to clean it up, but he ... but he—"

Victoria swiped at one tear, then another. They kept sneaking down her cheeks. "He pushed me into the mess, grinding my face—the left side, of course—into the broken shards of glasses and plates."

Harrison grasped her hand, his thumb coursing soft circles of reassurance on the back. His touch was one of safety and security, not fright, and it eased the confusing mix of emotions whirling within her because of that night's memory. Fear, shame, regret. Would fighting back have helped, or would it only have made Silas angrier and his abuse harsher?

"I moved to rise, but he kicked me again, his foot connecting hard with my abdomen over and over, alcohol sloshing all around as he still clutched the bottle." She'd been unable to catch her breath, her chest heaving with the attempt to take in oxygen as she'd prayed inwardly for him to stop what he was doing to her. To their unborn child.

She'd cramped and bled for several days afterward.

A sign of yet another thing she'd lost that night.

That was too intimate a detail to share with Harrison, however.

"By then, the spilled alcohol had seeped to the fallen candles. A fire ignited and spread, cornering him." A shiver raced down her spine at the final image she'd had of her husband—the wrath in his ice-blue eyes blazing hotter than the flames between them. "I—I turned around and ran out the back door. To get help." She licked her lips and took a shuddering breath, hurrying on, eager to have the tale over.

"But the fire spread with abandon, and by the time help arrived and put it out, it was too late."

Wracked by emotion, Victoria could no longer stop the tears nor the most remorseful disclosure yet. "I—I was so relieved."

She covered her mouth on a sob and dipped her head from Harrison's steadfast gaze. "It's so terrible to be grateful for someone else's demise, but I can't deny it. I still am. I can abide my face looking like this the rest of my life, knowing it was the price I paid to escape that living nightmare."

Harrison ducked his head to catch her eyes again, but she still couldn't face him. "Do *not* feel guilty, Victoria. You were an innocent victim in all of that. Silas"—Harrison spoke her former husband's name like a profanity—"was a monster. Plain and simple."

Wiping her eyes, she said, "I'm afraid I've turned into quite the watering pot."

"You have every reason to be upset. I give you full

permission to carry on as if I weren't here," he assured, as if her blubbering was of no consequence.

Reluctantly, she pulled her hand from his, reddening in embarrassment at the intimacy of all they'd shared. Searching for more neutral ground, she asked, "How is your head?"

"I find I am much improved. Thank you. And you?"

"Nothing like a good, messy cry to set oneself to rights, no?" She raised her chin but was still too abashed to turn to him head-on.

"We two are quite the pair, aren't we?" A rueful grin split his face, and she let out a small laugh.

"Yes, but I claim most physically marred." Her attempt at a clever rejoinder fell flat, and his expression sobered.

Slowly, he reached his hand out, took her chin, and gently angled her face toward him. Molten amber in the low light, his eyes roved over her face. She'd let no one so openly inspect her face before, and it was as frightening as it was freeing. She'd laid herself bare, open, exposed. How would he react?

"And that smile, like sunshine, dart/Into many a sunless heart/For a smile of God thou art." Painstakingly slow, his words pierced her heart.

Poetry. From Longfellow's "Maidenhood," if she wasn't mistaken. And if she wasn't careful, this emotionally complex, devilishly handsome, poetry-reciting man would be her undoing.

Harrison flicked his eyes from hers down to her lips and back again. She stared, too dumbfounded to decide whether to stop or encourage his intended actions. He leaned in ever so slightly, and she closed her eyes, angling her chin to his.

"Knock, knock."

Isabella. Finally, come to play chaperone. And just in time.

Harrison jumped to his feet before Isabella fully entered

the room, while Victoria took a renewed interest in confirming the contents of her valise were in order.

"Has Victoria's touch helped?" Isabella asked, sweeping into the room in a wave of deep blue muslin skirts.

Victoria's cheeks flamed with embarrassment at how close Isabella's innocuous comment came to the truth of what had happened.

Harrison raked his hands through his already disheveled hair, his response strangled. "The acupressure? Y—yes, my head is better." He offered Victoria his hand to help her up, and she took it, the warmth of his ungloved hand adding to the heat swirling within her.

"Good, good," Isabella said, turning to lead Victoria out the door. "Rest up, Harrison. We are back on the train tomorrow on our way to Detroit."

"Thank you again, Victoria," he said.

Isabella's eyebrows raised at Harrison's use of her given name. Isabella would surely interrogate her about it later. Harrison clasped his hands behind his back and gave another of his characteristic slight bows. "I wish you ladies a good night's sleep."

While Isabella gave a cheery "thank you, dear," Victoria kept her own reply to a reserved "good night." But how was she to sleep after all that had happened?

The din of the train car bound for Detroit prevented Harrison from doing what he really wanted to do—sleep. He'd hardly slept last night, the dank and dismal accommodations supplying only a small amount of his discomfort. Haunted by thoughts of Victoria, he'd tossed and turned for hours before finally falling into a fitful sleep.

What had he been thinking, nearly kissing her? Was he any better than her former husband, foisting himself on her after her vulnerable confession? Then again, had he misread the signals? Was she willing? Wanting? This was the very reason he set limits on his interactions with women.

He'd awoken near six, too beleaguered by his thoughts to try to sleep more. However, his early waking had given him ample time to send telegrams both to his stockbroker, with instructions on one of his investments, and to his father, with an update from the meeting with Mr. Peterson. The former being as enjoyable to write as the latter was depressing.

Harrison had just exchanged a few pennies at the railroad station's telegraph office for a promise the messages would arrive within a few hours' time.

He, Isabella, and Victoria now sat on the train that would take them east to Detroit, all of them the worse for wear from their two nights at the inn. The two women chatted quietly while he stewed. Victoria was back in one of her black daydresses, but her veil was notably absent.

A man boarded the train car and gawked unabashedly at her face as he passed by.

Harrison glared at him, allowing his eyes to convey his meaning instead of what he really wanted to use—his fists. *All a normal reaction when a friend was threatened, right?*

The man wasn't the first to stare at Victoria. Several people in the station and train car had done the same, some doing so more surreptitiously while others made no effort to conceal their blatant appraisals.

Victoria either didn't notice them gaping or pretended not to. The few times she had met his gaze this morning, they were timid petitions for assurance he'd still accept her as she was, scars bared and all.

And he did.

Yet with her uncanny ability to disarm his usual defenses, it was best to redouble his efforts to keep his distance. Hopefully, his unspoken communications to her achieved his intended balance of impartial validation.

Meanwhile, he fastidiously ignored the coils of desire winding within him whenever his eyes or his body detected her presence. Which was currently all too close, even sitting across from him in a railcar that was a duplicate of the one they'd taken west.

"Harrison." His given name on Victoria's lips sent another jolt through him. Why had he all but begged her to call him by his Christian name last night?

"Will you tell me more about your investments? I'm afraid I'm quite ignorant when it comes to such things," she said.

Isabella added her encouragement. "Oh yes, please do tell us. Our Exchange just moved into its new abode earlier this year, but that's about the extent of my knowledge on its doings."

With the expectant look both women wore, he relented. After all, they had at least ten hours of rail travel ahead of them.

As the train glided along the elevated wooden planks hugging Lake Michigan's shore, he gave them a brief overview of the New York Stock & Exchange Board. To their credit, Victoria and Isabella showed, or at least did a credible job of feigning, interest in his descriptions of stocks and bonds, and how the United States' growth and expansion fueled the rapid expansion of the Exchange.

Energized by the discussion, Harrison's enthusiasm grew as he explained the frenetic calls of the brokers who could barely keep themselves contained to the seats they had purchased, usually at an exorbitant cost.

Victoria asked insightful questions, a spark of genuine

curiosity in her eyes over a topic about which he was passionate. For the first time in who knew how long, someone supported something important to him. His father thought the investments were a waste of time and money. That Harrison should focus on a real vocation—the law.

"It sounds like quite an enthralling gamble," Victoria said.

He chuckled. "Yes, quite. It can make or break a man."

"Sort of like love." Isabella made her addition to the conversation with suspicious nonchalance. What were her machinations? He tried to catch her eye in warning, but she became suddenly all too interested in what was outside the window, which was the same prairie grass they'd been snaking through for miles.

Isabella's new topic drained his zeal for the old. Trying to keep the acerbity out of his voice, he responded, "I can only assume that's the case."

After all, he'd never been in love, and until recently—or maybe especially recently—he hoped he never would be. He was willing to gamble on stocks, but not on love.

Eleven

The weather threatened to turn just as foul as Victoria's mood. Storm clouds gathered in the western sky as she and Isabella, accompanied by a sullen and stiff-backed Harrison, made their way from their hotel to today's main attraction—the Michigan State Fair.

She shouldn't let another's actions influence her feelings, but her confidence—especially without her veil and with the last day's ordeals—was on increasingly unstable ground.

She'd engaged Harrison in a lively discussion about his investments at the beginning of their train ride yesterday, only for his mood, and that of the entire rest of their journey, to dampen once Isabella mentioned love.

He'd barely spoken after that, hiding behind a newspaper, or staring out the window at the seemingly unending prairie. Even when they'd stopped at another rickety wooden depot in the middle of nowhere for a meal of rather curious cuisine, he had no remarks to add to her and Isabella's uncertain commentary about the squirrels and buffalo hump served alongside the customary johnny-cakes and tea.

If his increasingly surly behavior was any indication, he clearly regretted the intimacy of the night before last. He was probably caught up in the moment then, and now, in the clarifying light of day, he was repelled by her scars—both physical and emotional.

But she wouldn't go back to cower behind her veil, especially not for the benefit of someone with such vacillating emotions. She would enjoy this adventure, Harrison's behavior aside.

Since they'd arrived at their hotel after dark last night, she was glimpsing Detroit for the first time this morning. Heading west, with their lodgings at their backs, the three joined the horde of other fair-goers in an unofficial procession down Michigan Avenue.

Moisture trailed down Victoria's back in the humid air. Thankfully, the clouds above shielded the sunlight from beating on her black daydress more forcefully. Now if only the onlookers would fixate less on her appearance.

She saw the pointed stares. Heard the whispers behind hands. But while she didn't hunker within her bonnet's brim, had she been too hasty in exposing her face to so many?

As if sensing her thoughts, Isabella squeezed her hand.

The hubbub prevented conversation with Isabella and Harrison, which was fine with Victoria. There was too much else to see and hear. Gleaming horses wearing equally shiny harnesses jingled by, drawing private carriages from which elegantly attired ladies witnessed the other classes' unadorned wagons and drays dashing and darting about ahead of the planned parade.

First the military band marched by, alternating between two spirited compositions, the names of which Isabella shouted over the synchronized notes of the wind and percussion instruments: "The Star-Spangled Banner" and "Hail, Columbia."

Next in line, the cavalry's horses felt the fervor too, snorting and prancing about with no regard for rank or order. The smartly dressed soldiers sat astride their wide-eyed beasts, uniforms neatly pressed and feathered hats bobbing, giving special attention to the young, attractive ladies. Unsurprisingly, they didn't give her any notice. The artillery was last, stopping to adjust the polished brass gun mounted on a rough-sawn wagon drawn by a quartet of mismatched horses.

With the parade over, they made their way to the fair's hub on Third Street. Harrison was her and Isabella's ever-present, silent shadow as the women explored the foreign sights and sounds of the fairgrounds. Four-legged animals in all their variety abounded, as did poultry.

"Why, Victoria. They have Cochin fowls here too." Isabella gushed when they were inside the agricultural exhibition.

In yet another display, the competition among the handicrafts and quilts appeared almost fiercer than the horse races being run around the adjacent dirt tracks. Kids of all ages repeatedly patronized the swings and merry-go-rounds in the far corner of the grounds, some running their own races with their hobby horses. All the while, bands of musicians played America's most patriotic ballads.

The trio paused outside a tent decorated in colorful signs touting P. T. Barnum's human phenomena. "Oh, my curiosity won't let me pass this one by," Isabella said, turning to face her and Harrison expectantly.

Fat water droplets fell from the leaden sky, compelling a rush of people inside the tent's relative shelter.

"I'll remain outside," Victoria politely declined. "It's far too much of a crush. But you go ahead."

"I will stay here too," Harrison said, earning a raised eyebrow from Isabella. She and Harrison would practically be alone if Isabella went inside.

Isabella hesitated, then said, "I'll be just a moment," before dashing into the tent, its flaps swallowing her tiny form.

The world was reduced to her and Harrison again—the first time since she'd performed the acupressure treatment on him. No longer among a throng of people, she couldn't easily ignore him now, though she still tried. The air between them grew as heavy as the rain-burdened clouds above.

A westerly wind picked up, stirring her skirts and whipping her bonnet off her head, though its strings thankfully remained tied around her neck so she didn't lose it altogether.

"Hoss!" The jarring male voice cut through the wind.

Victoria glanced up to find its source all too close. A hulking man stood before Harrison, jeering in her direction. Harrison tensed as he responded tersely, "How can I help you, sir?"

"You can send this here lass back in with Barnum's other freaks." The man cackled and, pointing at her face, said, "She'd be quite the draw in there with a face like that."

Mortification swarmed within her. She choked back hot tears with minimal success, and they joined the cool raindrops peppering her face in twin trails down her cheeks, the moisture on the left side navigating its rutted terrain more slowly.

Harrison, however, evidently felt a different emotion. He grabbed the man's collar with both hands despite the man outweighing him by a good many pounds. Face-to-face with the man, Harrison gritted out, "You are advised to disappear without another word."

Harrison released the man with a shove, and he stumbled back.

The man huffed another laugh. "I see now, hoss. She's yours and you want a fee for viewing her." Reaching for his pocket, the man said, "I can sure oblige you that, hoss—"

Harrison's fist connected with the man's jaw, interrupting whatever remaining foul words the man planned to say.

Victoria froze in horror.

And then the skies opened in an all-out downpour.

Did he just punch the man? Yes, there was his fist, still extended outward, his knuckles cracked and oozing blood. And through the torrential rain, the man's furious, bloody face. Although he'd never been too proficient at physics, Harrison knew beforehand—just as well as he knew now—his punch wouldn't have stopped that mammoth of a man. Which made his actions all the more absurd and dangerous.

"Run." Harrison grabbed Victoria's wrist and dragged her in his wake as he blindly sloshed between the booths and tents, seeking safety. The man bellowed behind them, but they possessed a speed and deftness the man's large size could never achieve.

After a few more twists and turns, the man's voice fading with every step, Harrison swung Victoria into a relatively sheltered gap between two tents. Their chests simultaneously rose and fell from the exertion, and they were both drenched from head to toe.

Victoria's bonnet was gone. Her hair spilled from its pins, the raven-black tendrils falling with abandon down her back. She looked stunning. And rather furious.

"That was a rather foolish thing, Harrison," she said, attempting in the tight space to tame her dripping hair back into a bun, all while glowering in his direction.

He flinched at the harsh way she'd said his name, so unlike the way she'd said it the few times before. His hackles rose in defense. "What would you have had me do, Victoria? Just ignore the way he was treating you."

She gave up on her hair and prodded his chest with her finger. "Ha. You're one to talk."

"What's that supposed to mean?"

"You've quite perfected the art of ignoring me."

"That's different."

"And pray tell, how so?" Her hands were on her hips now, her blue eyes a maelstrom of indignation.

He had steered their conversation down an uncomfortable path for him, and there was no way out. "It just is."

But as expected, she didn't abandon the topic. She didn't even need to speak. She just leveled her gaze at him until he crumbled.

"It's for your benefit that I keep away."

"And you're the expert on what's best for me, are you?" At the resolute set of her jaw, he nearly relented to this enticingly decisive creature before him.

"With this, I promise you I am," he bit out.

"And what do you think you're saving me from, Harrison?"

"Me," he said, sure his gaze was as piercing as the wind blustering through the gaps in the tent flaps.

The passing storm had cooled the air significantly, and a shiver coursed through Victoria's body. "And you're particularly villainous, are you? I don't believe you'd strike a woman like you just did that man. Although I haven't been too good a judge of character on that score in the past."

He winced at the self-loathing in her final statement. "This has nothing to do with you, Victoria."

"I feel like it has everything to do with me. If you're that repulsed by me—"

"My father treated women, especially my mother, with no regard for their feelings," he said, not letting her finish. She might as well know the whole truth of the matter. Let her judge him for who he truly was rather than conceal it any longer. He swallowed the distaste in his mouth. "The night of the accident. When my father claimed to have business in town. He was—"

Harrison paused a moment before releasing the shocking words. "He was with one of his mi—With one of his mistresses instead."

But she was confused, not horrified, by his revelation. "What does any of this have to do with your father?"

Was she serious? Wasn't it obvious? He'd have to spell it out for her. "All my life I've been told I'm my father's duplicate. We look the same, have the same mannerisms, and are engaged in the same career path."

An agitated expression finally crossed her face. Should he be happy or upset by it? She took a slight step back and flicked her eyes to the muddy ground and back at him, a hint of red blooming on her cheeks. "And you've—Have you acted like— like your father has? Toward women, I mean?"

"No, Victoria," he blurted, heat creeping up his neck. "I've never even gotten close enough to any woman to—" *This is going to pot in a hurry.* "What I mean to say is, I've vowed never to act like my father. And the easiest way to do that is to stay far away from the opposite sex. Well, easy, that is until you came along."

He released a breath of frustrated mortification. How pathetic his worst fear sounded when spoken aloud. But the truth of the matter was out now. Let her deal with it how she chose.

Seconds ticked by, during which Victoria searched his face with an expression akin to one working out a rather complicated math problem. Or a puzzle. It was all rather unnerving, but he determined not to let it show.

She stepped toward him, reigniting a heat between them, but one not sourced from anger this time. Did he not just explain why she should keep her distance from him?

"You know what I think?" she asked. Thankfully, she continued. He couldn't begin to guess what thoughts were circling in her head. "You're so afraid of *becoming* your father that you're keeping yourself from being the genuine you."

Her words were profound. He'd give her that. But they had one flawed premise, which he raised aloud, hoping his voice filtered out the vulnerability. "Except what if the real me is no better than he is?"

She paused for what seemed like an unending moment. "A few days ago, I might have agreed with you there." A wry grin quirked her lips, tugging unevenly to the right because of her scars. Still, she was beautiful. Even more so because she hadn't turned tail and fled by this point.

He let out a half-huff, half-laugh. "If you're hoping I'm comforted—"

"Harrison." Another small step and she reached out, placing her hand on his chest. "You've given me glimpses into what's really in here. You saved me and Isabella from a duel without thinking twice about your safety, and you've stared down everyone within a mile radius who has looked at my face."

So, his glares hadn't been subtle.

"You just punched a man who mocked me, for heaven's sake." She laughed. "And—"

"There's an 'and'?" he asked, braving a hopeful tone.

"Yes," she laughed again. "And you recite poetry."

He asked, "Poetry?"

"Yes, I've come to believe only the good-hearted read,

know, and especially write poetry." Another shiver wracked her body, her chattering teeth joining in.

He reached his hand to cover hers, stopping at the blood still trickling from his knuckles. "You're cold," he said at the same time she said, "Your hand."

She took his hand in her ice-cold one, examining the wounds more closely. Despite their disparity in size, her petite hand fit perfectly within his sizeable one. She withdrew a handkerchief from the pocket of her skirt and wrapped it snugly around his knuckles, muttering under her breath in a soft chastisement this time, "Rather foolish, Harrison."

He removed his topcoat and wrapped it around her shoulders, his hands snugging the collar in tight to her chin. Of its own accord, his right hand lingered on her shoulder, advancing to her neck, then her cheek. Her skin heated under his hand, and her eyes widened. His thumb traced over her lips, hoping to warm the hint of blue back to their usual rosy pink.

From her hair in a state that only a husband should see to the scent of her released by the rain's moisture, she was intoxicating. "I find I have many a foolish thought in my head today," he said, drinking her in.

But he'd acted too impulsively once already today, and he needed time to digest their conversation. To examine whether he shared her confidence in who he could be.

Summoning every scrap of resolve he possessed, he released her and stepped back. He took her hand again, which was slightly warmer now. "Come, let's find Isabella and get you two back to the hotel to dry off and warm up."

A different type of frustration crossed Victoria's face. Perhaps she was just as disappointed as he was that he hadn't kissed her, a fact which pleased him entirely too much.

Twelve

Victoria blinked her eyes open in the dark. She lay in bed at the National Hotel, her entire body veritably boiling. Last she remembered, Harrison had escorted her and Isabella back to the hotel, the three of them waterlogged and weary. Even with Harrison's coat around her shoulders, she had shivered uncontrollably while he explained what her body had experienced firsthand—a storm in this region of the country could drop the temperature by tens of degrees in just as many minutes.

Isabella had stopped Harrison at the door to their room at the hotel, assuring him she could handle things from that point. Victoria had discarded her sopping wet gown and donned a dry chemise, crawling under the covers while Isabella heaped her with extra blankets and whispered promises she would be her usual self soon enough.

She was now sweltering even though someone—Isabella, of course—had removed all but the top sheet in the intervening hours. What time was it? How long had she been sleeping? She tried to call out to Isabella, but pain seared her throat. Her head pounded, but it was nothing compared to the ache coursing through every joint.

A cool washcloth swept across her forehead, bringing fleeting relief to her scorching skin. She thrashed about in the perspiration-soaked sheets, turning on one side and then the other, glimpsing a dark mound under the covers next to her before sinking into oblivion again.

She woke an indeterminate time later to a still-dark room. The form beside her rolled over, kicking a leg into her shin. A hoarse and muffled "Sorry, Victoria" emanated from under the covers' depths. Isabella's voice.

Is she sick too? Then who's continuing to dispense the cool washcloths to her forehead? Surely not—

A second voice—hushed, but still strong and deep—spoke from her other side, near the night table.

Harrison. Was he talking to someone? Or perhaps reading something?

She squeezed her eyes shut. *Oh no. No, no, no, no.* He couldn't possibly see her in this state. Maybe if she just feigned sleep, he'd leave. *But how long has he been here?* She froze when he paused his quiet intonation and a chair—presumably the one he was sitting in—squeaked. He leaned over her, the smell calming. Reassuring. Alluring. He didn't touch her this time, though. He must be tending to Isabella too.

"Rather foolish, indeed," he muttered.

Another squeak of the chair told her he'd retaken his seat.

She held her breath. Would he continue his reading? Sure enough, he resumed his quiet, measured, one-sided dialogue. With her head still dazed, it took her a few moments to recognize what he was reading. Poetry.

His voice—typically contrived to be surly but now downright captivating with no pretense—only added to the heat coursing through her. With eyes still closed, she spoke the names of the poets in her mind as he recited their works aloud —Longfellow, Keats, Tennyson, and Wordsworth.

She wasn't sure how long he read, but she relished every moment. He finally stopped, snapping shut the book he'd been reading. She schooled the disappointment from her features, ensuring her face was still a mask of contrived sleep.

But he began again, reciting from memory since he hadn't opened another book. The words were foreign to her. She was well-versed in poetry, so why couldn't she work out which poem or poet this was? Granted, she wasn't at her finest at the moment.

> Four hooves conquer the hill's steep rise,
> A youthful beast still, yet with large churning
>   strides.
> From the mount, his dominion, he surveys,
> the rocks to bound over, the ripe fields to graze.
>
> Unbidden, his eyes, their brown orbs assess,
> the tree under which his dam took her last
>   breath.
> Gnarled limbs bursting with green leaves anew,
> the tree reminds he must begin again too.
>
> But a pounding behind draws his attention
>   back,
> to a steed with a coat—and a heart—of pure
>   black.
> His sire, whose blood courses through his own
>   veins,
> a creature so relentless that his son he chained,
>
> To a vile future, all dreams forced to forego.

And to anyone else, this would be a deathblow.
Yet to his colt, the sire unknowingly bestowed,
A stubbornness and a relentless resolve all
    his own.

A stubborn colt. Those words were familiar, yet the answer as to their source was just outside her reach. Harrison continued his recitation:

Hooves clash in a savage battle of wills,
Nostrils flare and teeth flash, aiming to kill.
Will father or son emerge victorious?
The youthful upstart, or the old hate so
    usurious?

Pure grit prevails, blood drips from each foe,
as the older limps off, defeated and slow.
A freedom so deserved, a hope so hard won,
over the tyrant father, and by his own son.

Victoria gasped—it was Harrison's poem. The one Isabella mentioned at dinner in Chicago.

Harrison abruptly stopped.

Her reaction must have been audible.

"You're awake," he said.

"I—er—yes," she croaked, her throat rough and raw. Embarrassment at her state of undress swelled to the forefront, and she grappled for the sheet, ensuring it was pulled all the way to her neck.

"You shouldn't be here." Her tone harsher than she'd intended, she continued, softer this time. "I mean, I appreciate your help, Harrison, but none of this is proper—that is, I don't know that you should—I'm not in a state where ..." Voicing aloud she was just two thin layers of fabric away from being entirely unclothed was even worse. And she likely looked atrocious. Did she even dare think about what she smelled like?

"I promise I acted the perfect gentleman while you were indisposed."

She couldn't quite read his tone. Was he jesting with her? Concerned his honor was being questioned?

"I didn't mean to imply you—"

"Victoria. It's fine. But I'm afraid Isabella isn't. She was right behind you in falling to the same illness. Soaked to the bone, just like you were."

Craning her neck in the opposite direction, she regarded Isabella's flailing form. "She's in for a rough time of it, is she?" How merciful she'd been unaware of all her body had endured.

"Unfortunately, yes."

Victoria turned back to Harrison. He was in a slightly rumpled white shirt, its sleeves rolled to his elbows, the top three buttons gaping open to reveal a glimpse of tawny skin underneath. She swallowed, wincing as fresh pain stabbed her throat. "How long was I—"

"More than a full day. It's"—he glanced at the watch fob he'd withdrawn from his trouser pocket—"just about four in the morning."

Victoria nearly sat upright but stopped when she remembered what she wore—or more accurately, what all she *didn't* wear. "But we are supposed to be on our way to Buffalo and Niagara by now. What are we to ..."

He reached out a reassuring hand, but again didn't touch her. He'd replaced her handkerchief bandage on his knuckles with a genuine one. "You can relax, Victoria. I've taken care of everything. We can stay here as long as we need for you and Isabella to recover. I've telegraphed ahead to our accommodations in Niagara, and they will welcome us when we are able. We can easily exchange our steamer tickets for new ones."

"Thank you, Harrison."

"Well, it's all my fault to begin with."

"So, you are all-powerful and can control the weather now, can you? If so, I have a request."

His husky chuckle at her quip sent her heart soaring.

"Sorry to disappoint you, madam, but I have no powers at all," he said, adopting a self-deprecating tone.

Her blue eyes captured his amber ones. "I beg to differ."

What on earth was she doing? Here she was, barely clothed, wrung out from her sickness, inches away from this all-too attractive man, and miles away from propriety, flirting. Or at least that's what she thought she was doing. Really, it was becoming too hard to tell as the circumstances threatened to overwhelm her again.

"I'm not entirely sure you've regained your lucidity, Victoria."

Okay, so she wasn't flirting. Or at least not as perceived by Harrison. A change of subject was the best remedy for her injured pride. "How are you? You haven't slept in this chair the whole time, I hope?"

"I wouldn't exactly call it sleep. More of a closing of my eyes for a bit here and there." He punctuated his assurances with a rake through his already ruffled hair. Still, he was inarguably handsome, even with the extra stubble prickling the defined planes of his chin and jaw and the half-moons shading under his eyes.

"You should really try to rest, Harrison."

"I'm all right. You first. I don't believe you're entirely through it yet."

She nodded her acquiescence, a sudden wave of tiredness washing over her.

"Is there anything you need?"

"More poetry?"

He raised an eyebrow. "You were supposed to be asleep."

A subject change had worked to her advantage before. "Water?" She didn't even need to feign the pleading in her eyes. Her throat was long past parched.

"Of course. My specialty." He rose, appearing even more towering from her reclined position on the bed.

He retreated to the door, his gait unhurried and assertive, his shirt taut over his shoulders and back. She must be on the mend if she noticed him so. When he shut the door behind him, she succumbed to sleep once again.

When Victoria next awoke, daylight filtered through the closed curtains in her and Isabella's room. A glass of water sat on the night table beside her, filled to the brim, while Harrison's chair was disappointingly empty. She must have been asleep when he'd returned with the water. But the additional sleep had revived her, though she was still somewhat weak.

She wiped the last vestiges of sleep from her eyes, then sat upright, preserving the sheet's position enough to drink without spilling water on herself. Harrison could re-enter the room at any moment. Her thirst quenched, her next two immediate needs—food and a bath—vied for precedence, but at a kick from Isabella's side of the bed, caring for her friend became first priority.

Except the door clicked open, halting her plans. She burrowed back under the sheet, ensuring she was entirely covered. If only she'd had a few more seconds' warning to at least comb her fingers through her hair.

Harrison's head peeked around the cracked door, and when his gaze connected with hers, his body followed. "You're awake."

She nodded. "But Isabella's still resting."

"That's good. Though I'm certain her stubbornness will get her over this in no time," he said with a wry grin.

A return smile split her lips. "I don't dare argue with that statement."

Silence pervaded for one beat, two beats, and she became all too conscious of her current state. What a fright she must look, but at least the unscarred side of her faced toward him. On the other hand, Harrison's borderline rakish state only amplified his handsomeness. Her stomach upended itself, and her need for food and a bath grew much less immediate.

As if reading her mind, Harrison said, more to his toes than to her, "I've ordered a tray and a bath for you."

Instinctively, her eyes traveled to the room's far corner, in which a large copper tub sat veiled behind a zig-zagged room divider. As if on cue, two maidservants bustled in.

"We've come to prepare your bath," one said, moving to light the gas furnace on the tank mounted to the wall above the tub.

"Th—thank you," she mumbled.

Harrison stayed near the door, which decreased the awkwardness in the air only slightly.

He paused, then cleared his throat. "I'll just …" He trailed off, gesturing over his shoulder before turning and slipping from the room.

Taking advantage of his absence, she scurried out from under the covers and behind the screen, her legs shaky with disuse and her head faint from rising suddenly.

The second maidservant released the valve on the water tank, piping hot water into the tub. She explained how to shut the valve when the tub was full, and after Victoria nodded her understanding and appreciation, both maidservants whisked out the door in the same efficient manner in which they'd entered minutes ago.

After availing herself of the nearby chamber pot while the tub filled, Victoria turned the valve to stop the water. With a single fortifying breath and a quick glance over her shoulder to ensure the door was firmly closed, she dispensed with her chemise in one hasty motion.

She stepped from the puddle of fabric on the floor into the water, first one leg, then the other, then finally her entire torso, stifling a sigh of pleasure at finally having a proper bath. She didn't want to risk waking Isabella.

Quiet settled over the room, broken only by the occasional splashes of water as she cleaned her hair and body with the soap powder the maidservants had left. The soap's stringent odor prickled her nostrils and raw throat, so unlike the soothing lavender aroma of her soap powder. Her powder, however, was across the room in her trunk, virtually inaccessible at present, so she made do with the hotel's.

Her ablutions complete, she reclined against the tub's sloping back, watching fingers of steam coil from the water's undulating surface. Cocooned in the water's warm embrace, she relaxed. Or at least as much as she could under the circumstances.

A crucial detail she'd previously overlooked niggled into her brain and all serenity fled. Her clean clothes were in her trunk along with her soap powder. On the other side of the room.

Thirteen

Uncomfortable didn't even begin to describe Harrison's current state. And it wasn't because he'd spent the last two days in the same rickety chair. No, rather, he was pacing outside the room where Victoria refreshed herself in an even more unclad state than she'd been in the past few days.

Not that he took unfair advantage of her in her sickness. Quite the opposite, in fact. He'd been exceptionally courteous, kept his eyes averted and thoughts benign.

But every man undoubtedly had his limits.

He pulled his watch fob from his trouser pocket. Twenty minutes had passed, though it'd seemed like ages. In all that time, neither a maidservant with a tray nor a fully clad Victoria had appeared at the door. *How long does it take a woman to ready herself? Surely she should be done by now?* After all, it took him less than half that time to dress.

As the minutes ticked on, his fears mounted. She'd been so fatigued. What if she'd lost consciousness in the tub? Or suffered some other trouble? With still no sign of another female to render him aid, he braced himself for the task that now seemed necessary. He wouldn't go in. He'd only knock and wait for Victoria's confirmation she was safe and alive.

He rapped his hand three times on the wooden door.

"Hello?" Victoria's whispered response contained an edge of trepidation. It also sounded far away. When he didn't initially respond, she continued. "Whoever it is, I need help, please."

His heart stuttered. She *was* in trouble. He cracked the door open, its hinges squeaking with the effort.

"Who is it?" her worried query originated not from a clothed figure on the bed, but from behind the screen. *She's still in the bath.* He had half a mind to close the door and turn tail, seeking the nearest maidservant he could find. But her anxious tone convinced him otherwise.

"Yes, Victoria," he whispered back.

She took a surprised intake of breath, but she said nothing further. Had he imagined her speaking in the first place? In his near sleepless state, perhaps this was all a deluded dream—no, nightmare—his mind had crafted. It was entirely within the realm of possibilities at this point.

"Would ..." she began, her teeth chattering. She had to be freezing by now. *What would influence her to remain in the tub for so long?*

Answering his unspoken question, she asked, "Would you mind retrieving me a clean set of clothes? I neglected to consider such a need."

Apparently, so had he. This was the most opportune time for a maidservant to return to assist. He waited a few breaths, but one did not appear. *Why weren't they present when they were needed most?*

Steeling himself for what the task would take, he kept his voice level, detached. "Yes, of course." In two quick steps he stood before her trunk, hesitating only a moment before opening it. She'd asked him to intrude into an area so private, after all.

Her lavender aroma wafted from the trunk's contents, and he closed his eyes and inhaled, ignoring what the scent was doing to his insides. Or at least he attempted to. *Focus, Harrison.*

True to Victoria's character, the trunk was well organized. He found a dress easily enough, bypassing the purple dinner dress for one of her preferred black ones.

Yet he couldn't make head nor tail of all the white, frilly pieces of fabric. Georgina was too young for him to have become familiar with women's clothing. *Are so many underclothes really necessary?*

"Any trouble?" she called softly from the corner.

He didn't want her to think he'd been dawdling, so he grabbed the dress and a fistful of the white garments. She could sort through what she needed. "Just finishing up," he said, hoping his voice conveyed a nonchalance he didn't feel.

Crossing to the screen, he arched the armful of clothes over the divide, keeping his eyes resolutely on the floor. As she took the bundle from him, her hand brushed his. Though he retreated to the doorway in two quick steps, he couldn't outrun his racing heart. He was in trouble.

Victoria couldn't get dressed quickly enough. Thankfully, Harrison had managed to retrieve everything she'd needed—and then some—but their stilted exchange from their respective sides of the screen when he'd handed her the clothes only compounded the flaming of her cheeks over what she'd asked him to do.

As the water drained from the tub, the door clicked open, followed by the clipped stride of a maidservant. "A tray, sir?" was the maidservant's polite inquiry.

"I—er—yes," Harrison started. "For the lady. The one behind the screen. Not the one in the bed. I'm just going to—I need to—I'll be back later." The door snapped shut on Harrison's strained response, and Victoria released a breath. He was gone. Now she could have a bit of time to regain her composure.

Fully bedecked and buttoned again, she rounded the screen and smiled at the young maidservant, gesturing for her to place the tray on the night table. "Thank you."

The maidservant curtsied her acknowledgement, then click-clacked out of the room. Ravenous, Victoria settled into Harrison's chair with the tray on her lap, and—with the benefit of no observers—devoured the tray's contents of a strong broth and yeasty slice of bread in a rather unladylike manner.

On returning the tray to the night table, however, the silverware slipped from the plate and clattered to the floor. Isabella released a startled grunt from the bed, and Victoria held her breath, waiting for Isabella to settle again.

"Victoria?" Isabella croaked.

She sighed. Luck was never in her favor. "I'm here, Isabella. I'm sorry about the noise," she said, picking up the silverware and returning it to the tray.

Isabella emerged from her nest of covers, hair and clothes in disarray, but with the usual gleam back in her eyes. "Praise be—I'm alive!"

Victoria laughed, pleased her friend was feeling plucky again. "Yes, so it appears."

"You look reinvigorated, dear," Isabella said as she finger-combed through her tangled dark tresses, wincing when she snagged a knot. "Rather rosy in the cheeks and all that. A good bath, I take it?"

Certain her cheeks were freshly flaming after her memorable bath, Victoria could only manage an "mmm hmmm" in response.

"Well, P. T. Barnum would be pleased his tent was worth all this fuss. I haven't been so sick since the measles at ten years old. I was worried for a moment, there, that we might have caught cholera at the inn in Chicago. But never mind, we are on the other side now. And Harrison seems to have been spared, thankfully." She took a breath and peered around the room as if just now registering his absence. "Wherever has he gone?"

If Isabella expected Victoria to answer, she didn't give Victoria time to do so. "We do quite owe him, don't we? I had managed tending to you until the chills had me shaking so badly that Harrison ordered me abed. He even used his feigned sternness, so uncooperative I was." She let out a small laugh and waved her hand in the air. "Sure, he was a bit off-putting at the beginning of our journey."

Victoria nearly snorted at Isabella's understatement.

"But I'm so glad you have been able to see through it, Victoria. I daresay *you* may have even caught *him* off guard."

"My scar has a tendency to do that," she said, reverting to the ever-familiar self-effacing tone.

Isabella waved her hand again. "Pish-posh. Not in that way, dear. I'm surprised—no, no, that's not the correct word." Isabella scooched her way to the edge of the bed, placed her hand atop Victoria's, and squeezed. "I'm so pleased at seeing the real you—well, for lack of a better word—unveiled. This self-possessed Victoria is rather remarkable."

Victoria's cheeks burned with a new type of discomfiture. She'd never been able to handle praise with grace before, even as scant as it had been in her past. "Thank you, Isabella," she managed, turning her hand upward to squeeze Isabella's in return. "I do feel changed." Then, with a tease to her tone, she added, "Now, whether it's for the better or for the worse, remains to be seen."

Isabella's mouth curved into a grin, her eyes glinting with mischief. "I know of one gentleman for whom it's been for the better."

"You, my friend, are clearly mad with hunger. I'll go ring for a tray." Victoria made to stand, to avoid the uncomfortable turn the conversation had taken, but Isabella held her hand fast.

"I know Harrison. And I know you. Why, maybe I should take offense if you think I'm so thick-headed not to have noticed." Isabella's tone contained jest, but Victoria still squirmed under her pointed inquisition.

She met Isabella's eyes. "Yes, but you know what limits my situation imposes on any potential husband."

Isabella opened her mouth to answer, but the click of the door interrupted whatever she was going to say. Victoria glanced over her shoulder. It was a maidservant, not Harrison, and her stomach dipped in disappointment.

"Oh, miss, I would simply love a bath drawn and a food tray too," Isabella said, taking her usual command of the situation. "Thank you, dear."

The maidservant cleared Victoria's tray from the night table, and Victoria thanked her before she whisked out of the room again.

Isabella climbed out of bed, stretching deeply and collecting clean clothes from her trunk before disappearing behind the screen. They wouldn't be continuing their earlier conversation; the moment was lost. As was any chance of an answer to the question now burning in Victoria's chest—how would Harrison feel if he knew it wasn't just her face she'd concealed from him?

~

"I'm so glad I convinced you to get the green one," Isabella said, nodding to Victoria's new dress. Victoria stood with Isabella, Harrison, and three hundred other passengers queued to board the *Mayflower* for the overnight trek across Lake Erie.

She fingered the satin sapphire of her new gown, marveling at the way the setting sunlight danced across the fabric in prismatic waves. Clad also in the fresh bonnet and pair of cream, kid leather gloves she'd unearthed from the bottom of her trunk, she advanced along the steamship's wooden loading platform as turned out as ever. Which only served to churn her already agitated stomach that hadn't even had a full day to recover from its illness.

After waking from their sicknesses without Harrison— who'd begged off, claiming he had work to do—she and Isabella had spent the rest of the afternoon together. Still, there'd never been the right opportunity to revisit their earlier interrupted conversation.

Instead, at Isabella's persuasion, they'd patronized the modiste around the corner from their hotel and had both come away with new dresses. Victoria had spent far more than she'd planned to at the shop; her usual penny-pinching ways as cast off as her veil. But then again, she was long overdue to replace her fading mourning wardrobe. She and Isabella had fortuitously found dresses that fit well enough without custom tailoring. And although the necklines didn't reach as high as those of her mourning clothes, her new dresses weren't nearly as revealing as her purple dinner dress.

Harrison had reappeared shortly after the women's trip to

the shop, seeming surprised to find them dressed and packed, ready to board that evening's overnight steamboat to Buffalo. Isabella had waved off his repeated queries about whether they were feeling well enough for the journey, shooing him out the door to pack his things so they wouldn't miss the eight o'clock departure, all the while explaining she'd already negotiated the exchange of their tickets with the front desk attendant. It seemed no one could avoid Isabella's persuasion.

Or her walking stick. Even now, as everyone clambered aboard the *Mayflower*, Isabella brandished it to keep their fellow travelers from crushing too close. Victoria claimed the least crowded spot on the metal railing, and Harrison and Isabella came to stand on either side of her.

Harrison was altogether too close and too far at the same time. He seemed to need to meet her eyes as much as she needed to avoid his, but he had come out the victor yet again, trapping her gaze with his. "Are you certain you're all right, Victoria? We could have deferred this trip another day."

At his gravelly whisper and unrelenting gaze, her stomach engaged in a rather absurd form of acrobatics, adding an embarrassing breathiness to her reply. "We both know it would have taken more effort to have disagreed with Isabella than to have crossed Lake Erie tonight."

Humor sparked life into his amber eyes and tugged a wry half-grin from his lips. "No truer words, madam. No truer words."

She recalled Isabella's remark earlier about how she'd been able to see through Harrison's "feigned sternness." But Isabella was wrong. It wasn't her who had seen through anything. Rather, it was Harrison who was letting down his usual barriers. For her.

Whether from too little food during her sickness or too much familiarity with Harrison, her midsection now resided somewhere near her throat. A state exacerbated every time Harrison's elbow brushed her arm in the crush of bodies on deck.

She willed away the memories of her stomach's mutiny during her last water voyage and took a few, deep, fortifying breaths. Surely an inland lake wouldn't be nearly as turbulent as the open ocean, right?

Fourteen

Apparently, Victoria would never get a full night's sleep in this country. Terrified screams pitched with the *Mayflower*'s lurching, preventing any rest whatsoever.

She finally abandoned her efforts at slumber and sat on her bottom bunk, gripping the metal bars for stability. Her eyes slowly responded to the dimly lit surroundings, the ship's turbulent rolling and rocking only adding to her disorientation. Isabella was already up and out of the top bunk, attending to their two cabinmates, comforting them with, "It'll all be over soon, dear."

They elicited slightly quieter shrieks with the next sway of the ship.

One woman whispered in a rich Southern accent what Victoria took to be prayers, while the other was alarmingly quiet in between screeches.

Isabella whispered another reassurance, "This two-thousand-two-hundred-ton ship will get us through this gale."

Calmed somewhat, they settled, but their saucer-sized

eyes remained wide, the whites almost luminous in the intermittent lightning flashes.

Victoria stumbled across the confined quarters to the cabin's sole circular window, stifling a rise of queasiness at the movement. Would that she could keep control of her stomach this time around.

Thankfully, she'd taken the stewardess' advice earlier that evening to remain dressed overnight. Waves higher than any she'd ever seen in the ocean battered the *Mayflower*'s flanks, causing the ship to groan and creak in eerie harmony with the roaring winds and crashing waves.

A retching noise followed by the smell of sick reminded her she wasn't alone. Victoria turned to find the Southern woman in an all-too-familiar position with a bucket, crying uncontrollably in between bouts of sickness.

The other woman was still unnervingly silent.

Not wanting to upset the Southern woman further, Victoria refrained from covering her nose, trying to breathe through her mouth instead. She also didn't want to meet the woman's same fate. She must distract herself. Her oils would help both her and her cabinmates. Ginger would curb the nausea and vomiting, along with maybe a dab or two of peppermint. And lavender, of course, to help with the nerves.

Victoria scanned the small cabin, but her small leather valise with her acupressure supplies was nowhere to be found. Not under the bunks or within her or Isabella's trunks or valises. The ship tilted to the right, sending her stumbling. She caught herself with her elbow, wincing at the painful contact that would surely leave its mark. Assuming they survived this night.

Despite the tumult inside the cabin, her head cleared long enough for her to remember her valise's location. During the hubbub of boarding the ship, Harrison had offered to take the women's hand luggage with his and deliver it later to their cabin. Her small valise had likely been left behind in his cabin. She shouldn't wake him, though without the valise, the women would go unaided. She couldn't sit by and let that happen. Not when she had the means to assist. She must ask Harrison for her valise. Besides, how could anyone be sleeping through such turmoil?

Her mind made up, she called to Isabella. "I'm going to retrieve my acupressure supplies from Harrison's cabin. I won't be but a moment."

Without waiting for a response, Victoria left the cabin and staggered down the narrow passageway, her hands held fast to the twin metal rails on either side as she navigated the twists and turns within the ship's underbelly in what scant light the deck prisms refracted from above.

She lost her way a time or two, turning around and retracing her steps each time. She must have covered all two-hundred-and-eighty-three-feet of the *Mayflower*'s length by now. And why did her mind choose at such a moment to recall these precise details from one of Isabella's travel pamphlets?

She turned another corner and down a passageway marked with doors numbered in the one-hundred-twenties. Yes, she was close now, recalling the cabin number Harrison had offhandedly told them as they were boarding—128. The doors on the right-hand side were even-numbered. 122, 124, 126. There—128.

The *Mayflower* plunged in two different directions at once —up and to the right—too quickly for her to brace her fall with an outstretched arm or elbow. Instead, her head connected with Harrison's door with a resounding *thump,* and her world flickered to black.

～

A loud thunk woke Harrison, and he lay in his bottom bunk, hopelessly willing sleep to return. His bunkmate, a grizzled, former sea captain, still slumbered, according to his snuffling snores above.

But the noise against his door sat discordant against the storm's other sounds. It was of a different tone and origin, and it lacked the repetition of a knock.

His curiosity overruled his inertia, and he blundered his way to the door like a man too deep in his cups.

But no one stood outside the door. That's odd? Why would someone play a trick at a time such as this?

He was closing the door when his eye snagged on a flash of blue on the floor.

Within the puddle of blue fabric were milky white limbs and coiled strands of glossy black hair.

Victoria!

Kneeling beside her, he registered the rise and fall of her chest and expelled his breath. Good, she was still breathing. But what had happened? Had the noise against the door been from her?

With one hand under her shoulders and the other behind her knees, he swooped her up and—with little contemplation—settled her into his bunk. Curled on her left side, she bled from a small gash near her right temple. Harrison withdrew a handkerchief from his pocket and staunched the trickle of red.

Her hair had wrested itself from its pins, and he brushed a wayward strand behind her ear as his eyes slipped to check for a pulse. Thankfully, it thrummed strong and steady. A good sign, even though she hadn't regained consciousness. But he'd witnessed Georgina in a similar condition far too many times over the last few years to be fully comforted.

Victoria appeared peaceful, at least. And downright beautiful.

Another noise struck his door—this time a real knock—and he crossed the room and opened it. Isabella stood on the other side, drumming her fingers impatiently on her skirt.

Before he could speak, she peeked around his shoulder despite her small size to where Victoria lay on his bunk. Her eyes rounded in shock, and she pushed past him to Victoria's side. "What happened?"

"She must have lost her balance," he said, hoping to convey the very rational reason Victoria was in his bed. "And hit her head. She was unconscious when I found her."

"Oh. Poor dear. No wonder she was gone for so long. I was getting worried. Well, we mustn't move her. These head injuries can be quite serious, you know." A pitch in the ship sent Isabella grappling for the metal bars of the bunk. "I'm afraid I have my own invalids to tend back in our cabin. I trust you can care for her here." A loud snort from above drew Isabella's attention upward.

"Captain Ernest Delaney," Harrison said by way of introduction to the sleeping man.

Isabella pursed her lips. "Well, chaperones are typically older *women*, and an awake one at that, but I suppose we can't be too picky in times like these." Her eyes alighted on something across the room. "Ah. Victoria's valise. What she— and now I—came for." Case in hand, Isabella strode to the door, calling over her shoulder. "Come for me immediately if she takes a turn." Then, she was gone.

Harrison returned to Victoria's side. Her head had stopped bleeding, but she'd still not awakened. Gingerly, he sat at the end of the bunk and eased her head into his lap, careful not to jostle her too much. He gently tucked a stray tendril of hair behind her ear and then trailed his fingers over her cheek. At least some color had worked its way back into them. The ship rocked less forcefully now, and fatigue washed over him. He relaxed his head back against the cabin wall and closed his eyes.

I'll just rest for a minute.

∼

Victoria awoke enveloped in a safe, contented warmth she'd never before experienced. Where was she? The last thing she remembered was falling into oblivion. Is this what the afterlife felt like? Had she and the three hundred others aboard the *Mayflower* met their untimely demise last night at the hand of Lake Erie's fury?

But surely her head wouldn't be throbbing so if she were in non-earthly realms. She must be back in her bottom bunk aboard the ship. Yes, there was the usual calm rocking that confirmed they were still afloat.

No longer able to contain her curiosity, and although doing so would surely exacerbate her head pain, she fluttered her eyes open. This wasn't her cabin, and this wasn't her bunk. Her pillow was a pair of legs—*Harrison*'s legs.

She made to sit up, but a weight over her shoulder blocked her. And did it—? Yes, it did. It imperceptibly tightened. Harrison's right arm was the weight slung over her, holding her firmly, almost possessively. A slight wiggle from her and it pulled her even closer to his solid frame. His *warm*, solid frame. A responding warmth swirled in her belly. Self-reproach for the impropriety swiftly followed. She had to move.

"Harrison," she whispered.

No response other than the rise and fall of his chest against her told her he slept on.

She pushed against his legs, trying to extricate herself, but he only tightened his hold in response. Still, he slept, oblivious to their current state.

Her body, however, was all too aware.

His warmth, his smell, his commanding presence even in sleep. It was too much for her already swirling head.

"Harrison," she said, louder this time, and accompanied with as much of a shove as she could manage against his legs.

He startled awake, then released her. Her motion, combined with his, sent her careening off the bunk and into an ungraceful heap on the floor. She landed hard on her bruised right elbow and sucked in a sharp breath at the fresh stab of pain. Her vision swam, her head spun, and her stomach churned.

"Victoria, are you all right?" Harrison's voice was thick with sleep as he peered, bleary-eyed, over the edge of the bunk to where she was sprawled. "Why ever are you on the floor?" His face was one of innocent concern. Did he truly not know of their imprudent state just moments ago?

Her body heated, likely from having to explain what had transpired between them. But wait, no, this was another kind of bodily instinct. "I'm going to be sick," she croaked.

Harrison leaped into action, retrieving the washbasin just in time. As her stomach purged its contents, Harrison gathered her unbound hair away from her face. "Shh," he murmured, rubbing circles on her back. Though they were small movements—just a few inches at most—they were having far too large an impact on her already mutinous stomach.

When she finished, he discreetly removed the washbasin from her lap, and she brought her knees to her chest, crossed her arms, and buried her face in them. Now that her humiliation was complete, she fought her body's next reflex— tears. Hadn't everything else he'd witnessed on this trip been lowering enough? Apparently not, for this was much, much worse.

"Aye, this one ain't got her sea legs yet I see."

Victoria raised her head in alarm at the strange voice, quashing another wave of nausea as her head spun with the sudden movement. *Who on earth?*

An older man scrutinized her from the top bunk, his beard and hair an untamed, wiry white. A few gold teeth glinted from within his smile of friendly jest.

"Captain Delaney, ma'am," he supplied in answer to her unspoken question. "Yer chaperone." Another toothy grin. "And mostly a good one at that." He paused to scratch his beard, presumably where his jawbone lay hidden underneath. "Yep. You two were mighty cozy a bit ago, but still above board by my reckoning."

Victoria's gaze snapped to Harrison's, and his features transformed from confusion to understanding. "Victoria, I—" He swallowed, his Adam's apple bobbing with the effort. "Nothing untoward happened. You hit your head. I put you here." He gestured to his bunk. "Isabella said not to move you, I —I sat here at the end and had your head in my lap so I could assist you when you awoke. I must have drifted off to sleep—"

Victoria held up her hand and dipped her head to her lap. She really needed to stop moving her head so quickly. "Harrison. No, I'm sorry. I imposed. Over stepped. You've lost quite a lot of sleep on my account already on this trip." She let out a half-huff, half-laugh. "I'm like a needy newborn child who can't seem to leave you be."

"Victoria."

She wouldn't—couldn't meet his eyes. Unshed tears lumped in her throat. She toyed with the fringe on her dress. Oh, if only Lake Erie really had swallowed her last night.

"I've always avowed that raising Georgina has been more than my fill of being a parent," he bantered. Then, in a more serious tone. "This is not that. I promise you."

His words held more comfort than he could have known.

Still, she couldn't stay another moment. She needed time to recover her composure—both physically and mentally. She teetered to her feet, steadying herself on the bunk railing. "I must go check on Isabella and the others." At least her voice only cracked a little. Harrison reached for her, but she waved him off. "I'm quite recovered. Thank you, Harrison. Good day, Captain Delaney."

"At least let me escort you back," Harrison said.

She reluctantly nodded, then walked out of cabin 128 with as much false dignity and balance as she could muster. She didn't take his arm, though. Nor did she slow her pace to walk beside him. Mercifully, she found her cabin again with little trouble.

Harrison trailed her the entire way, and she thanked him over her shoulder and under her breath before crossing the threshold. The other women's excited chatter barraged her.

"Are you feeling better?" Isabella asked. "I trust Harrison took good care of you?"

"Y—yes," she managed. "Though I'm feeling quite ill myself now." It wasn't a complete lie. "Please if you don't mind, I would like to lie down and rest."

"Of course, dear. Don't let us stop you," Isabella reassured.

Victoria tumbled into her bunk and burrowed her face into her pillow. At a not-so-quiet whisper of "Was she with a man?" tinged in a Southern accent, Victoria let loose the flood of tears.

Victoria's stomach had yet to fully recover from its riot a few hours earlier. Very few other passengers had appeared for dinner, not more than a third of the *Mayflower*'s passengers, by her guess. Perhaps they'd also been seasick and were still recuperating. As she scanned the *Mayflower*'s Gothic grandeur, her breath hitched anew, even after almost twenty-four hours aboard the ship.

The long saloon boasted soaring ceilings that arched into gilded grapevine moldings. Quite the contrast to the porcelain spittoons that nearly outnumbered the green upholstered chairs and sofas on the room's outskirts.

"Why, it's vanilla ice cream, Victoria." Isabella bounced in her chair at their meal's final course served in cut-glass bowls with tiny silver spoons.

If only she could mirror even a small fraction of Isabella's ever-present enthusiasm.

Victoria gave a noncommittal noise of approval, then glanced from her ice cream to where Harrison conversed with the Southern woman from her cabin—a Miss Emily Jameson—

who had made quite the miraculous turnaround from last night.

A quintessential Southern belle, Miss Jameson was all golden ringlets and grace, packaged in a startlingly bright pink and shockingly low-cut dress with nary a blemish or scar on her porcelain-white skin. Victoria frowned and turned her head away, catching her reflection in one mirror flanking the end of the saloon. The light emanating from the chandeliers hanging above cast her scar in deeper relief and tinged her purple dinner dress toward drab. She averted her eyes from the grotesque sight to the rich, velvety carpet cushioning the waiters' footfalls as they went about their business.

But when Miss Jameson tittered at something Harrison said, Victoria's gaze strayed their way again. Miss Jameson rested her hand on Harrison's forearm and leaned forward to provide him with a view of what was already so prominently displayed.

Victoria's gut knotted and her heart wrenched, and she instinctively raised a hand to ensure her hair hadn't escaped the twist she'd wrangled it into. She was being ridiculous. What right did she have to feel anything about Harrison's attentions toward another woman?

In rebuttal, her rebellious mind recalled this morning's events—waking with Harrison's arm wrapped around her. The smell, the feel, the warmth of his body pressed against hers. Desire swelled in her belly, fighting—or was it joining forces? —with jealousy.

Her whole body flushed hot, and she spooned a bite of the cold, buttery yellow confection to quell the heat.

"However do they keep it frozen?" Isabella questioned.

Ah, Isabella was still on the topic of the ice cream.

"We are in the middle of a lake, by all means," Isabella continued in between spoonfuls.

Victoria would focus on Isabella's question instead of the Miss Jameson and her motives toward Harrison.

"Why, Mr. Wright, you must tell me all about New York City," Miss Jameson's sultry voice cooed from across the table. So much for vowing not to listen in.

If only the surroundings would prove a more steadfast distraction.

Victoria forced her eyes to the engine situated in the very center of the room, where it and its inner workings could be viewed from the twin glass windows enclosing it.

Remarkably, the assortment of cranks, levers, gears, and dials all performed their intended duties with no human instruction or intervention. They too gleamed of polished steel or bronze and mechanically whirred and hummed in oddly comforting harmony.

"A lawyer. Why, how admirable." Miss Jameson's crowing broke the engine's trance over Victoria.

Victoria glanced across the table, her eyes first registering Miss Jameson's hand on Harrison's forearm again before rising to Harrison's face. Inscrutable to those who didn't know him, his face was a mask of polite acquiescence to Miss Jameson's remarks, though he clenched his jaw slightly and tightened his grip on the dessert spoon. Miss Jameson, however, appeared unaware of her unintentional blunder in fawning over Harrison's occupation.

Victoria suppressed a smug smile. Her emotions this evening were indeed ugly. But she wasn't about to interject.

Let Isabella and her perpetual garrulousness save Harrison from Miss Jameson. Except Isabella was in animated conversation with the man wearing a palmetto-hat to her right.

Victoria sighed. She would have to intervene after all.

A uniformed steward blew one short call on a whistle

looped about his neck. A timely interruption. "And now, we dance," he announced, sparking a flurry among the passengers as they rose and congregated to the couches and sofas on the periphery. Dozens of uniformed crew members swooped in and cleared away the dinner dishes, pushing the tables and chairs to the fringes. Meanwhile, a four-piece orchestra entered and, after taking their seats in the far corner, began tuning their instruments.

Dancing? Aboard a ship? Would she ever be unsurprised by American customs? She turned to her right to gauge Isabella's reaction to the evening's entertainment, but her friend was no longer there. She scanned the room but couldn't find Isabella in the chaos.

She did, however, see Miss Jameson. The woman guided Harrison away to the far corner of the saloon, casting a triumphant smirk over her shoulder at Victoria. Quite a vitriol-laced expression for someone supposedly possessed of southern charm.

Still, Miss Jameson possessed more than enough skin-deep beauty and youthful energy, which most men would favor over a scarred, on-the-shelf widow. While Harrison didn't seem like most men, she hadn't known him long. Perhaps she'd misinterpreted his American gentlemanly manners as interest.

Spirits low, Victoria turned to the other corner of the room and sank into a chair beside two silver-haired women. They scrutinized her, their eyes lingering longer than was truly necessary on the left side of her face. She sighed, mindlessly roving her hands over the chair's carved arms, fingering the ridges and grooves in the cocoa-brown wood.

The orchestra struck a lively tune, and Victoria's eyes unwittingly strayed to Miss Jameson. She flitted over the dance floor in Harrison's arms, beaming. Victoria didn't recognize the dance, but one of her neighboring matriarchs remarked it was the American-made-famous "Portland." It appeared to mimic the polka, but then again, she hadn't had too many opportunities to become well-versed in dances.

"Aye, and here I thought the man had eyes for you." The gravelly voice to her right caused her to jump.

Captain Delaney. While his beard defied taming, his hair had obeyed a comb, and he was dressed in tan slacks and a faded navy coat with at least one missing button. No elaboration was needed to translate his comment, for he, too, watched Miss Jameson and Harrison.

"Well, Captain, as you can see, he's found a far prettier companion." Had she effectively concealed the acerbity in her voice?

"Strange, that." He scratched at his beard, still not taking his eyes from the couple on the dance floor. "Usually, I have a knack for these sorts of things. Seen many a besotted man in my day. Hate to think my gift is failing in my old age."

They both fell into silence for a moment before Victoria composed herself and changed to a neutral topic. "Are you here for the dancing, Captain?"

He guffawed, the sound echoing deep in his belly. "Aye, no, my dear. My left leg still hasn't been right since the *Montgomery* ran aground in '12." He pointed one gnarled finger toward the offending appendage before continuing. "I came above deck to refill my 'liquid courage.'" He opened his coat and gave her a glimpse of a small silver flask in his inside pocket.

"Liquid courage." She couldn't help but smile. "Well said, Captain. If only I had some."

With a gleam in his eye, Captain Delaney slipped the flask from his pocket and held it out to her. "What's stopping ye, aye?" The flask glinted in the saloon's chandelier lighting, beckoning to her.

Well, why shouldn't she? She was here for an adventure, after all. She hesitated only a moment more before taking the flask from Captain Delaney's outstretched hand and tossing back a large swallow, studiously ignoring the sidelong glances of the women to her left.

The liquid seared the back of her throat, clawing its way into her nose. Tears sprang to her eyes, and she coughed once, twice, three times to clear the burn within her.

Captain Delaney laughed again. "Aye, it'll getcha that first time for sure. The second time'll be better."

She handed the flask back to him. "Thank you, Captain, but once was enough for now." Maybe forever. Her throat had to stop burning at some point, right? The captain bid her good night, and with one last glance at the dancers, he limped to the stairwell leading below deck.

The music slowed into the romantic strains of a waltz, and despite her self-admonitions to the contrary, Victoria couldn't keep from watching Miss Jameson and Harrison as they performed the intimate, three-beat dance with undeniable grace. They made a handsome pair. Miss Jameson's fair hair was in stark contrast to Harrison's dark mop, her petite frame fitting well within his large one.

Harrison's gaze connected with hers from across the room, and she startled, dropping her gaze. He'd caught her staring. She'd only met his eyes briefly, too short a time to decipher how he felt about having a woman such as Miss Jameson in his arms.

Her whole body flushed hot. Whether from embarrassment at being caught gawking, or from the crush of bodies in the room, or from the lingering heat of Captain Delany's liquid courage, she needed cool air. Immediately.

She stood and exited through the double glass doors of the saloon and into the refreshing early October air, heaving a sigh of relief that the deck was empty. She made her way to the railing. The water churned and splashed below in a constant clash with the *Mayflower*'s wooden hull.

"Victoria, are you all right?"

She'd know that voice anywhere. Slowly, she pivoted.

Harrison stood several feet away as if he knew she wanted space. He tried to catch her gaze, but she won out this time, averting her eyes to the wooden planks of the *Mayflower*'s deck. She didn't need to remind him of her blemishes when he had just been looking upon the youthful, flawless face of Miss Jameson.

"Quite all right, Harrison." Her voice quavered only slightly. "I thank you for your concern, but as you can see," she gestured with her hands, "I'm all in one piece. You may return to dancing with Miss Jameson now."

"Are you sure? You appear a little green." He took a step closer. She shifted back in response, her back now flush with the ship's metal railing.

She had nowhere to go.

"I can assure you, Harrison, I'm not feeling sick anymore."

Silence filled the space between them. Finally, she raised her eyes. He studied her with a rather amused smile.

What does he find so humorous?

He arched his brows, the scar above his right eye disappearing beneath his hairline. "No, not sick. I was referring to a different type of green. That of the envious type."

Victoria's mouth gaped. Had her feelings been so obvious? In any case, she wouldn't shy away from the topic. Especially with the fortification from Captain Delaney's flask. "Well," she assumed an air of nonchalance she didn't feel. "Miss Jameson possesses attributes in quite an abundance and to a degree which most women couldn't compare." Gesturing to her face, she continued, unable to mask the acerbity in her voice. "Myself included."

Harrison's cheeks colored slightly. Ha. So, he had noticed Miss Jameson's attributes. She made to turn around, but stopped when Harrison cleared his throat and said, "A woman with a keen mind is far more attractive to me."

She all but scoffed. *Yes, just the way to make herself more becoming in his eyes.*

Harrison stepped closer and continued, "and one with courage and pluck."

Another step closer and her traitorous heart thumped harder. He was within arm's reach now. "And one who cares deeply for others. And helps them selflessly."

A final step and they were toe to toe. Her breath came in deep, uneven puffs, her heart all but hammering out of her chest now.

His scent hung in the air, heady and far more intoxicating than the liquid in Captain Delaney's flask. He raised his hand and cupped her cheek, the warmth of his touch plunging all the way to her toes. "And who is, without a doubt, unassumingly beautiful. Inside and out."

His gaze pierced hers, the amber of his eyes molten with unspoken want. She stood there speechless, breathless, as he dipped his head toward hers.

Harrison's thumb explored ahead of his lips, first tracing her jawline, then moving down her neck's smooth expanse. It skimmed back and forth over the defined ridge of her collarbone, his calloused fingers surely grating over her impossibly soft skin. His fingers dove into her hair, undoing whatever elaborate style she'd put it in.

When his lips found her ear lobe, her gasp fanned the smoldering heat in his belly. He needed more of her.

Determined to savor her, he trailed kisses along her jawline, but as restraint gave way to impatience, his pursuit of her lips took precedence. She, too, had become impatient—she turned to meet his lips.

What a delusion to have thought finally kissing her would tamp his desire. That he wouldn't want even more of her. Certain he was crushing her, he mustered one last scrap of self-control and pulled back slightly. Victoria communicated her displeasure at the minuscule separation by closing the distance again, pressing all of herself into him.

The blaze in his stomach was now an all-out inferno. He was acting as if he were a small child off leading strings for the first time, stumbling headfirst into danger. Danger. The warning bells clanging in his head—the ones he had resolutely been ignoring—reached a crescendo and he broke the kiss, resting his forehead on hers. Victoria's ragged breathing mirrored his, his right hand deep in her ebony curls, his left hand ending perilously close to danger on her right ribs.

His hand rose and fell with her short and shallow intakes of breath, her warmth seeping through the fabric of her gown into his fingertips. The smell of lavender, of her, permeated everything and further warmed the pool of desire within him.

Yet he refrained from going back in for more. He'd lost control, been too forward. Humiliation burned through him.

"Victoria, I—I'm sorry," he said, his voice hoarse and his eyes unable to meet hers. The only way he could regain his grip on his decorum would be to release her. So he did. And then he turned and dashed into the welcome abyss belowdecks.

Sixteen

Back in his cabin, Harrison could almost pretend the last half hour hadn't occurred. That he hadn't just kissed Victoria. Thoroughly kissed her. A more pleasant endeavor than even when he'd had his arm wrapped around her this morning.

Unlike Miss Jameson, who was quite the unpleasant dinner and dancing companion. Miss Jameson, well, the only way he could put it, was *counterfeit*.

He paced back and forth across the small cabin, surely creating a rut in the ship's floorboards by now. *What had he been thinking?* Clearly, he hadn't been thinking at all. Foolish indeed. This was why he stayed far away from women. Yet, the past few days in Victoria's company had been some of the best he'd ever known, even with sicknesses and storms and little-to-no sleep. He could truly be himself around her.

But what must she think of him now? How dim-witted to have charged off after that kiss? At the memory of his lips on hers, her body molding to his, heat flushed through him, and he shed his coat and rolled up his shirtsleeves to tamp it down.

Pushing the distracting thoughts aside, Harrison threw himself onto his bunk. What was he to do next? Unfortunately, now was not the time to go to her. They'd be docking at Buffalo within the hour. Plus, Miss Jameson would be in Victoria's cabin too. No, it'd be better to wait until they had a moment alone. Later.

Raking his hands through his hair, he leaped back to his feet and spun on his heel for another trek across the cabin, jumping at a flash of navy from the top bunk. Captain Delaney. In his haunting introspection, he'd all but forgotten about the man's existence.

"Good evening, Captain." Hopefully the man registered his dismissive tone and would leave him to his thoughts.

"Ya kissed her, eh? Made up for your blunder earlier, dancing with the other one. The young chit?"

Harrison sighed. He couldn't begin to unravel the layers of Captain Delaney's perceptiveness. How in the world had the captain deduced so much? "Mrs. Clarke and I"—Harrison cleared his throat—"We reconciled."

"Aye, I'll say." Captain Delaney grinned. He was far too enthusiastic about this topic. "So why are ye in here instead of still out there with her?"

"I—er. I extracted myself. To restore propriety."

"Oy, mate. You're a daft one. So how ya gonna make it up to her?"

Harrison had no answer, and he let the question hang. Still, it dominated his thoughts as he alternated between packing and pacing in the final moments of the *Mayflower*'s trek across Lake Erie.

As he, Victoria, and Isabella joined the three hundred others disembarking at Buffalo in the fading light of dusk, the question still plagued him. Thankfully, when he bid *adieu* to Captain Delaney on the pier, the older man didn't probe the topic further. Rather, he simply gave Harrison a hearty handshake and a knowing look.

After they boarded yet another train car destined for Niagara, he tried to catch Victoria's eye, but she dodged his glances. The more it happened, the more intentional it seemed. If only he could find a moment alone with her to discuss what had happened, but people overloaded the railcar.

He huffed out a frustrated breath. He'd finally connected with a woman, only to have thoroughly mucked it up. Right now, he was more a "forlorn and shipwrecked brother" in Longfellow's "Psalm of Life" than one "with a heart for any fate."

And it was all his fault.

Victoria's emotions vacillated between frustration at herself for letting Harrison kiss her in the first place, to anger at him for breaking the kiss so soon and then running away.

And what a kiss it had been. Harrison's true personality revealed itself in his affections—bold and daring in declaring his wants, yet still attentive and considerate of her needs. Physical intimacy with Silas had always been on his terms, with his comforts and pleasures in mind. Never in her years of marriage had her body craved another's affection as it had during the fleeting moments of Harrison's kiss. The skim of fingertips, the brush of lips, the whisper of endearments—it'd awoken something within her, something that told her the small morsel of what they'd shared wouldn't be enough. For her, at least.

Harrison, on the other hand, had broken the kiss and then said he was sorry. Sorry he'd kissed her? Did he truly not feel even an inkling of the magnetism she'd felt between them? Or was she such a terrible kisser that he had no other choice than to end it and escape? After all, having only kissed Silas and now Harrison, she was woefully inexperienced.

He'd tried to catch her eye a few times since they'd disembarked from the ship earlier that evening, but she had to remain resolute. She didn't need to hear it from his lips—the kiss was a mistake.

He regretted it.

Which is why the best course of action was to ignore him and the incident completely. They could go back to loathing each other for the next several days before parting ways forever —he, remaining in New York, and she, returning home, an ocean's distance away.

For the last two hours on yet another train, she'd craned her neck to the window and the black nothingness beyond at her left, trying her hardest to ignore Harrison's commanding presence an arm's reach away.

Isabella had piped in now and then with travel information, to which Victoria could only muster a nod here and there in acknowledgment. Harrison, conversely, had been completely silent. He was probably sleeping, blissfully unaware of her inner turmoil. She wasn't going to risk a peek to find out.

"We'll exchange the rail here shortly for a carriage, which will take us across the suspension bridge to the Canadian Province and the Clifton House." Isabella's confirmation that this interminable train ride would soon be over provided a small reprieve from the despondent thoughts circling in Victoria's head.

In the absence of any response from her carriage mates, Isabella warmed to her topic. "It's unfortunate the top portion of the bridge isn't open quite yet. Then we could take the train all the way across instead of traversing the lower portion via carriage. We're just a few months too early," she finished with a laugh that fell flat on its audience.

Silence pervaded their transfer from the train to the carriage. Thankfully, Isabella sat next to her again. However, the usual trouble of Harrison's long legs resurfaced with him seated across from her. Especially when they jolted down what had to be the worst road in America. When the carriage wheels weren't deep in a hole or rut, they were rolling rather unsuccessfully over tree stumps. She clutched the seat, gritting her teeth each time her knees collided with Harrison's.

If only her body weren't so aware of him, so tuned into his every move. She couldn't even escape his scent. It lingered in the confined space and did traitorous things to her heart.

The carriage climbed in elevation, plunging headlong into the pitch black of night. At least, the carriage's lantern light wasn't strong enough to illuminate the steep drop to the river below. Though, it would be nice to see the waterfalls instead of only hear them. As their carriage lurched ever closer to the bridge, the falls' unceasing plunge rose from a low reverberation to a resounding roar, vibrating deep in her chest.

At the suspension bridge's entrance, the driver pulled the horses to a stop. Then, after they paid the sixty-cent toll and assured the customs officer no one in their party was a smuggler, the carriage wheeled onto the bridge's slightly less-bumpy wooden planks and into the air between America and the Canadian Province.

Isabella jittered with excitement next to Victoria. "We are now over two hundred feet above the river," she blurted, pointing out the window on the falls side of the carriage. She'd likely been waiting most of their journey to share that fact. "And the river below us is over two hundred and fifty feet deep. Can you fathom that?"

Victoria pictured plummeting off the not-yet-complete

structure to the churning rapids below. Her vision swam, and she closed her eyes, breathing deeply. As they rattled across the bridge, something brushed her left hand, which was sitting atop her knee. The touch was so light. Had she imagined it? But no, there it was again.

She peeked her eyes open.

Harrison's right hand brushed her left again in a silent question.

Her eyes rose to his. Though he still faced out the window, he caught her gaze sidelong. A boyish grin that didn't entirely conceal a mischievous undertone hitched the right side of his lips. Lips that, not too long ago, had been on hers.

His actions went beyond those of an unaffected acquaintance, didn't they?

Regardless of where his affections stood, though, she'd been wrong about being able to ignore him and the kiss they'd shared. She could never go back to the way things were before. This captivating, complicated man irreparably changed her. Now, hopefully he wouldn't shatter her heart completely.

Seventeen

By mid-morning the next day, Victoria sat in the window seat at Clifton House, just across from the river, peering through the thick clouds outside. She had yet to see the falls they'd traveled so far to see in person, and now the weather threatened to also cancel their Behind the Sheet Tour scheduled for that afternoon.

Isabella barely contained her frustration at the predicament. "What a disappointment. I am beyond eager to see these infamous falls. Ever since landing in America, everyone I've spoken to has been in raptures over them. And now this." She paused in her pacing and gestured outside the window to the foggy blanket that had entrenched itself in the gorge.

She dropped with a sigh onto the window seat beside Victoria. "I suppose I should stop my complaining. I need a diversion. Tell me, dear, what is the latest with you and Harrison?"

Victoria's cheeks heated at Isabella's change of topic. She must not have seen Harrison take her hand in the carriage last night. Where to begin? Victoria swallowed, stalling. "He seemed to enjoy dancing with Miss Jameson."

"Pish. She was a ninny."

Victoria snorted at Isabella's frankness, and Isabella grinned before schooling her face into a more serious expression again. "My dear, some women will go to great lengths to get attention from a man, even if it isn't favorable. To those such as Miss Jameson, any attention is as good as none. I do expect Harrison to know the difference." Isabella paused and thought for a moment before continuing. "He didn't make any advances, did he?"

"Not where Miss Jameson is concerned, as far as I know," Victoria hedged.

Isabella arched an eyebrow. "Interesting choice of words. I do feel as though you are leaving something important unsaid, my friend."

Victoria's eyes darted out the window and then back to Isabella. "Well—he—er, we kissed."

Isabella squealed and squeezed her in a hug. "My dear. This is an exciting development." Isabella released her and scrutinized her face. "But then what about yesterday's tension between you two in the train car? You both act as though I don't notice these things," she chided.

"I am just as puzzled as you, Isabella," she said. "After the kiss, he ran away."

"Harrison, Harrison," Isabella tsked. "What are we to do with him? I'm certain he was just scared."

Victoria gestured to her face, not hiding the sarcasm in her response. "Yes, I know I am quite terrifying."

Isabella waved away her self-deprecation. "Stop that, will you? No, I mean, he fears how he feels about you. In all the time I've known him, he's kept himself distant from women. It's all his father's doing, really, serving as such a poor example of a doting husband and father." She rose and began her pacing again. "We need a plan."

"Isabella, I don't think—"

"Well, clearly I can't leave this to the two of you to sort out. There's less than a week remaining in our trip together."

What was Isabella's intention? Panic rose in Victoria's throat, but she stifled it, trying a different approach. "I think Harrison and I just need a chance to talk. Any scheming would only work to frighten him further, don't you think?"

Isabella paused in her pacing and nodded. "Yes, yes, quite right. Our travel arrangements lately haven't allowed for that. I'm an ever-present third wheel. I'll do my best to make myself scarce, dear." A gleam sparked in her eyes. "While still serving as a chaperone, mind you."

She blushed, and Isabella grinned. "I'm mostly teasing. Just know how happy this makes me for you both." The sun split the clouds and filled the room with radiant light, capturing Isabella's attention to the window. Her smile beamed as bright as the sun's rays. "Well, if that just isn't a sign, then I don't know what is."

Squinting through the brilliance, Victoria's breath caught. Her imaginings fell short of the truth of a hundred-foot tall, half-mile wide wall of raging water. The trees were clad in their autumn attire of crimson and orange leaves, and a rainbow arched across the river, as if Mother Nature were making up for not cooperating earlier. Mesmerizing didn't come close to describing what was before her.

"Those are the American Falls directly across," Isabella chimed in, pointing her finger against the window glass for emphasis. "And those," she moved her finger to the right where the cusp of another falls began, this one taller than the last, "are the Horseshoe Falls. Simply magnificent, aren't they?" Then, after a brief pause and a single clap of her hands, she said, "Well, what are we waiting for? Let's get closer."

~

Victoria ate lunch with Isabella and about twenty others in the dining room. According to the proprietor, the Clifton House had settled into a quieter state now that the peak summer season was over, so most of the room's three hundred seats remained vacated. But Victoria preferred it that way. Harrison was notably absent, but she did her best to ignore the empty seat to her right.

The usual American flair for expediency accompanied lunch's service, and after dining, they were ushered out onto the Clifton House's green front verandah and into a melee of carriage drivers all vying for their business.

Shouts, insults, and even a few punches were hurled about, multiplying Victoria's trepidation. A hand grasped her elbow, and she startled. She glanced over her shoulder to find Harrison just behind her.

"I'm here," he whispered.

Her mind rushed back to the last time they'd touched, and her whole body flushed. She retreated one tiny step to quell the reaction.

Still, his presence in the tumult comforted her. How had this man so quickly gone from the root of her terror to her source of safety?

He guided her and Isabella behind him, taking command of the situation. "You there," he said, selecting the least sinister-looking driver over the one offering the cheapest fare.

The driver gave a gap-toothed grin and collected the coin Harrison proffered him. Victoria approached the carriage, warily eyeing the step and splashboards attached by only a rope. What other parts suffered similar dilapidation? Would the conveyance even survive the trek back across the suspension bridge?

Harrison held out his hand expectantly, and Victoria had no choice but to get in. Isabella entered the carriage after her and, scheming woman that she was, claimed the entire rear-facing seat. "I'd like to see the view from both windows," she explained all too innocently.

Harrison entered and took the only spot left, next to Victoria. Though she squeezed against the carriage wall as much as possible, his large build consumed all the remaining space—and air—next to her.

Harrison rapped twice on the carriage roof, and it sprang to life, carting them down the narrow, serpentine drive from Clifton House. As their carriage hugged a precipice hundreds of feet above the churning Niagara River, Victoria clung to the handle inside the carriage. Perhaps last night's journey in the dark was preferable to what the light revealed today. Now she could see the true danger of traversing such a road with no barricade. Especially in their ramshackle carriage.

She wiggled in her seat, trying to find the spot with the most stuffing while repeatedly brushing a hanging piece of roof fabric out of her eyes. Harrison's right leg was directly adjacent to hers, and his right hand perched rather nonchalantly on his knee. How was he so unaffected by everything?

They reached the suspension bridge once more, this time headed eastward, and Victoria closed her eyes and held her breath, pushing the fingers of her right hand into the hollow behind her ear to curb the mounting vertigo. She needed her lavender oil.

Someone took her left hand, and she startled, opening her eyes to find Harrison leaning into her. His touch conveyed what words in that moment could not—*Trust him*. With a caress that was hesitant at first, he turned her hand over, palm up, and nudged the cuff of her dress sleeve down a few inches. At his touch, gooseflesh prickled along the exposed skin, her body overcoming in an instant the mental bulwark her brain had taken painstaking effort to build.

He held her hand slightly aloft and skimmed his thumb down her wrist a few inches before settling it firmly against her skin. Belatedly, she recognized his intent. But how did he—how could he—?

A small, knowing smile quirked his lips. "A book from your valise," he whispered in answer to her unspoken question. "It fell out in my cabin on the *Mayflower*."

Not only had he read about something important to her, he'd actually remembered the acupressure remedy for vertigo. "May I?" He let go of her left hand and gestured to her right, which, in her shock, remained frozen behind her ear.

She nodded. "Thank you, Harrison," she whispered, turning toward him slightly and proffering him her right hand. He repeated his actions with this hand, taking more time than was truly necessary in grazing his thumb across the sensitive skin of her wrist to find the correct location. He held his thumb and her gaze steady, his rugged jaw and tousled hair alluring.

He released the pressure of his thumb, and she made to pull her hand away. But he held fast to it, dipping his head and pressing a single kiss to the warm spot where his thumb had been. A delicious shiver traveled the length of her. *Mercy.* Her head spun, but not because of the vertigo this time. He released her right hand and snagged her left one again, and she nestled her hand in his. They'd both neglected to put on their gloves, so the full warmth of his hand flush with hers melted into her.

Victoria turned her head to enjoy the view out the window,

hoping to hide the giddy smile cracking her lips. But she hadn't been fast enough, and she caught Isabella's perceptive smirk *en route*. A scheming woman indeed.

~

Harrison held fast to Victoria's hand in the carriage. But were his actions enough to convey what his words could not yet? He still hadn't found time alone with her to explain himself.

This morning, he'd been engrossed in responding back to his stockbroker's favorable news from his earlier telegram. An exciting turn of events, Harrison didn't want to raise any false hopes without hearing the stockbroker's confirmation first. Having entirely overlooked lunch and nearly missing the carriage, he'd had no opportunity to speak with Victoria, especially with the ever-present Isabella.

Last night, he'd had to settle for taking Victoria's hand in the nearly silent carriage ride. He'd more boldly claimed it in the daylight just now—had even given in to the impulse to kiss her wrist. But the touches left him needing more.

This had to differ from his father's affectations toward women. How could it not? After all, Miss Jameson had nearly thrown herself at him on the *Mayflower*, but she'd held no allure for him.

With Victoria's hand now settled in his, a myriad of emotions—some more frightening than others—traversed him, all of which pointed toward a growing attraction for her, if his heightened pulse and swirling stomach at just being near her were any indication. That flash of a smile she'd tried to hide after he'd kissed her wrist renewed his grin. How had he gone from brooding to besotted in just a few short days?

Their carriage trembled to a stop, interrupting his ruminations. It was for the best, though. If given enough time, his mind would entertain the thoughts circling the periphery of his consciousness. The thoughts that asked the sensible, reasonable questions, like what could truly become of this connection between them? And what could he truly offer her besides a broken man with an unfulfilling career in partnership with a father he loathed, and with a dependent adolescent sister to boot?

Victoria withdrew her hand from his—a natural reaction given they'd reached their destination—but his intruding thoughts gave the movement a sense of agreement with his internal reproof. His smile sobered into a grim line, and he exited the carriage, handing Victoria, then Isabella, down. How much were he—and she, for that matter—willing to gamble on something with such low odds of a favorable outcome?

Eighteen

Victoria stood at the brink of more than one powerful thing that could entirely destroy her, her thoughts as turbulent as the "Hell of Waters" to her right. Perched on the tip of Luna Island between the rushing Bridal Veil and American Falls, Mother Nature's tumultuous beauty cascaded below her. The water's vibrations echoed in her ears and chest as it plummeted unceasingly over the precipice at her feet, flinging drops of spray back into her face. The October day had warmed, and she angled her head to soak in the sun, closing her eyes against its brightness.

Unbidden, her thoughts strayed to the other disastrous force she was up against, one she didn't—couldn't—name. It was too fragile, too fleeting, as evident in Harrison's ambivalent attentions in the carriage. One moment, they'd been holding hands, and in the next, he'd released himself from her with a scowl. It was as if crossing the arched overpass to Goat Island had brought him back to the bleak reality of their situation. What conclusions had he drawn? And would she ever have the opportunity to add her input before he dismissed the notion altogether?

His aside about Georgina on the *Mayflower* had given her some small measure of hope at any rate.

Isabella's excited chatter reached her, and she turned to find her friend rounding the corner of the walkway on Harrison's arm. Isabella had taken the short footbridge to Goat Island to check with the tour company on their departure time, somehow roping Harrison into her errand too. Victoria had stayed behind for a final few moments alone with the view and her thoughts.

As the duo approached, her eyes, as usual, pivoted to Harrison. He'd slowed his gait so Isabella could keep up with his long stride, and Victoria used the extra few seconds to take him in. Attraction buzzed within her. Yes, he was undeniably handsome, especially in a custom-fitted jacket and trousers perfectly cut to his figure. But what lay within fueled the pull on her, what he normally kept hidden from others versus the outward appearance he couldn't conceal.

He glanced up and met her eyes.

She smiled, well aware that doing so would pucker her scar unnaturally. She really should have practiced smiling in front of a mirror before now.

He replied with a small smile. It wasn't much, but it was better than the scowl he'd had when they'd disembarked from the carriage.

"I know I could stare at that view forever too, dear," Isabella called as she released Harrison's arm and joined Victoria at the railing. She scanned nature's panorama before them. "Beauty and terror have formed a perfect combination here, have they not?" Isabella sighed deeply. "But, alas, we must go. Our guide confirmed that he is ready for us. We don't want to miss our Behind the Sheet Tour after coming all this way."

Isabella squeezed her hand and swiveled. Victoria couldn't turn from the magnificent view to walk with her friend until a few moments later, but Isabella was nearly to the footbridge already, having bypassed Harrison, who stood a few paces back.

"She's quite quick when she wants to be," he said as Victoria approached. Amusement glinted in his eyes, and he proffered his arm, which she took. His warmth seeped through the fabric layers separating them, a welcome sensation, especially as they left the sunny outcropping for the wooded path back to Goat Island.

"A veritable force of nature," Victoria added to their stilted exchange. Silence pervaded, interrupted only by their shoe heels clipping across the footbridge running above the rapids. Isabella was far ahead now, a flurry of green skirts on a very determined mission. They had limited time before joining a crowd again, so she tried for a more neutral topic. "Have you visited the falls much, them being half in your home state?"

"Sadly not." An edge crept into his voice. "My work travel has not led me to such exciting places as we've seen on this trip."

"This trip has had more excitement than I believe any of us had bargained for," she quipped, blushing at the implication her words could have. "Duels and storms and punching men in the face," she added, trailing off, intentionally leaving out any mention of their kiss.

Harrison chuckled, the sound raising her spirits. "The latter rather deserved his punishment, I do believe."

"Rather unsporting of you not to give him a chance to defend himself."

"I prefer my face intact, thank you." He froze, the lightheartedness gone. "Victoria, I—I didn't mean—"

He had meant no aspersions on her appearance by his remark. She placed her free hand on his upper arm. "Harrison. It's all right."

"I'm sure you're feeling rather like punching me yourself now." His voice was thick with self-reproach.

"No. I much prefer your face intact too," she replied, hoping he caught her jest. She took far too much pleasure in the red creeping his neckline at her unabashed teasing.

"I do believe that must mean you find me handsome." His cheeky grin was back, and she let out a small laugh at how quickly he'd gone from humble regret to mock boasting.

"I do. As does every other woman within a half-mile radius of you."

"That's where you're wrong."

"Oh, really?"

"Yes, I'm certain it's only a quarter mile."

She nudged him playfully with her elbow. "And your modesty surely only attracts the women more."

He halted, turning to face her, wearing a serious expression. "Victoria, you must know, you're—"

"There you two dawdlers are." Isabella rushed toward them, a ball of frenetic energy.

Victoria reluctantly tore her gaze from Harrison's, his unspoken words left hanging. Isabella and her inopportune timing.

"Here, take an oilskin." Isabella ushered them into a small wooden building where rows of black slickers hung waiting.

Victoria chose a relatively dry one and donned it, the oversized garment nearly swallowing her entirely. The oilskins were apparently only one size. Like Victoria, Isabella drowned in hers, and they both rolled the sleeves to free their hands.

Meanwhile, Harrison pulled rather unsuccessfully at his cuffs trying to cover his wrists, but to no avail. A few inches of his coat sleeves remained exposed underneath.

Victoria stifled a chuckle at their seal-like appearance.

"Come on," Isabella said, tugging her arm and dragging her to the opening of a staircase clinging to the edge of the sheer cliff face eight stories above the jagged rocks below.

Though enclosed in wood, the staircase renewed Victoria's vertigo, and she gripped both sides of the railing. Having likely seen more than its fair share of Niagara's elements, the timber clawed through her gloves and threatened to leave slivers in its wake.

"It's okay, dear." Isabella's attempt at soothing held the smallest morsel of exasperation. "Biddle's Staircase has stood for over twenty-five years. Not even that boulder in '47 could bring it down. It's solid. One step at a time, my friend, and we'll be at the bottom in no time."

Victoria couldn't ruin her friend's excitement. Isabella had traveled all this way and had already been more than patient with her other misgivings and missteps during the trip.

As if having yet again sensed her distress, Harrison came up from behind her and squeezed her shoulder, whispering in her ear. "You can do this. I'm right here."

She wished he would continue speaking, perhaps even finish what he'd been about to say earlier when Isabella had interrupted. But no, now wasn't the time to try to continue the conversation, for her present circumstances afforded little opportunity for anything other than survival. She closed her eyes and inhaled a deep breath, holding it for a few seconds before releasing it with a whoosh. She opened her eyes. Yes, she could do this. She would.

As she edged down the steps one at a time, Harrison never once expressed frustration over her slow progress, and Isabella kept her impatience mostly concealed. Victoria, however, declined to peek through the periodic portals in the enclosure. She did not need to see just how high she was. Isabella's intermittent exclamations of the view beyond were enough.

Finally, her feet hit rock instead of wood, and she cast a triumphant smile over her shoulder at Harrison.

He squeezed her shoulder and leaned in close. "I knew you could do it."

Isabella's voice cut through a horn blare. "The *Maid of the Mist*! We must hurry!" She took off, scurrying over the rocks with extraordinary agility to where the rest of the group waited on a rudimentary dock several paces away.

Victoria winced and forged ahead, trying to catch up. But she kept slipping on the slick rocks underfoot, only keeping upright because of Harrison's steady arm catching her elbow. When they finally joined the group, everyone else was already aboard the paddle-wheeler.

"Another boat," she groaned, steeling herself for leaving dry land yet again.

Harrison gave her hand a reassuring squeeze. "It's a short journey. Come, let's make Captain Delaney proud with our sea-prowess, shall we?"

She sighed, then muttered, "In America, the capabilities of English ladies are very much overrated."

Dipping his head to hers, he whispered, "I happen to highly rate your capabilities."

How had he heard her over the commotion of their surroundings? And had anyone else heard his remark?

He straightened and ushered her onto the boat with a nonchalance belying his flirtatiousness moments earlier.

The rascal. Ducking her head so she wouldn't subject the others to a beet-red *and* scarred face, Victoria turned and squeezed next to Isabella on the boat's starboard-side railing.

Isabella raised an eyebrow in her direction, which Victoria studiously ignored.

Harrison pressed himself into the last remaining spot on her right, and she willed her body to calm itself. Just when her pulse quieted somewhat, the boat angled left, furnishing her first unobstructed view of the entire Horseshoe Falls cataract and sending her heart rate soaring again.

As the *Maid of the Mist* chugged into the panorama of towering, tumbling water, the roar grew thunderous, drowning out the other group members' excited chatter. The colossal column of mist created at the water's convergence soaked her hair, face, and clothes, permeating the gaps in her oilskin with little effort.

She swiped her face clear of the moisture again and again, and the coiffure she'd painstakingly pinned together this morning was now a sodden, tangled mess. So much for trying to impress Harrison. He, however, still appeared so becoming, even while drenched. Drops of moisture clung to his obsidian hair, glinting when the sun's light captured them at just the right angle. He raked his hands through his hair, sending the locks into a devilish state of damp disarray. She permitted herself one small moment to gaup before Isabella's clutch on her arm brought her back to reality.

A huge grin split Isabella's lips as she shouted over the cacophony. "The front view is the only one for Niagara. Simply splendid!" Despite being just as water-logged as Isabella, Victoria laughed at her friend's unfailing enthusiasm.

"Yes," she said in a return holler, smiling and wiping a fresh layer of spray from her face. "Simply splendid."

The *Maid of the Mist* angled her bow westward and, a few minutes later, paddled abreast another dock. Isabella clucked with dismay. "We've arrived at Table Rock all too soon. But at last, we are ready to go behind the great sheet." She winked and released Victoria's arm, and they shuffled off the boat after the other group members.

Harrison came up behind her, placing a reassuring hand on the small of her back. Even through the drenched oilskin, his touch scorched her skin.

He leaned down to her ear again. "Do you have one more staircase in you?" he whispered.

Innocuous as his comment was, her heart involuntarily stuttered at his warm breath on her neck. They reached yet another spiral staircase twisting down a sheer cliff face, and her heartbeat notched even higher.

"Harrison, we ascend that afterward, not now," Isabella chided, her eagle ears as perceptive as ever. "Come, you two, hoods on."

Victoria put on the oiled calico hood Isabella proffered and stood before the dark chasm of rock.

She followed behind Isabella and Harrison, navigating the narrow path snaking along the cliff face. Shale fragments crunched beneath her boots, and the incessant rush of cascading water grew its loudest yet. After a few minutes, she startled to a stop. She now stood behind the great sheet of water Isabella had so raved about.

It was mesmerizing in a terrifying sort of way. Mother Nature's unchecked power descended a mere arm's length away—a power that could sweep her off her feet in an instant and into the churning whirlpool several stories below.

The wind gusted through, pelting her with yet more moisture. The hood was a useless device, for the spray blew everywhere—in her eyes, ears, mouth, up her sleeves, and down the back of her oilskin and, yes, even her dress. Under all her layers of clothing, her skin erupted in gooseflesh, and she staggered and shivered her way along, her loyal half boots squelching with each step.

She'd lost sight of the others but followed the path as it veered right, away from the sheet, and widened slightly, affording an increasing reprieve from the tempestuous scene directly behind the sheet. After what seemed like an interminable trek, but was likely only a few hundred feet, she reached a larger opening in the rocks where the other group members milled about, chatting quietly with each other.

Her ears hummed in the relative quiet following the past several minutes of deafening noise. Dropping her hood to her shoulders, she spotted Harrison and Isabella near the back of the group, closest to the rock wall, and picked her way in that direction.

She caught Isabella's whisper to Harrison of "leave it up to me" before Isabella turned to face her and beamed. "Well, dear, what do you think of Termination Rock?"

"It's er—appropriately named," she supplied cautiously, suspecting Isabella had been scheming again.

However, Isabella's face was a mask of innocence. "You are quite the joker when you want to be, dear." She laughed, then, swiping a rivulet of water out of her eyes, she patted the wall and continued, "Quite the impenetrable piece of limestone, no?"

Victoria wasn't quite sure what more could be said about the rock.

"I'll just go ask the guide a quick question," Isabella continued, sparing Victoria the trouble of responding. "You two take your time." Isabella gave Harrison a not-so-subtle, pointed look before scampering off toward the guide.

An awkward silence hung in the air between them. For once, Harrison avoided meeting her eyes. He scuffed his boot toe along the loamy dirt path and opened his mouth as if on the verge of saying something, before shutting it again. He glanced over his right shoulder—and her gaze followed his—

to where the group members were making their way out of the Termination Rock tunnel. If he wanted to speak, time was running out.

Isabella trailed the others about halfway down the tunnel, then turned back and gestured with her hands in what appeared to be a *go on* motion. Isabella could be insufferably embarrassing sometimes.

Victoria returned her attention to Harrison, who was now raking his hands through his hair, a sign he was flustered. "Harrison—" she started, at the same time he blurted, "Victoria—"

He let out a strained laugh, cleared his throat, and said, "This is not a time for ladies first." He cast another peek over his shoulder before finally meeting her eyes. Unchecked vulnerability swirled therein, and her heart lurched in anticipation of his next words.

"Earlier. Above ground, near the staircase. The first staircase," he amended, reaching up and tucking a wayward lock of her hair behind her ear. His hand lingered, trailing down to cup her face, scars and all.

Victoria swallowed, certain her beating heart drowned out the falls' reverberations in the cave.

"You must know there are no other women. That you're the only woman I've felt—that I've ever had these types of feelings for."

He'd laid his heart bare, his eyes equal parts expectant and hesitant as he awaited her response.

But words would fail her, travel-weary and dripping wet, tens of feet deep in a cave below a churning waterfall.

No, now was not a time for words. Now was a time for action.

Victoria clutched Harrison's oilskin coat and pulled his lips down to hers.

Nineteen

Harrison stood stock-still while his brain comprehended what his body was sensing. Thankfully, the wait was short, and his body made up for lost time, pulling Victoria tight against him. Her body, initially timid and rigid, melted into his, and he angled his head to deepen the kiss.

Victoria's once-cold lips were now warm and pliable under his and far from shy in declaring her desires. The fact that she'd initiated the intimacy, that she'd boldly claimed her want for him, especially after his admission, made him only crave her more.

Victoria took his bottom lip between her teeth, and he emitted a rather ungentlemanly-like groan. But then again, the feelings swirling within him were far from gentlemanly, and besides, she'd smiled against his lips at his reaction. Well, two can play at that game. He freed his lips and sent them on a journey of her jaw and neck, rediscovering the cavity just below her ear, a place he'd learned was a favorite of hers.

She rewarded his efforts with a gasp of "Harrison" in his ear and a tangle of her hands in his hair. Her cry held a note of displeasure at no longer being in control of the situation, and if he could speak right now—which he couldn't—he'd admit he was no longer in control either. No, there was a more powerful force at play here that they'd both succumbed to when their lips had met, and it'd completely undone him.

He was just making his way back to her lips, rather intent on and eager for the task before him, when he registered an "ah-hem" in the periphery and felt Victoria freeze.

Reality crashed down, bringing with it a tide of embarrassment. Here he was, essentially ravishing the very woman he was supposed to be serving as an escort for, and in a dark corner of a dank cave like some sort of menacing, gothic-novel-type monster.

He reluctantly pulled away from her. But Victoria didn't appear regretful, maybe a bit embarrassed like he was that Isabella had caught them in *flagrante delicto*, but definitely not remorseful the kiss had happened. "Sorry," he whispered, feeling anything but. "I—ahem—got a bit carried away."

"Are you going to make it a habit of apologizing every time we kiss?" she asked, her voice husky and her breathing still erratic.

He grinned. "Does this mean you intend to kiss me again?"

Her cheeks flushed further, and her lips curved into the most becomingly bashful smile he'd ever seen. Her lips were swollen from his kisses, and a jolt of possessiveness shot through him. He made them that way.

As bold as he was acting, he expected a demure response from her, but she said, with mock dispassion and formality, "I believe that was much too pleasurable not to be repeated, Mr. Wright."

"I concur, Mrs. Clarke," he said, adopting the same mock formal tone despite the grin expanding on his face. "I wholeheartedly concur." His eyes lingered a second longer on her before he reluctantly released her and turned to face their chaperone.

Isabella stood silent, her crossed arms just barely peeking out from under the oversized oilskin sleeves. How could a woman he had an advantage of both age and height over give him such a thorough reprimand with a single look?

"Isabella, we were—we are—" he began.

"Are you two quite finished?" Isabella finally spoke, her voice echoing in the near-empty cavern.

He couldn't quite tell what Isabella was thinking from her tone of voice. From the evidence before her, however, it probably wasn't in his favor. When he'd asked for Isabella's help earlier to find a few moments alone to talk with Victoria, he had not intended for things to go in the direction they had. Victoria had initiated the kiss, after all. Not that he could tell Isabella that, though. No, he was supposed to be the gentleman, and the responsibility for what had happened rested entirely on him.

He glanced over at Victoria to gauge how she was faring under Isabella's scrutiny, ready to act the hero falling on his sword. Yet, when he met Victoria's gaze, her eyes glittered with mirth, and her hand—the one he didn't have still grasped in his—pressed to her lips to conceal a smirk.

She was trying not to laugh, a feeling that became quite contagious the more he fought it. They both ceded seconds later, falling into fits of laughter at the absurdity of their situation. Here they were, grown adults, both nearly into the third decade of their lives, acting like young lovers stealing kisses in whatever dark nook or cranny presented itself.

Incapable of words, Harrison merely shrugged sheepishly at Isabella, who seemed to be trying her hardest to avoid the humor herself. Isabella's lips twitched, but she kept her face schooled into one of utmost propriety. "If you two are quite done gazing upon Termination Rock—" She paused while he and Victoria completed another round of involuntary snickers. "Then let's go get our certificates before the tour guide gives us up as having gone over the edge, and I lose out on the piece of paper I've worked so hard for."

Isabella, a black oilskin specter gliding along, led the way out of the Termination Rock tunnel, back behind the great, roaring sheet, and up the metal spiral staircase to Table Rock House. There, they exchanged their borrowed, soaking-wet oilskins for a souvenir of dry, overpriced woolen blankets and a certificate, signed by the proprietor, Thomas Barnett, declaring they had "passed behind the Great Falling Sheet of Water to Termination Rock, being 230 feet behind the Great Horse-shoe Fall."

By the time they emerged from Table Rock House to hail a carriage back to Clifton House, dusk had settled. As a result of Isabella's continued cunning, he and Victoria sat side-by-side again. Ensconced in her blanket, with her hair a tumbled mess and her eyes sparkling with shared humor and affection, she'd never been more beautiful.

He itched to pull her in for another knee-buckling kiss, but given the bystander within the carriage, he settled instead for tucking her in next to him. As she nestled her head on his shoulder, with his arm around her, her loveliness and a hint of lavender enveloped him. He could grow quite accustomed to this comfortable intimacy with her.

A companionable silence pervaded the carriage, all of its occupants presumably spent from the day's excitement. Or lost in thought, like he was. Harrison replayed in his mind the kiss with Victoria—numerous times—and the inanity of their young-lover-like cavorting in the cave. True, they both might no longer be young. But were they in love? How was a man who'd never experienced such a state to know?

Another day, another early train ride, but Victoria was quite enjoying this one for a change. The ambiance still left much to be desired. The benches were just as hard and wooden as those on the other train rides. The train floor was just as covered with apple-cores, chestnut-husks, and streams of tobacco-juice. And the passengers were just as eccentric in their amusements of storytelling, whittling, smoking, and singing "Yankee Doodle."

Rather, it was one passenger in particular who made this leg of her journey pleasurable, and he just so happened to be sitting beside her. Even now, Harrison's nearness ignited a visceral reaction within her, likely the one responsible for her wanton actions in the cave yesterday. Every time she recounted her boldness in claiming his lips, embarrassment joined the swirling within her belly. She pressed her gloved hands to her cheeks, hoping the coolness of the kid leather would douse the heat flaming therein.

"How are you faring, Victoria?" Harrison's murmur near her ear did little to help her gloves' assignment.

She dropped her hands to her lap. "Quite all right, thank you," she replied, meaning it, except for her body's uncooperative ability to recall their kiss with nary a prompting.

He took her hand in his and rubbed circles on her palm

with his thumb. She liked it—very much indeed—but it did little to keep her thoughts focused on where they should be. At least, their current seating arrangement on the train afforded a bit more privacy.

They'd been unable to find four seats facing each other in the packed train car from Buffalo to New York City, so Isabella had volunteered to take the seat across the aisle from her and Harrison. Victoria appreciated how her friend had sanctioned her budding romance, even allowing one small good-night peck in the Clifton House hallway before ushering Victoria into the room, mother-hen like.

Even now, Isabella kept a watchful eye and ear from across the aisle. From the way her mouth quirked into small smiles after her every-so-often, corner-of-the-eye glances their way, she also conveyed her support and encouragement.

"And how does our spectator fare? Not too lonely, I hope?" Harrison must have caught her peeking at Isabella and vice versa.

"She appears content with her new companion," she replied honestly. Isabella was chatting animatedly with the young, bespectacled woman seated to her left, and affection for her friend swelled in Victoria's chest. Isabella could truly befriend anyone.

An impish thought arose in her mind, and before sense could silence her, she spoke it aloud. "She's probably grateful to be away from your mooning over me."

"Yes, and also your habit of kissing me at any reasonable opportunity." Harrison's response was quick, and just as dryly delivered as hers. Oh, how she loved witty banter.

"Don't forget the unreasonable opportunities too," she countered.

Harrison laughed aloud, and she loved how the low timbre

of his voice echoed in his chest. "Yes, the cave was most definitely that."

"A habit usually implies something needing to be stopped, no?" She delivered her question with just the right amount of airiness despite being deeply invested in its answer.

"I rarely correct beautiful women, but I feel as though I must in this case. Don't forget, a person can make a habit of good things too, and *that* kind of habit is definitely one that shouldn't be stopped."

She blushed at his calling her beautiful and waited for him to continue and say the obvious next thing. But he let the silence linger, toying with her.

The scoundrel was waiting for her to come right out and ask it.

Well, it would be a test of wills, then.

"So, the particular habit we have of kissing, Harrison. Good or bad?"

His hand gripped hers. "Most definitely the former."

"Too bad so many people are around now."

His voice was almost strangled as he continued, "Yes, now would be a highly unreasonable time. Perhaps later?"

"Yes," she whispered in answer before lifting her head off his shoulder. He smelled especially delicious this morning. She grasped for what would hopefully be a more dispassionate topic. "Are you eager to arrive back home?"

He stiffened slightly beside her.

Despite her efforts to the contrary, she'd unintentionally hit a nerve.

"I am eager to show you New York City," he said. "It's a metropolis full of every amusement imaginable—theatres, museums, monster hotels, and even more monstrous stores. Its industry is unmatched, as is its extreme wealth and, unfortunately, its abject poverty too." He appeared to choose his next words carefully. "But I'm afraid I'm not looking forward to returning to the reality of my profession there."

He'd hinted at his unhappiness at being a lawyer before. Would he feel comfortable divulging more about it now? "If a lawyer isn't your first choice of vocation, then what would be?"

He thought for a moment. "Assuming money is no object? Philanthropic work."

"Handsome *and* generous. Quite the irresistible combination." She gave his hand a playful, reassuring squeeze.

After a somewhat abashed smile and blush, he continued, "It's all my mother's doing, really. She took notice of the extreme need in the city. Her benevolent efforts reached as far as they could with our family's modest means. I had always hoped to be more like her, that if my work as a lawyer couldn't help people directly, the income would allow me to help in other ways."

"But that hasn't been the case?"

Harrison let out a sardonic laugh. "No, my father has made quite sure of that."

Victoria leaned her head on his shoulder and took her turn trailing her fingers over his hand.

He seemed to relax a bit at her touch, enough so he went on. "For all that my mother was good, my father is not."

She'd gathered as much from what he'd previously told her of his father. "It must be aggravating to work so closely with someone of such disparate convictions, especially family."

"Utterly. My father specializes in barely legal, seedy deals with equally dodgy clientele whose source of payment shouldn't be questioned too much. I took over the firm's accounting a few years ago and mostly put things to rights, but doing so drove a larger wedge between us, and there are times when I know he still hides things from me, especially money."

"How frustrating." Poor Harrison. Victoria's ire rankled at

his father's misdeeds. It was no wonder he dreaded returning to New York.

"Beyond vexing. And wearying. I've thought about a fresh start on my own, which is quite intimidating."

"Understandably so," she said, her heart weighing with the burden of Harrison's troubles.

"Made more so because my father knows I've had such thoughts too and has essentially threatened to 'be my professional undoing' if I tried to start my own practice."

"Hence the Stubborn Colt poem?"

"Well, I'm more of an obstinate nag at this point but, yes, I guess you could say my father was the inspiration for the poem."

His father sounded like an intolerable man, one who would probably get along well with hers. Now that she was dwelling on her impending reality, its bleakness weighed further on her.

As if he could read where her thoughts were heading, Harrison asked, "What about you, Victoria? What would you do if money were no object?"

She didn't need long to think of her reply. "Something with children."

His "hmm" vibrated in his chest. "You and my mother would have been fast friends. She adored children. Her charitable work typically centered around them. Quite the baby soother too, like you on the train with that little one."

She laughed softly. "I believe that was luck acting in my favor for once."

"Well, I wish I'd had even a portion of that luck those nights after my mother died, when Georgina was inconsolable."

Victoria's heart splintered for both brother and sister. For Harrison and the burden of immense responsibility he'd had to shoulder, and for Georgina who unexpectedly lost the person around which her entire world revolved and who was much too young to comprehend any of it.

She squeezed his hand again. "You've done admirably in handling it all. Truly."

"When you meet Georgina, you may change your mind on that score." He cast her a wry grin, pride underlying his tone.

She let out a soft chuckle, liking how his use of "when" instead of *if* meant he considered the meeting an inevitability. "Does she have a bit of her older brother's temperament?"

"Georgina's passion, if you will, is all her own creation. Despite all that forewarning, I do hope you get a chance to meet her. I telegraphed ahead to see if she and Mrs. March, the governess, would be at our city residence, but I received no reply before we left Buffalo."

"I hope so too," Victoria smiled, trying to picture this three-year-old little girl she'd heard so much about. "No one can top my two nephews' reprobate nature, though," she added.

Harrison chuckled. "That insufferable, huh?"

"My family specializes in miscreant members."

"Surely no one is as bad as my father?" He said drolly.

"Not individually, no, but perhaps collectively my family members may be your father's equivalent, sad though it may be."

Before she could lose her nerve, she dove into the full dossier on each of her family members. "My father hasn't spoken to me since Silas's death—as the one who'd orchestrated the marriage, he blames me for causing the fire, and unfair as that conclusion is, I have slowly come to accept I cannot change his mind."

Harrison emitted a grunt of displeasure, but he didn't interrupt her.

"My mother's nerves, on the other hand, not only keep her abed most of the time but also from ever going against her husband's edicts, including his tacit directive to essentially shun me."

His grip tightened in unspoken encouragement for her to continue unburdening herself. So, she did.

"My sister, Arabella, is older than me by only eighteen months but has never missed an opportunity to remind me of her superior status and knowledge as the older sibling. Nor the fact that our parents had given her a name which means 'answered prayer.'" She gave a sardonic laugh. "Though Arabella has allowed me to live with her and her husband, Percy, and their sons since the accident, it's an unbearable arrangement on the best days, intolerable on the worst. But I suppose I should be grateful I have somewhere to live at all."

It'd taken courage to share these most vulnerable feelings and experiences with him. But it'd also lifted a weighty burden from her. Hopefully, Harrison didn't perceive her comments as wallowing in self-pity.

To lighten the mood, she transitioned to tales of her over-indulged nephews' misbehavior and indiscretions, trying to cast the source of Benjamin's and Daniel's antics as to that of youthfulness rather than the trait they were developing from their parents—selfishness.

In return, Harrison recounted memories of his less-nefarious antics with his younger brother. Despite the sorrowful undertone in Harrison's voice over his too-soon-departed sibling, they both laughed at the exploits.

Their conversation lulled for a few moments. Harrison appeared ready to speak again, yet hesitant to do so.

"Did you—were you and—" He cleared his throat, his voice a low whisper of inquiry as he continued. "No children came from your first marriage?"

She didn't begrudge Harrison his curiosity about the

matter. The topic had to arise at some point, and it was a natural segue after all their discussions of children.

"No, except—" she started, but the train lurched to a stop. Amid the upheaval, the moment vanished. Rail hands dismantled the train and hooked the individual cars to four-horse teams that clattered into the heart of the urban metropolis.

They'd arrived in New York City.

Twenty

It was quite intimate being in Harrison's house, traversing the same halls he'd navigated for years, peeking into each room, seeing how he liked things arranged, what books he had on the shelves, what artwork he liked, whether he was messy or tidy. Not that Victoria was nosing about. Merely curious.

They'd arrived late and after dark the night before, which hadn't afforded the time nor the light by which she could truly take in her surroundings—both the city itself and Harrison's three-story brownstone. He had been a most accommodating host, making sure she and Isabella had everything they needed before retiring to his room a floor below their rooms. There'd been no good-night kiss, though, most likely because Harrison's housekeeper, Mrs. Jones, had been a bystander to the somewhat-awkward exchange in the top-floor hallway as she and Isabella retired for the evening.

Victoria had slept remarkably well, appreciating the indulgence of a room to herself for a change. And a stunning one at that. The ceiling soared at least a dozen feet high, and the room's breadth expanded wider still. With hot and cold water running to a bathroom down the hall and heated air blowing from a furnace somewhere in the brownstone's underbelly, every comfort was thought of, every want met.

After rising early, she'd readied herself quickly and was now tiptoeing downstairs to see if she could trouble Mrs. Jones for a cup of tea. Victoria's hand trailed along the stairs' polished walnut balustrade as her eyes roved the intricately carved moldings and cornices adorning the walls and doorways. Stunning indeed, but not in a gaudy or overdone way. Had Harrison's mother chosen the understated white paint for the walls? They were a perfect backdrop for the sapphire blue damask upholstery and curtains. Or had a designer's hand been at play?

She paused on the second-floor landing and eyed the closed door she guessed led to Harrison's bedroom. At the thought of him just a few paces away on the other side of the carved wooden slab, perhaps still abed, a heat stirred within her. She suppressed the sudden, strong desire to peek into his private quarters, but *that* would surely cross the line from curiosity to nosiness.

Intent on her tea, she reached the first floor as noiselessly as possible and rounded the corner into the dining room, halting when she found it already occupied. Piercing eyes the same golden hue as Harrison's, but on a much shorter and younger frame, watched her from the dining table with a mixture of wariness and interest.

Georgina.

She was as handsome as her brother, with the same determined set to her jaw, but surrounded by youthful, cherub cheeks. Her hair was lighter too, more molten chocolate to Harrison's obsidian locks. If Victoria's scars frightened Georgina, the girl didn't show it. How was it a three-year-old could have better manners than most grown adults?

Victoria recovered from her initial shock and smiled in what she hoped was a reassuring manner. "Good morning, Miss Wright. I'm Mrs. Clarke, a friend of your brother's."

Georgina didn't reply. Rather, she snuggled the stuffed animal in tighter to the crook of her elbow. A ragged rabbit, if Victoria interpreted the folds of fabric correctly. Georgina sat before an empty plate, clothed in a pale pink nightdress edged in creamy lace.

"Might I join you?" Victoria asked.

No response.

She took the silence as assent and sidled into a chair at the foot of the table, away from Georgina, not to frighten her by getting too close. "And what is the name of our third breakfast guest?" she asked, nodding to the rabbit.

"Cat." Georgina's voice rang with the sweet innocence of youth.

"Quite an intriguing name for a rabbit, no?"

"Catherine was my mother's name."

Victoria winced inwardly at her blunder. Not even five minutes in this little girl's company, and here she was, bringing up the poor child's deceased mother.

Victoria opened her mouth to reply—with what words, she didn't yet know—but was spared by Mrs. Jones, trotting into the room, and a woman Victoria hadn't yet met, trailing behind the housekeeper.

"Oh, Mrs. Clarke," Mrs. Jones stopped a few steps in. "I didn't know anyone else had awakened yet. I'll get the kettle on and see how soon breakfast will be ready. We can have Georgina eat in her room if you'd prefer. The child is still in her nightclothes. I'm so sorry—"

"Really, Mrs. Jones," Victoria interjected, "please don't have

Georgina leave on my account. We were just getting acquainted."

Mrs. Jones smiled approvingly, then gestured to the woman behind her. "This is Mrs. March, Georgina's governess."

Mrs. March was as tall and angular as Mrs. Jones was short and plump. Mrs. Jones had immediately set Victoria at ease with her near-constant grin and hooting laugh. On the other hand, Mrs. March was standoffish, if not downright dour. The governess merely nodded in greeting, her eyes lingering on the left side of Victoria's face longer than was appropriate.

"I must apologize for the state of Georgina's appearance," Mrs. March spoke with a sigh. "I've tried my hardest to raise her properly, but her will is to do otherwise."

Why did propriety require a three-year-old to be dressed by seven in the morning? But Victoria kept the thought to herself. "Well, if I had known it was the day to wear nightclothes to breakfast, I would've remained in mine." She gave Georgina a conspiratorial wink, which earned her a glower from Mrs. March.

"Shall we do so tomorrow morning, then?" The baritone behind her could only be one person.

Harrison.

Victoria turned, and her heart leaped to her throat. Though not in his nightclothes, he was in more casual clothing of a shirt, sans necktie, tucked into tan trousers. Harrison wore them—and the mantle of homeowner—well. His was a quiet authority.

Mrs. Jones certainly esteemed him highly, perhaps even considered him more son than employer, while evidently he hadn't won over Mrs. March. Her face had pinched into a sour expression at his comment, and she'd yet to recover.

Georgina lit up at her brother's entry, and, pushing away from the table, she ran into his open arms. "Harrison!"

He lifted her into a hug and twirled her around, her pink nightgown taking flight too. Victoria fought back the tears springing to her eyes at the joyful reunion before her. But now wasn't the time to turn into a watering pot.

Harrison propped Georgina onto his hip and greeted the other women in turn, saving her for last.

"Victoria," he said, his eyes all but begging to add a good morning kiss to his words. Victoria cast her eyes to the tablecloth, trying to quell the heat rising in her cheeks and school her face into a mask of innocence like he'd managed.

"Good morning." Isabella called moments later, bursting into the room and joining the throng. "How is everyone this fine day?" She greeted everyone in turn, including the still-taciturn Georgina. Meanwhile, Mrs. Jones bustled about setting the table for breakfast, which was delivered shortly thereafter by another older woman whom Victoria presumed was the cook.

"Shall we?" Harrison asked, gesturing for the others to take their seats at the table. Isabella sat to his right, while the pinch-faced Mrs. March seated herself to his left. Harrison took the chair at the head of the table across from Victoria and nestled Georgina into his lap.

He met her eyes, a contented smile splitting his face, and Victoria's heart constricted at the happy glimpse of domesticity before her. But absent a particular question from Harrison, that's all it'd ever be—only a glimpse. With nothing currently preventing her departure, she'd be gone in just a few days' time, as would any chance at such future happiness.

～

Harrison huffed out an exasperated sigh at the mess he'd made of his necktie and undid it for the third time. *There are altogether too many people in this house.* Though that wasn't the reason for his sudden inability to dress himself, it did explain his short temper. He shouldn't be complaining about a situation most people would be grateful to be in, being surrounded by family and friends as he was. But at every turn, there was someone else there, preventing him from any meaningful interaction with Victoria.

After dining together at breakfast yesterday, the motley band of females under his roof had divided. Isabella and Victoria had toured the city, while he and Georgina remained back at the house, Georgina under Mrs. March's tutelage. He immersed himself in work obligations, with one quick errand outside the house. They'd all reconvened for dinner, followed by a conversation in the parlor, before retiring early for the evening.

It was downright torturous, though, having Victoria there in his house, almost always an arm's reach away, yet in a position where he couldn't give in to his desire to reach for her, hold her, kiss her. At least today, he'd be able to spend the day with her, but perhaps that would only exacerbate his problem.

Georgina was coming with them on their excursion, and he'd managed to convince Mrs. March to take the day off. She was his father's hire, and the woman was far too surly for his liking. He didn't discount her teaching abilities, but she was often harsher with Georgina than was truly necessary, especially of late as Georgina's spirited personality revealed itself more and more.

He made a mental note to search out a new governess for Georgina, but then again, if what he'd been devising in his mind came to fruition, doing so would be entirely unnecessary.

A knock sounded on his bedroom door, and Georgina

bounded in a moment later without waiting for permission to enter.

"Hurry, Harrison. We are going." Adorned in a pink pleated dress, ruffled pantaloons, and curled ringlets, she appeared every bit a young lady.

"Well, a good morning to you, Georgina."

"You will make us late." She flounced onto the footstool near his bed and crossed her arms.

He stifled a laugh. She was like a tiny dictator on her throne.

He returned to face his mirror. "I just need to finish my necktie, and then we will be off. Did you sleep well?"

"Mrs. March snores."

Harrison didn't doubt that. The woman's room adjoined Georgina's, and apparently the noise was loud enough to traverse the walls.

"I'm sorry to hear that, sweetheart. I will see what I can do about it."

"I bet Mrs. Clarke doesn't snore."

Harrison had long given up trying to follow a child's course of thought, especially Georgina's. He muttered a noncommittal "hmm" in reply and pulled out his necktie yet again.

"What happened to her face?"

He momentarily abandoned his task and kneeled before Georgina, taking her hands. "You have had such wonderful manners, Georgina, by not asking in front of the others. You see, sweetheart, Mrs. Clarke had a terrible accident that left her face scarred."

Georgina thought for a moment. "I think she's pretty. And nice."

His smile grew, and he squeezed her hands. "Yes, how right you are."

"There she is!" Georgina pointed through the open

doorway to where Victoria now stood, halted in her trek downstairs. "Mrs. Clarke, tie Harrison's tie. Please. So we can go."

Harrison stood again and gestured for Victoria to enter, studiously ignoring the fact that he'd just invited her into his bedchamber. With color high in her cheeks, Victoria acquiesced to Georgina's politely delivered command and stepped into his room.

Victoria's deep emerald dress swished as she made her way over to him, her eyes darting about the room before meeting his. Lavender enveloped him as she neared, sending his pulse skittering. Her deft fingers worked the silk strip of fabric, occasionally brushing against the bare skin of his neck. He sucked in a breath, grasping for a new level of self-control.

At Mrs. Jones's faraway call of "Georgina," Georgina sprung from the footstool and dashed out of the room, tossing a "Goodbye" over her shoulder.

While the door remained open, the delicacy of their situation—unmarried, alone, and in his bedroom—wasn't lost on him. What was lost, however, was the self-control he'd had in front of their miniature chaperone.

He cupped Victoria's face with both palms, smoothing his thumbs over her cheeks. "How are you?" he whispered.

"Quite all right, Harrison," she whispered back, "but certainly we should be going." Her tone held more question than command, as if hoping he'd disagree with her. Which he did.

He cast a quick, furtive glance out the door. "I miss you."

She chuckled softly. "I've been right here the entire time, Harrison."

"Yes," he admitted, rubbing one thumb along her now-parted lips, "but I haven't been able to do this." He dipped in to claim her lips in a much-too-cursory kiss. It wasn't enough to satiate his few days' famine from her last kiss, but he'd have to make do with this clandestine sign of affection.

"Harrison," she breathed, which again sounded more like a petition to continue rather than stop.

Oh, how he wanted to concede, to encircle her in his arms and never let go, but he couldn't risk anyone discovering them, nor risk his self-regulation failing when the temptation was so strong.

Instead, he took her hand and guided her to the doorway, peeking out to ensure it was free of prying eyes. Mercifully, the house full of people appeared to be concentrated on the main level at present. He ushered Victoria out the door with a squeeze of her hand. "I'll be right behind you. I just need to retrieve my coat."

She nodded, then disappeared down the hall in a swell of lavender and green skirts. He donned his frock coat, giving its right pocket an extra pat, and took one final glance in the mirror. Victoria's handiwork—a long, vertical tie instead of a bowed one—was a stretch of fashion for him, but one he quite liked.

At Georgina's trill of "Harrison!" from below, he finger-combed his tousled hair and tried to school the silly grin from his face. It would betray to everyone that he was a besotted fool, but he didn't quite care anymore whether he concealed his true feelings for Victoria.

Twenty-One

Victoria was smitten, plain and simple. As she descended the stairs following her interaction with Harrison, she couldn't entirely quell the blush flaming on both cheeks. Worse still, she wasn't as remorseful as she should be over such an audacious action. And in his bedroom of all places.

His desire emboldened and enlivened her.

Here was someone in her life who actually wanted her. Who didn't shy away from her imperfections and idiosyncrasies. And one who was considerably handsome, generous, and possessed of a dry wit that added levity to life's tumult. What an undeserved good fortune Harrison was, and she would not look too closely in this gift horse's mouth.

"Good morning." Mrs. Jones beamed when Victoria reached the first-floor entry hall. Georgina stood beside the housekeeper, demurely clutching her hand. Thankfully, Mrs. March and her perpetual frown were absent.

"Is Isabella still unwell?" Mrs. Jones asked.

"Yes, unfortunately. I just administered acupressure and

ginger oil to ease the stomach discomfort, but she still looked quite pitiful."

Mrs. Jones clucked. "Poor thing. Those oysters can be nasty business if you get a disagreeable one. Good thing you abstained, Mrs. Clarke."

Victoria nodded.

Yesterday, she and Isabella had traversed what felt like Broadway Street's entire extent. They'd passed the palatial Metropolitan and St. Nicholas hotels, toured the New York Hospital's cupola-clad building, and lunched at the marble-adorned Taylor's Saloon. Isabella fulfilled her usual responsibility of providing unprompted, informative tidbits about each landmark.

After a shopping excursion to Stewart's Dry Goods, which was a rather unassuming name for the very opulent edifice, Isabella had decided, and Victoria agreed, they could skip P. T. Barnum's New York Museum, since Isabella had seen his tent in Detroit. However, Isabella had insisted on stopping at an oyster saloon.

If the subterranean level in which the allegedly edible victuals were sold hadn't been deterrent enough, their slimy, gelatinous appearance had confirmed Victoria's decision to recuse herself from their consumption.

Isabella had waved her off with a "Pish" before tossing back another shell's raw contents. Unfortunately for Isabella, the bivalves had proved uncooperative in digestion, rendering her unable to come along on today's journey.

"Shall we?" Harrison asked, joining them in the entry. As he swooped Georgina into his arms, he cast Victoria a private smile.

Her pulse beat double time as if it'd been hours or days, not mere seconds, since she'd seen him last.

"Where are we going?" Georgina asked, one hand clutching Cat, the other wrapped around Harrison's neck.

"That, my dears, is a surprise," he said, hoisting Georgina higher on his hip, then wishing Mrs. Jones a goodbye. He led the way to a hired hack sitting ready at the curb. Excitement—and nervousness—seemed to underlie his motions.

Georgina, however, was downright enthusiastic. She sat squarely between Harrison and Victoria, unaware of just how much her presence served as chaperone for the two adults. She chattered about this and that, occasionally pointing at something outside the carriage that caught her eye, all the while Cat the rabbit remained burrowed in the crook of her arm.

In the day's slightly cooler October weather, the three huddled under the carriage's thick wool blankets, and when a stiff breeze blew, Georgina nestled in closer to Victoria. The child had quickly endeared herself to Victoria, and vice versa.

"Mrs. Clarke?"

"Yes, Georgina? And please, you may call me Victoria."

"Mrs. Victoria, you will like Wiley."

Victoria glanced over Georgina's head at Harrison for some clue as to who Wiley was, but Harrison merely shrugged.

"If you like him, I bet I will too." She gave Georgina a warm smile.

Georgina's all-too innocent eyes blinked up at her. "He's sometimes naughty, but I still like him," she continued, punctuating her statement with a nod.

Victoria hugged her closer. "It's wonderful you see the good in others, Georgina."

"Mrs. March doesn't like him."

Victoria didn't doubt that, and her heart twinged when Georgina's tone soured every time the governess was mentioned.

"Georgina," Harrison cut in, "where did you meet Wiley?"

"Our country house."

Suspicion grew in Harrison's tone. "Does Wiley happen to have four legs and fur?"

Georgina nodded.

Harrison sighed, "Georgina, we've talked about the animals. We can't possibly give them all a home."

"He was sick but is better now. He purrs really loud."

This time Harrison directed his comments to Victoria. "Georgina's heart has more room for stray animals than our house does, even the one in the country." Then, to Georgina, he said, "We'll talk more about this later, sweetheart. I'm sure Wiley is wonderful, but—" He cut himself off when Georgina wiped a tear from her cheek. He patted the blanket over her legs. "We'll talk more later."

Victoria's heart swelled for this little girl, who had already lost so much in her short life. It's a good thing Harrison had some fortitude, for at this point, she was ready to give Georgina an entire litter of kittens.

"Mrs. Victoria," Georgina sniffled. "Do you have animals?"

"No, dear, no animals at this point. I have two young nephews, if they count," she teased.

Georgina giggled, and the sound sang within Victoria.

"Children?"

The inquiry, though entirely innocent, stabbed the ever-tender spot in Victoria's heart that would never truly heal.

"No, dear, no children either," she said, hoping her voice still conveyed a lightheartedness she didn't feel.

"You don't want children? Like Harrison?"

Harrison startled back into the conversation. "Georgina, sweetheart, we've talked about this."

"You did say that."

"No—well, yes, but not those exact words," Harrison

fumbled. "I was overwhelmed and had little sleep in those early days." He put his arm around Georgina's shoulder and squeezed her to him. "I love you, my little sister. I'm so grateful we have each other."

"And Wiley."

"Yes, and apparently another cat too." Harrison chuckled.

"Look." Georgina pointed out the carriage toward a tall, gray-walled structure, having easily abandoned the current topic for a new one as the young were liable to do. "A castle!"

Victoria followed Georgina's gaze to a rather castle-like building.

"Ah, that, Georgina, is a reservoir," Harrison supplied.

Georgina appeared rather unimpressed by his explanation.

"If your Aunt Isabella were here, she'd tell you all sorts of fascinating information about it. But you'll have to settle for my account. It holds the city's water that comes from many miles away. The water even crosses over a river to get here."

"There are people on top." Georgina seemed to gain interest now.

"Yes, there are. We can go up there sometime, if you'd like."

Georgina nodded eagerly.

"Then we shall." The carriage turned right, and Harrison narrated the sights of what had to be a previously unexplored area of the city for Georgina. The briny smell indicated they were nearing the water, but the typical port sounds and sights were absent.

Instead, the hack weaved along a narrow dirt trek between farm plots, cresting a hill before dipping down into the most delightful little cove. The East River churned beyond, with the occasional ship mast drifting past, but within the cove itself, the water was still and serene.

"Turtle Bay, ladies," Harrison supplied with a sweep of his hands.

Georgina clapped with delight, and Victoria grinned. She never would have expected such a pastoral scene just a few minutes' ride from the city's commotion.

Harrison helped the women down from the hack before grabbing the blankets and asking the driver to return in an hour.

Victoria tentatively stepped onto the sand, her boots sinking further with each step. Georgina, on the other hand, shucked off her shoes within seconds of landing and took off at a run, a stream of chocolate ringlets and pink muslin behind her.

Oh, to be so young and carefree.

Harrison spread a blanket on the sand, sat, and patted the spot next to him.

Victoria obliged and sank down next to him. When he rolled his trouser cuffs a few inches up and stripped off his shoes and socks, Victoria's eyes strayed to the exposed stretch of skin. She quickly ducked her head and averted her eyes from the sight only a wife should see.

"Now it's your turn to remove your shoes, Victoria."

She warmed to Harrison's nearness and his suggestion. "That would be rather unladylike."

"How else are you to make footprints?"

She registered his implication a moment later—Longfellow's "A Psalm of Life."

"I did have to go quite out of my way to find sand in this city," he teased.

What lengths *had* he gone through to arrange this surprise? She took a fortifying breath, then slowly unlaced her boots before finally slipping off her stockings, trying to keep her feet concealed under her skirts during the process.

Harrison rose and offered her a smile and his hand.

Taking it, she gingerly edged onto the sand, sucking in a breath. "It's so cold."

Harrison chuckled from beside her. "October typically isn't the best beach-going month."

"Noted," Victoria said, wiggling her toes. Beneath her, the sand readjusted with her every movement. "It tickles," she laughed, then met Harrison's eyes.

He was grinning too.

"Thank you, Harrison." But those two words were wholly insufficient to convey the depth of her gratitude for such a meaningful gesture.

"My pleasure. Come, let's walk closer to the water where you can really see the footprints." He guided her to where the water lapped at the shore, the sand molding to the contours of their feet.

The cold water nipped at her toes, and when a rogue wave from a passing ship on the river sent a tremor through the bay's water, she released Harrison's hand to clutch her skirts higher.

Victoria cast a glance over her shoulder. Behind them, twin trails of indentations in the sand—one with longer, larger depressions than the other—marked the journey she and Harrison had taken together.

Footprints, that perhaps another, ... seeing, shall take heart again.

Her eyes met Harrison's, and a smile of pure delight broke across his face. Her heart bloomed with a happiness she'd never known, and all because of this man before her.

Not long ago, she'd all but loathed him. And now—well, now, she was fairly certain she loved him. How quickly it had snuck up on her, but then again, she'd never loved Silas, nor any other man for that matter, so was it any surprise she hadn't quite recognized it at first?

But did Harrison feel the same? And would he act on it before she departed?

He released her hand and held his arms out to Georgina, who splashed over to them, cheeks and nose rosy. He swooped her up, then pretended she was slipping from his grasp, except he caught her just before she reached the water. Repeating the action several times, he sent her into squeals of part-fright and part-delight.

Georgina tired from cavorting near the water's edge, and Harrison carried her to the blanket where she laid down, snuggling Cat beside her. He tucked a second blanket around her and sat before turning his attention to Victoria again.

His gaze brought a welcome heat to her now-frigid limbs. He beckoned her over with another pat beside him on the blanket.

Conscious of his gaze on her, she picked her way back to the blanket and settled next to him.

He wrapped his arm around her, and she nestled into what was now becoming her favorite spot. Here, she felt safe. Here, she felt secure.

Harrison enfolded them both in the third blanket, and, combined with his body heat, warmth seeped back into her extremities.

As she fought to keep her eyelids from drooping closed, she now understood Georgina's fatigue upon being inert after a romp in the sand.

She must have been unsuccessful, because an indeterminate time later, Harrison's voice awakened her. "Victoria."

He sounded almost alarmed, or at least anxious, and his heartbeat thumped rapidly in his chest beneath her ear.

She quickly roused herself fully, her own heartbeat ticking

up and her eyes darting to Georgina. "Is everything all right?" she asked.

But Georgina was burrowed under the blanket, still fast asleep.

Harrison pivoted to face her, rearranging the blanket around her shoulders. "No—er, I mean, yes, everything is all right, I'll just—" But his nervous actions said otherwise. He cleared his throat and fidgeted with his necktie before reaching into his coat pocket. "I'll just read it."

Was it a new poem he'd written? Sharing his poetry with her had made him uncomfortable before, but he now turned awfully pale. Did he in fact have bad news? Afraid her speaking would interrupt his course of thought, she simply nodded to indicate she was listening.

He pulled a small piece of paper from his pocket. Judging from its creases and tattered edges, it'd been folded and refolded many times. He cleared his throat, straining her curiosity to its breaking point until, finally, he spoke:

> I, a once forlorn and shipwrecked brother,
> a soul then dead, it fully slumbered
> with an empty dream, until another
> could reverse my fate, I wondered.
>
> Taking heart again, this hero in strife
> is earnest now for a life sublime,
> but only beside you, Victoria, as my wife,
> walking life's sands together for all time?

Spoken in his low timbre, the verses entranced her. He'd transformed Longfellow's words into something entirely his own, and she was still interpreting his words when he reached into his pocket again and withdrew a small velvet box.

Her pulse stuttered, and her breath caught. Did it truly mean what she thought it did? In answer, he opened the box. Inside, a pale oval sapphire on a gilded band winked out at her, the embodiment of possibilities promised today and vows to be declared in the future.

Tears—happy tears—lumped in her throat and blurred the timidly expectant expression on his face before her. He needn't have fretted though.

She knew with certainty her answer a second before it left her lips. "Yes, Harrison, yes!"

Twenty-Two

"You're engaged?" Isabella burst into the dining room where Harrison had just sat at the head of the table beside Victoria, Georgina on his other side. "Am I to be the last person to know?" But her tone conveyed more elation than admonishment, as evident when she squeezed him and Victoria into a hug on both sides of her.

He, too, was having trouble accepting he was an engaged man. He'd never even conceived such a situation would happen at all, but this was the right course for his—well, their—future. Together.

"How are you feeling?" he asked, but Isabella waved him off.

"I'm up and about, aren't I?" she said, seating herself next to Victoria. "Now, for the more important questions. Where did you propose?"

Before Harrison could answer, Georgina piped up. "We went to the beach."

"Oh, how delightful," Isabella crooned, giving him a nod of

approval. "I didn't know New York City had beaches. You're very daring, visiting one in October."

"We kept warm enough." Harrison's gaze swept to Victoria, who dipped her head in a blush at the insinuation in his statement. What he wouldn't do to be able to pull her into his arms again now. Later, if his favor held.

"It's still all so fresh, I know," Isabella continued, "but have you decided on a wedding date?"

"As soon as this lovely woman will have me," he said, earning a smile from Victoria and a laugh from Isabella.

The cook entered and delivered their plates, while Mrs. Jones hovered in the doorway, watching the exultant scene, handkerchief clutched in her hand, eyes misty with tears.

Harrison's eyes burned, and his throat constricted. Now *he* was turning into a waterpot. He cleared the lump from his throat and swigged a mouthful of water for good measure.

"Mrs. March is leaving." Georgina bounced in her chair as she delivered her announcement. It was the most animated he'd seen her in a long while, which did nothing to help the squeeze in his throat and chest.

"If I'm here," Victoria supplied, "we can send Mrs. March on to a more suitable post."

Isabella's eyes brimmed with tears. "So, you'll make New York City your home, then?"

Victoria nodded. "England holds no future happiness for me. Other than you, of course, my friend."

The pressure in Harrison's throat intensified. Victoria's life in England had been rather disheartening thus far. Still, she was giving up the only home she'd known to be with him.

"Well, this just gives me even more motivation to come back and visit again," Isabella said, a forced cheerfulness in her tone. She rose from her chair, glass held aloft. "I would like to propose a toast."

Harrison reached for Victoria's hand, but she was already reaching for his.

"After a somewhat rocky beginning—" Isabella paused, and Harrison chuckled, as did Victoria. Isabella's grin widened. "You two have found true happiness in each other, and for that, I am pleased. Do you know, I almost gave up on you two?"

Another round of chuckles from her captivated audience.

"But I'd gone through too much trouble already to concede defeat so easily. You both know me better than that."

Suspicion arose within him. Had Isabella been scheming all along? He opened his mouth to ask, but as if sensing his pending interruption, Isabella plunged ahead. "Harrison, Victoria is one of the most wonderful women I know. Your mother's tenderheartedness carries on in you. You've given glimpses of that, so don't be afraid to let it show even more as Victoria's husband."

The burning in his eyes returned, especially at the mention of his mother, so he simply nodded at Isabella's directive and squeezed Victoria's hand to convey his commitment to be the husband she deserved.

"Now, Victoria, my dear friend. Harrison will test even *your* perpetual patience."

Victoria laughed beside him, and he couldn't help smiling as well. It was true, after all.

"But he is good and kind. He will give you his whole heart and more. My only regret"—Isabella paused, her voice thick with emotion as she continued—"is that you, my friend, will no longer be near me." Next to him, Victoria sniffed and wiped her eyes with the hand not holding his.

"But enough with the histrionics. Let's drink to a happy future." A chorus of "here, here" and clinking glasses ensued. The party then migrated to the drawing room, with Georgina climbing into Victoria's lap to read a book, while he and

Isabella talked about her subsequent travel itinerary to her cousins, which would take her back to Canada for a few weeks.

"It was the plan all along for me and Victoria to part ways in New York," Isabella explained. "Only now, she gets to remain here, with you, instead of returning to England."

The drawing-room door opened, with Mrs. Jones at its threshold. "Sorry to interrupt, but, Georgina, we better get you off to bed—" A flash of black and white streaked past her legs, and she shrieked.

"Wiley!" Georgina cried. Then, to the non-animal occupants in the room, she said, "See, he is sometimes naughty."

Harrison made the connection a second later—the kitten. But why was it—how did it get here? Wasn't it at the country house? He mentally reviewed the earlier conversation with Georgina. She had said she'd *found* the kitten at the country house but hadn't gone so far as to say she'd *left* the animal there.

"Oh, I'm so sorry, Mr. Wright," Mrs. Jones said, joining Georgina's efforts to corral the tiny kitten in a place other than under the settee, which was where he'd currently hidden. "This is all my fault. See, the little thing hitched a ride in Georgina's bag, and when she got here, I couldn't turn the poor thing away. I told her I'd keep him in the kitchen, but somehow the door was left open and—"

The woman was working herself into a state over what was becoming an increasingly humorous situation. "It's quite all right, Mrs. Jones," he cut in with a smile. "Georgina pulled the wool over our eyes with this one." By now, Georgina had coaxed the kitten out from under the settee and had him cradled in her arms, cooing in hushed tones to him. She really did have a way with animals.

"Come, let's see the little thing," he said, crouching and

taking the kitten from Georgina's arms. Amber eyes, almost the same size and color as Georgina's, blinked up at him. Well, he couldn't very well deny this lost soul a loving home now. It appeared the Wright family would grow by yet another member. Two in one day, he mused inwardly.

"Wiley Wright, nice to meet you," Harrison said. As if to convey acquiescence in being admitted to the family, the kitten mewed once—a squeak really—and purred. *Look at where tenderheartedness got me.* He delicately gave the vibrating bundle of fur back to Georgina.

"I can keep him, then?" she asked, expectancy and hesitancy etched into her tiny features.

"Yes, sweetheart. We can keep Wiley."

"Thank you, Harrison!" she squealed, then carried Wiley over to Victoria and Isabella—who'd moved to the settee in all the commotion. The two women took turns fawning over the creature.

"You're a good man, sir." Mrs. Jones's voice startled him from his reverie. He'd all but forgotten she was there. "I'm so glad you've found your happiness." She dabbed her eyes with her handkerchief again.

"I just didn't know it would also include a cat," he quipped.

Mrs. Jones guffawed before growing serious again. "Animals have greatly comforted Georgina. She's too often alone, especially for a sprightly girl her age."

Harrison's heart ached with the truth of Mrs. Jones's statement. While he'd done his best to support her, Georgina had lived a rather solitary existence in her almost four years of life. His proposal to Victoria comforted his conscience with the improved circumstances it would provide. For all of them.

"I don't mean to pry, but what will become of Mrs. March?" Mrs. Jones asked.

As if conjured by the mention of her name, the woman

appeared in the doorway, causing Mrs. Jones to jump beside him and clutch her hand to her heart.

Mrs. March scanned the room with her piercing gaze, reserving an especially sharp glower for Wiley. Her mere presence dampened the once-jovial scene.

"Georgina," Mrs. March admonished. "It is past time to retire. You know what happens if you overtire yourself. We do not need a fainting episode."

Harrison flinched at Mrs. March's tone. The dreadful task of her dismissal still loomed before him, but he couldn't stomach doing it tonight. Not on his engagement day.

Georgina, who moments ago was all unadulterated gaiety, snapped into sobriety. "Yes, Mrs. March."

"Don't worry, dear," Mrs. Jones soothed, retrieving the kitten from Georgina's arms. "I'll get Wiley his bedtime snack and put him to bed. He loves that spot in front of the kitchen fire."

Georgina nodded and kissed Wiley's head before dipping a curtsy to the room's occupants and murmuring, "Good night."

Harrison snagged her into a hug. As Georgina had done with Wiley, Harrison pressed a kiss to the crown of her head. "Good night, Georgina."

"Good night, Harrison." Her high-pitched response assuaged his guilt only somewhat.

Mrs. March led the solemn procession out the door, Georgina trailing behind her governess with Mrs. Jones and a squirming Wiley taking up the rear. Silence pervaded the room upon their exit, the ticking of the mantel clock the only sound for one second, two seconds, three seconds.

"Well, shall we liven things up with a game?" Isabella asked.

Isabella's enthusiasm sounded somewhat forced, but he appreciated her efforts to lighten the mood.

She continued, "Have either of you ever played The Rhymes? I daresay with your fondness for poetry, Harrison, you will be a natural."

He plastered a smile on his face and took a seat in the chair opposite the settee and rubbed his palms together sportingly. "Let's see if Victoria can keep up, shall we?"

Victoria cast him a sincere smile in return. It held a glint of challenge, though. So, she must be as competitive as he was. The fervor of competition rose within him.

"The rules, lady and gentleman"—Isabella stood and paced the room, never one to sit still for long—"are as follows: you ask a question of a person in the room—I daresay it will still be fun even though we only have three in our party—and that person must then ask their question of another. But the caveat is, the first word of their question must rhyme with the last word in the question asked of them. Everyone understand?"

He and Victoria nodded, and Isabella continued, "I'll go first. And I'll start easy. Harrison, how are you *tonight*?"

"*Quite* all right."

"Ooh, a double rhyme. This will be fun, just as I thought." Isabella returned to the settee and sat, waving him on. "Now, your question."

"Victoria, how do you find New York, my future *wife*?"

She blushed at his endearment, as he'd hoped she would. But she answered after only a slight pause, not entirely thrown off guard. "*Rife* with amusements, I do say." Oh, how he loved her quick wit. "And you, poor Isabella, do you forgive the city for making you *ill*?"

"*Until* my dying day, dear." Isabella hooted at her cleverness before adding her question. And so the game continued around the room for quite some time, the questions becoming more cunning, the answers more absurd.

He tried to stump Victoria with a question about whether she was "ready to live in this *chaos*," only to have her quip back with "*Naos*, it is, actually." A consultation with the dictionary proved it was not only a word, but a fitting one since it meant *temple*.

After answering Victoria's question of her, Isabella asked him, "And Harrison, did you ever think you'd be *engaged*?" He didn't let on he'd asked himself the very same question this morning. Rather, he raised the stakes by voicing aloud the thoughts that'd been circling in his head of late.

"*Waged* against me, did you? Well, Victoria, what do you say to not only a husband, but a son or daughter with eyes of *blue*?" Victoria visibly startled, which was odd since he'd given her a rather easy word to rhyme with.

Granted, he was asking a rather personal question before another, a question which they hadn't quite broached together yet. But Isabella was more family than friend, and they were all of the age to know children typically followed marriage.

Victoria cast Isabella an agitated glance, and his stomach dropped to his toes. Something was terribly, horribly wrong.

Victoria didn't know what hurt worse—her heart splintering or that she'd be shattering Harrison's heart with the words she should have voiced sooner.

Isabella squeezed her hands and rose from the settee. "I'll just go check on Georgina," she said before exiting the room in a few quick steps.

Harrison crossed to the settee and took Isabella's place next to Victoria, his brow creased with worry.

Victoria couldn't meet his eyes any longer. Instead, she focused on her hands knotting themselves in her lap.

"Victoria. If I said something wrong, please forgive me. I must have gotten carried away with the game." He took one of her hands in his. "Will you tell me, darling?"

The endearment—the first time he'd said such a thing—only fractured her heart more. She swallowed, then spoke, her heart cracking along with her voice. "You—you want children?"

"Perhaps it was a funny way to say so, but yes, I suppose I do."

"But before. You'd said a few times that raising Georgina was—is—enough parenting for you." After what he'd just said, it was too much to expect this was still true, but she needed him to confirm his intent.

"It took me by surprise too." He exhaled a breath. "My mother always warned me it would, though. She was adamant that as soon as I found the woman I wanted to spend the rest of my life with, the desire for children would follow, and she was right once again."

Her eyes settled on her hand in his—the last time it'd ever be there. "I'm not that woman, Harrison."

"Yes, you are. I thought I'd made that clear earlier today, when I asked you to be my wife." He fingered the ring on her left hand as if to further drive his point home, his tone edging on jesting, attempting to lighten the mood.

Dizziness swept over her, and her stomach knotted. She undid her hand from his, rose from the settee, and crossed the room, trying to gain as much distance from him as possible. She couldn't be drawn back in. Not for her sake, but for his.

"But at that point, you didn't know—" Tears welled in her eyes, and her breath came in shallow gasps. "I—I can't have children, Harrison." Her great secret passed her lips on a whisper.

He rose from the settee and approached her. "Surely just

because you and your first husband weren't successful in—er —such things, doesn't mean we won't be." His voice was soothing and sure, and he brushed her shoulder, but she shrugged him off and retreated to the fireplace, the blood in her veins ice-cold despite its warmth.

"I *was* with child. Silas's child." She turned to face him now, the surprise evident on his face. Questions were forming there too, along with what looked like hurt, emotion he had every right to feel. She swiped a tear from her cheek. *It won't do to belabor the matter. Best to get it over and done with.*

"That night. When he—when he gave me these scars." She gestured to the left side of her face. "I lost—I lost the baby." The agony of that night, and every day thereafter that she'd had to live with what he'd done to her, finally spilled over. Between heaving sobs, she managed the rest of it. "The doctor. He saved me from bleeding to death that night, but only by taking from me the ability to ever mother a child."

Harrison stood stock-still, clearly shocked. And why shouldn't he be? She hadn't meant to harbor so great a secret. She had only assumed from his comments that it wouldn't prove to be pertinent. Oh, how wrong she'd been. "So, you see, Harrison," she said, her voice only wobbling a bit. "I cannot be the woman you marry and have children with."

With trembling hands, she removed the ring—his ring— and laid it on the marble-topped end table, its clink of metal against stone the only sound in the room. Then she swept past him and exited without a backward glance.

Twenty-Three

How could a woman—one who'd been staying in his house, no less—disappear without a trace? It had to be the thousandth time the thought had crossed Harrison's mind during the last eight torturous hours. He heaved himself into his leather desk chair, the worn cushion sighing almost as heavily as he did. He removed the ring from his trouser pocket and turned it about in his hands, replaying what had gone wrong.

Victoria had certainly surprised him with her admission in the drawing room. He understood why she hadn't told him sooner, but he was still upset. Over what Victoria had lost then, and over what could never be for her. Or for him. His anger at Silas rekindled stronger than ever.

Harrison should have gone to Victoria immediately, but he'd needed time to mull over what she'd said. And he hadn't expected her to flee. He had remained in the drawing room for an hour or so, his thoughts as erratic as they were weighty.

In the end, after reaching no answers, only more questions —mostly of himself—he'd knocked softly on her door. After no response the first time, he'd knocked again. And then again. After still more silence, he'd cracked the door open to find her valise absent and the room empty of all but her trunk.

With his gut and mind churning, he'd awakened Isabella and alerted Mrs. Jones, and the three had scoured the house to no avail. He'd managed to flag down a hack around midnight and directed it to the police station, but the officers there had been unconcerned with what they deemed as a "mere missing woman" when they had mobs of "rowdies" armed with concealed firearms and stilettos to deal with.

He'd returned to the house thoroughly irritated and despondent. After urging Isabella and Mrs. Jones to retire to bed, he'd sequestered himself in his office. Despite the overwhelming exhaustion weighing him down, sleep—or any sort of rest for that matter—had evaded him.

The stately grandfather clock in the corner chimed four times, marking the start of yet another hour of not knowing where Victoria was or whether she was safe.

He re-pocketed the ring, then rose, striding to the sideboard and stopping with his hand poised above the whiskey. No, a lapse in judgment would make him more like his father. He poured a glass of water instead, every swallow only reminding him more of Victoria and the water he'd brought her along their trip. He was living a nightmare, one he could never wake from.

"Wright men turn to whiskey over a woman." It was a voice he knew all too well, delivered with its usual air of unsympathetic authority. And it belonged to a most unwelcome interloper—his father.

"To what do I owe the pleasure of this visit, Richard?" Harrison made sure sarcasm dripped off his words as he returned to his desk chair.

"How many times have I told you to call me *Father*?"

Without an invitation from Harrison, Richard poured himself a generous glass of whiskey and sat in the chair opposite Harrison's desk.

Harrison clenched his jaw and tightened his grip on his glass of water. His father had a talent for reappearing at the most inopportune times, and this moment was no exception. "Ah yes, well, that is a title that must be earned."

If his barb had met its mark, it didn't show. Richard's face remained a mask of indifference as he slurped down a swallow of whiskey. "I heard you'd had a bit of trouble with a woman."

Thick with lack of sleep, Harrison's mind spun. Who'd tattled to his father?

"You're wondering how I knew, no? Don't think I don't have eyes on you at all times. Mrs. March has served me well," his father boasted.

Of course. His father had hired the dreadful woman in the early days after the accident. Harrison inwardly cursed himself for not dispensing with her sooner, but his father had stated in no uncertain terms that if Mrs. March went, then Georgina would be sent to a boarding school.

"I came to offer my advice," Richard said.

Harrison let out a derisive laugh. "Your history proves you the *least* capable person of rendering advice on matters of love."

"Love? Is that what you thought it was?" Richard laughed now, more of a scathing snort, really.

Harrison downed the rest of his water, determined not to be baited by his father. Silence was usually the best option when his sire was involved.

But Richard took the silence as acquiescence to continue. "I've told you before that where women are concerned, detached dalliances are favored. Prevents these sorts of ... messy complications of the heart, if you will."

Harrison ground his teeth and bit out, "What about Mother? And me, Alfred, and Georgina? Were we simply 'messy complications' of your heart?"

"Ah yes, you've always had a soft spot for your mother. And Alfred and Georgina." Richard finished off his whiskey and sat back in the chair, crossing his right ankle over his left knee and fingering the golden ring he habitually wore on his left middle finger. "I did my best to make you a man, but your mother's doting made you soft. Buck up—a plethora of other women are out there, ready. And willing. You have my looks. You could have your choice of any—nay, all—of them."

The man was truly irredeemable. "I only want her."

"An aging, scarred widow?"

Mrs. March had evidently been nothing but thorough in her report to his father.

"It must be impossible for you to comprehend faithfulness and devotion to a single woman, so I won't even attempt to explain it."

"So, what went wrong? Did she see you for who you truly are? A chip off the old block? If she insisted on having you all to herself, then it's a good thing you sent her—"

"Enough!" Harrison shot to his feet. "I won't have you disparage her good name in my presence."

Richard held up his hands in a show of mock capitulation. "Calm down, calm down. I see the male Wright temper is alive and well in you. You have every right to be upset. A nobody chit of a girl walking out on the likes of my son in that manner. Come, tell me why."

"She is unable to have children," he said, the truth slipping from his lips at barely above a whisper. He slouched in his chair again, defeated. Had he admitted the truth because it might hasten his father's departure? Or had it been the lack of sleep? Most likely a mix of both.

Richard's laugh held more mirth this time. "Ha. Well, then I see where she has merit. Fewer entanglements. But then why —oh, don't tell me, you want children now? I thought you were wiser than that." Cunning as he was, his father had puzzled it out himself.

Harrison propped his elbows on his desk and kneaded his forehead, cursing the head pain brewing. If only Victoria were here. She had successfully soothed his last one—right before he'd been breaths away from kissing her in Chicago. At the memory, his misery compounded. "Fathering children may have been your life's greatest disappointment, but it is a common desire among gentlemen my age, and younger, even."

Richard scoffed. "So, your mother has more of an influence on you, even beyond the grave, than your parent sitting right before you?"

Of course, Harrison's father would make the entire ordeal about himself. "Shouldn't I emulate the one most worthy of honor?"

"Now listen here," Richard flared. Harrison had finally bristled his father, but the victory was hollow. "You have not wanted for anything in your life. Daily you walk by those less fortunate than you. You're well educated, with an established career. *I* made sure of that."

"You're right," Harrison responded. Bewilderment crossed his father's face, and Harrison almost laughed. For once, his father spoke the truth, but not in the words his father likely expected. "There are others less fortunate than I, which is why I'm conceding my interest in the law firm." He hadn't entirely sorted that final bit out before now, but upon uttering the words, his heart confirmed it should be his path forward.

Richard sputtered. "Are the ramifications of that knock on the head in the carriage accident finally manifesting themselves? Certainly, there's no other reason for such daftness, especially from my son."

"I won't be practicing law anymore." Harrison's confidence in his decision only grew the more he repeated it.

"And pray, how will you maintain the lifestyle to which you've grown so accustomed without me? You need an ongoing income to do so." Richard gestured around the room, a knowing smirk on his lips.

"A fact of which I am well aware." Harrison's growing calm seemed to only fuel his father's fury. "I own this house and the country house outright. I bought them from you when you needed funds to bail yourself out of whatever drunken debt or dilemma you'd crawled into, remember?"

"But what will you do instead?" Trained lawyer that he was, Richard laid claim to the alternative argument. "Don't think for an instant any paternal affections on my part will save you from a traitor's fate. No law firm will touch you after I'm through." His golden eyes lit with barely contained ire as he spat out the words.

"Practicing law was always *your* dream for me." How freeing to finally voice these complaints he'd harbored for years. "I find philanthropic work will align quite nicely with my interests and passions, like Mother exemplified."

"Well, the law firm hasn't quite been prosperous enough to create that rise in station for you."

"Having been the one to keep the books recently, I'm well aware. You've made quite sure any excess was immediately squandered."

"But how will you earn money?" His father enunciated each word.

With his father, it'd always been about greed and gluttony, both in his professional and personal pursuits. What a sad existence. Thankfully, Harrison could escape a similar fate.

Instead of voicing his answer, Harrison rifled through the papers on his desk. He found the one he sought and slid it across to his father, playing his final card, one showing he had the upper hand. His father's face morphed into incomprehension, his mouth flapping open and shut, guppy-like. Was it wrong that Harrison somewhat enjoyed baiting his father in this manner? He almost felt bad for the old man. Almost.

Harrison registered the gleam developing in his father's eye. Perhaps he shouldn't have shown his father the exact payoff amount of his stock investment. But the action couldn't be undone.

From experience, it was better to keep the upper hand with his father. "I propose a deal," Harrison continued. "I will cut you a check right now for this amount"—he paused to write a number in the paper's margin and show it to his father—"if you agree to two things. First, you will willingly and expeditiously sign the papers allowing me to legally adopt Georgina. And second, you will leave and never show your face in my presence again."

Richard fingered his chin before taking up the pen, crossing out Harrison's number, and scrawling his own, significantly higher sum. Greed and gluttony indeed. But Harrison had anticipated his father's avarice and had made his initial offer for a lesser amount, so the increase, even substantial as it was, wasn't ruinous.

Harrison made a show of mulling over his father's quantity before giving a single nod of acceptance and reaching for his checkbook. Both father and son were silent as Harrison's pen scratched over the check, the entirety of their relationship amounting to only a few numbers on paper.

Silence pervaded the office as Harrison's pen moved from the checkbook to the notepaper. On a single signed page, he conveyed his interest in the law firm to his father. While the ink dried on that sheet, he rifled through his drawer until he found the documents he'd had waiting for a while now—the adoption paperwork for Georgina.

He summoned a sleepy-eyed Mrs. Jones. She had the discretion not to ask about the circumstances surrounding her early morning rousing and stood quietly while witnessing him and his father wordlessly sign the papers.

"That will be all, thank you, Mrs. Jones," he said when they were finished. She ducked her head in acknowledgment before whisking from the room.

"I believe this concludes any and all business we have together," Harrison said, rising and meeting his father's amber eyes. Still so like his, but no longer wielding power over him or his future.

His father stood. "If this all goes south, don't expect any assistance from me." The warning hung in the air as his father strode to the door. But Harrison didn't deign to answer. He'd claimed his future, and with such a right came the acceptance of any consequences—good or bad.

The door banged shut behind his father, for what would hopefully be the last time, and Harrison puffed out a relieved sigh. He'd gained far more than he'd paid out. Self-realization. Liberation. Closure. Peace of mind. Georgina.

But while he'd decided much about his future in the last hour, his already weary mind spun with too much discomfort and too little sleep to unravel what to do about a particular Englishwoman. She could grant one part of his heart's desire but couldn't fulfill another.

Whatever was he to do?

～

The sun crested the East River and the Brooklyn peninsula beyond, chasing the night's chill from Victoria's clothing and casting the New York City harbor in a somewhat-less-nefarious light.

Following her impulse to leave last night had been headlong. But once she'd returned to her room after the encounter with Harrison, she couldn't stay in his house a moment longer. Abandoning her trunk, she'd quickly packed her valise and tiptoed past the drawing room's closed door and out the home's back entrance.

Mercifully, she'd flagged down a hack a block from Harrison's brownstone, the driver appearing unconcerned about his coach's occupant and destination at that time of night.

The night had been harrowing, but necessary. She dug within her valise and retrieved her peppermint oil to help enliven her senses, at least enough to get aboard a steamer bound for England.

Harrison shouldn't consign himself to a life with her, one he'd certainly regret when she couldn't give him what he truly wanted. The impasse of their disparate realities was no way to start a marriage and would only breed future contempt. Harrison deserved better. And if the parade of elegant American ladies before her at the dock was any indication, he'd have an abundance of women from which to choose his future wife.

The pier's clientele had shifted with daybreak. Gone were the smudged, weary faces of the overnight dockworkers and disembarking emigrants, replaced by the whisk of imported Parisian silk on slight, youthful female frames. Balanced on the arms of equally impeccably dressed gentlemen, with shining hair and luxuriant complexions, the graceful creatures far outshone her.

In her black daydress, she'd never been shabbier, more unseen. But wasn't that what she wanted? Regardless, it was what she deserved.

She fingered her scars, the shrill blast of a steamship whistle interrupting her maudlin musings. Those waiting at the docks queued for boarding. Hefting her valise, Victoria rose from the bench that had been her makeshift abode for the night. At least she'd found a safe, tucked away corner of the Cunard port to attempt rest.

She deferred to her rightful position near the back of the crowd and clutched the ticket guaranteeing her a spot aboard the RMS *Asia*. It'd taken no small amount of persuading last night—not to mention an additional, yet not outrageously large fee—to convince the ticket clerk to exchange her ticket for later in the week to one departing the next morning.

The same ticket clerk periodically glanced her way throughout the night, eyeing her scars warily. Even now, his scrutinizing gaze bored into her turned back. Oh, if only she'd taken the time in her haste last night to retrieve her veil from her trunk.

But she had to look ahead now. To the life she had resigned herself to once before. She could do so—*would* do so—again. Pausing only momentarily at the gangplank's apex, she took a steeling breath before crossing over the threshold and onto the *Asia*'s deck, bidding *adieu* to dry land for at least another ten days.

Twenty-Four

"Harrison, come quick! It's Georgina!"

Harrison jumped awake at the panic in Isabella's voice. It took a few moments for the grogginess in his head to clear. Still seated at his desk, his mind quickly filled in the gaps. His father. The check. Victoria. He must have finally succumbed to sleep in the wee morning hours, but it'd been a very short one, for the hands on the grandfather clock were barely past eight o'clock.

Certain he must look frightful but not caring one whit, he stumbled to his feet and raced after Isabella to Georgina's room. Georgina lay in her bed, an unnaturally still speck almost entirely consumed by the frilled white folds of the bedsheets. He was at her side in an instant, gingerly taking one spindly arm, finding the weak pulse thrumming under her wrist, and heaving a relieved sigh.

Still, these episodes rendered Georgina's condition perilous, so he called over his shoulder to Mrs. Jones, who'd entered the room moments behind him and Isabella. "Send for Dr. Livingston at once, please."

Eyes wide, Mrs. Jones nodded and made a hasty exit.

To Isabella, he asked, "How long has she been like this?" His tone harsher than he intended, he added, "Thank you for calling me."

"About five minutes. As I've been told by Mrs. Jones, Georgina was playing with the kitten when he scampered into —into the other guest bedroom." Harrison didn't miss Isabella's careful rewording of Victoria's room. Isabella paced at the foot of Georgina's bed. "Georgina found him hiding under the armoire in the room." Isabella paused then, both in her walking and talking, and he steeled himself for impending bad news. "Georgina also found something else. A letter from Victoria."

He shot a glance at Isabella, but she'd ducked her head to avoid his eyes and resumed her pacing. "Georgina took the letter to Mrs. March."

He groaned aloud.

"Yes, I know," Isabella agreed. "Apparently Mrs. March was most unkind—and untruthful—in conveying the contents of the letter to Georgina. Mrs. March said Victoria left, which is true, as you know. But—Oh! This is really quite awful." Isabella stopped walking and met his eyes, dropping her voice to a whisper despite Georgina's continued unconsciousness. "Mrs. March said Georgina was the reason Victoria left."

Harrison hissed through his teeth while Isabella hurried on. "Georgina ran, crying, past my room. I tried to comfort her, but her emotions took over, and then, she fainted. I managed to get her settled in bed, but she hasn't come to."

Pure, unadulterated rage coursed through him. Mrs. March was just as heartless as his father. No wonder the two were in collusion. "Where is Mrs. March?" His voice had gone severe again. Isabella was only trying to help.

She crossed to him and laid a calming hand on his forearm.

"Mrs. March is gone. And I don't believe she'll be back. Mrs. Jones told me so just moments ago. She'd heard it straight from Mrs. March."

Harrison puffed out a breath. Well, at least the woman's departure had taken care of itself. Still, it would have been satisfying to tell her off like he had his father. Calmer now, he recalled one part of Isabella's words. A letter. From Victoria. "Where is the—"

But Dr. Livingston entered the room, cutting off the remainder of his question. Harrison begrudgingly gave up his post by Georgina's bedside to the doctor while he and Isabella both supplied the man with a summary of what had happened.

Harrison still hovered close by as Dr. Livingston silently examined Georgina. Why wasn't the man saying anything?

Dr. Livingston retrieved a vial from his bag and held it under Georgina's nose.

She stirred, then blinked her eyes open and then shut them again, a whimper escaping her lips.

"There now," Dr. Livingston said, giving the bedcovers a reassuring pat. "She should perk up in the next few minutes. I saw no issues from the examination. A rather lengthy episode, was it?"

Harrison nodded.

"Brought on by strong emotions again?"

Harrison nodded again. The doctor didn't even know the half of it.

"At least it'd been a while since she'd had one," Dr. Livingston said as he repacked his bag.

Harrison clenched his jaw. Dr. Livingston had been the family doctor for decades, but he could be annoyingly optimistic about Georgina's fainting spells.

The doctor snapped his case shut and shook Harrison's

hand. "Call again if she takes a turn." Dr. Livingston crossed the room, pausing at the doorway and calling over his shoulder. "Oh, and Harrison. More sleep." As he exited the room, he chuckled at a joke funny only to him.

Harrison clenched his fists and forced himself to take a deep breath. He was thoroughly wrung out, but none of it was Dr. Livingston's doing. Harrison shouldn't take his anger out on the aging fellow.

"Harrison?" Georgina's timid voice panged his heart.

He rushed to her side.

Isabella retrieved the cane-back chair from the corner and brought it to him.

He nodded his thanks as he sat. "How are you, sweetheart?"

"Dizzy."

"We'll have Mrs. Jones fix some food. Buttered bread?"

Georgina nodded, color flushing its way back into her cheeks. That was a good sign.

"It's so wonderful to see you refreshed, dear," Isabella said. She squeezed Georgina's hand and smiled. "Now, let me go see about that bread for you."

The door clicked shut behind Isabella, and Georgina blinked up at him with wide, innocent eyes. "I'm sad Mrs. Victoria left."

He gave Georgina's hand a squeeze. Hopefully, the action would stave off another swell of emotion—the usual culprit of Georgina's fainting spells.

"Yes, I am too," he replied. He wouldn't deny Georgina the truth, especially not when it had the power to heal. "But it had nothing to do with you. Mrs. March wasn't being truthful."

Georgina gasped, the shock of a young child learning for the first time—and the hard way—adults were flawed.

"Why *did* she leave?" Her brows furrowed.

"Well, sweetheart, I suppose it was because of me."

She scooted to a sitting position and assumed her hands-on-hips position of defiance. "Well, then say sorry so she will come back."

So much for the goal of keeping her calm. "It's more complicated than that."

Mrs. Jones bustled in then, tray in tow, providing a much-needed interruption to the weighty conversation between siblings. "Here we are. Bread fresh from the oven and a bit of melted chocolate drink too."

"Hooray!" Georgina clapped, and Mrs. Jones set the tray on the bed. Isabella came into the room a moment later, a black and white bundle in her arms.

"Wiley," Georgina cried around a mouthful of bread.

Isabella set the kitten on the bed, and he scampered about, delighting in the novelty of uncharted territory. He chased after Georgina's moving legs under the bedcovers and even licked at the butter on Georgina's bread.

"No, no, Wiley," she lovingly corrected him, distracting him with the ribbons on her nightgown.

"Thank you, Mrs. Jones, Isabella," Harrison said. He even nodded a silent thanks to the kitten for its unsurpassed powers of distraction. Unfazed by Harrison's hard-earned gratitude, the kitten gaped a huge yawn and curled beside Georgina, blinking its eyes closed. *Lucky thing, surrendering to sleep so easily.* But then again, why should he be jealous of a kitten? He really did need to follow Dr. Livingston's advice and sleep. But not when Victoria was still missing and Georgina's health hung in the balance.

Isabella finished a hushed exchange with Mrs. Jones, then motioned for him to follow her out the door. After he'd clicked the door shut behind them, Isabella pulled him into a hug and said, "Oh, Harrison. How unendurable the last few hours must have been for you."

He gave an acquiescing grunt over Isabella's head. His head spun, and his stomach roiled.

Isabella set him at arm's length and squeezed his hands. "Good news, though. We know where Victoria is. According to her letter, she's taken a Cunard back to England."

He turned, ready to bolt downstairs, out the door, and to the harbor as quickly as he could find a hired hack to take him there. But Isabella—with both speed and sobriety on her side—snagged his shirt sleeve. "The first Cunard ship departed forty-five minutes ago, Harrison."

"Please, Isabella," he croaked. "I need to at least try."

"Assuming she isn't somewhere on the Atlantic Ocean right now, what would you say to her if you found her?"

He opened his mouth, ready to reply, but no words came. He inwardly cursed Isabella's perceptiveness. *How does she always know my thoughts better than I?*

"I thought as much," Isabella said, her voice sure, but not unkind. "Take time to—to compose yourself, if you will. You have some weighty thinking ahead of you." Her voice choked with emotion. "I'm truly sorry, Harrison, if I—if I encouraged things between you two. I didn't know your feelings on children and I—"

"Shh. It's okay, Isabella." He swallowed around the lump forming in his throat. Lack of sleep was doing nothing to help his fortitude against tears. "I apparently didn't know either, until recently."

Isabella nodded and swiped at her eyes. "Do you want me to stay longer? I can telegraph my cousins and tell them either I'll no longer be able to make it up north to them or I'll be a week later—"

"No, no. There's no need to adjust your plans on my

account." He raked his hands through his hair and puffed out a sigh. "You're right, it's all on me to have a thorough talking-to with myself."

His quip garnered a small chuckle from Isabella. "Don't be too harsh on yourself, please."

"I'm feeling rather tyrannical at present, especially after my father's visit a few hours ago."

"He was here?" Isabella's expression turned gaping. Oh yes, she didn't know yet. The exchange with his father already seemed ages ago, rather than just a few hours. He quickly relayed all the details of Richard's unannounced arrival, with Isabella making appropriately timed noises of commiseration, both of anger at his father's audacity and of triumph at his liberation from his father's negative influence. "You've always been your own man but are even more so now," she said. "You are truly free of him, Harrison. Remember that."

He didn't miss Isabella's deeper meaning. She'd expressed these sentiments numerous times to him in the past, but they were ones he'd only recently come to believe as true. But that was the thing about life. One had to usually learn these sorts of things for oneself. "Thank you, Isabella. I will," he said with a nod.

She reached into her pocket and withdrew a folded paper, pressing it into his hand and closing his fingers around it. "Now, tempted as I am to tell you what you should do about a certain Englishwoman, that is also for you to search out in your heart." She laid one hand over her heart in demonstration. "But I will say this. Longfellow captures it most eloquently, so I will use his words, ones which you know too: *'Trust no Future, howe'er pleasant! ... Act,—act in the living Present! ... With a heart for any fate.'*" She gave his hands one final squeeze before relinquishing them—and Victoria's letter —to him.

He pocketed the paper in his trousers, fighting the emotion lumping in his throat again. If only Isabella—or someone, anyone—would tell him what to do. But he had to make the decision for himself, regardless of how muddled the ideas of love and happiness and sacrifice all seemed at the moment. He took a fortifying breath and tried for a smile, sure it came out more grimace than grin. "Does this mean I'm the hero Longfellow spoke of?"

Isabella arched one brow. "In strife, mind you."

"This has all felt rather strifeful, I'll give you that," he said, his tone a toying attempt at self-pity.

"And now you're making up words. Go on. Your first priorities are sustenance and sleep. Then, decide the entirety of your future."

"Sounds easy enough," he said dryly.

Isabella simply acted as though he hadn't spoken at all. True to form, she knew when he was being obtuse. "My train doesn't leave until six o'clock, if you have a *real* need of me between now and then. I'll also be back in a few weeks before my steamer to England."

They parted ways, Isabella ascending the stairs to her room and he turning toward his. As he walked down the hallway, he loosened his necktie and yanked the wrinkled piece of fabric from around his neck. It would likely be unsalvageable, but with it gone, he was already less stifled, less strangled by the task before him. He toed the door shut and dispensed with the rest of his crumpled formal wear in a discarded heap on the floor, not bothering to retrieve and fold them as he normally would. He did, however, retrieve Victoria's note from his trouser pocket.

A wooden rectangle perched on the foot of his bed caught his gaze—a food tray—and he paused in opening the letter. Bless Mrs. Jones and her foresightedness. He devoured the tray's contents in an impromptu picnic on the floor, right at the foot of his bed, then finally opened Victoria's parting words.

Between the explanation she was boarding a steamer back to England and her name, she'd only written: "You deserve your heart's desires, Harrison. I do not want you to live in regret." How disappointingly brief. It contained no insight into why she fled or how she felt.

He set the empty tray near the pile of cast-off clothing in the corner and crawled under the bedcovers, still clutching Victoria's letter. The letter had left him with more questions than answers, and his thoughts pulled him in all directions. To love and hopes and dreams and regret. But as fatigue followed the fullness in his belly, sleep pulled harder, luring him into a welcome, long-overdue oblivion.

Twenty-Five

Harrison sighed and set aside the papers before him, papers he hadn't absorbed a single word of despite looking at them for at least fifteen minutes. Isabella had popped by yesterday after two weeks in Canada to check in on her *lovelorn friend*. Since reading Victoria's letter, he'd composed one in response. Which was currently on a steamship with Isabella somewhere east of New York.

He was going mad not knowing in return Victoria's thoughts, her desires. His errant thoughts still drifted to her every few seconds, even though he'd had much in the intervening weeks to keep him distracted. He had filed the adoption paperwork with the court, finalizing Georgina's adoption, and with the profits from his stock investment, had begun investing in the philanthropic causes most dear to him, namely those involving orphaned or less affluent children.

Harrison was just returning to the philanthropy-related papers on his desk when the door creaked open, and two sets of amber eyes peered through the crack. "Come on in, Georgina."

She entered—Wiley clutched in one arm and the raggedy stuffed rabbit in the other—and padded over to his desk in her pink nightdress and matching satin slippers. "We've come to say good night."

He pushed his chair back and held out his arms to her. "Well, come on then."

Georgina set Wiley on the desk and clambered into Harrison's embrace. She smelled of sugar and youthful exuberance, with just a hint of something citrusy. Orange, perhaps? Mrs. Jones must have allowed Georgina to indulge in a scented soap powder at A. T. Stewarts during their earlier outing.

He was beyond indebted to the housekeeper. She'd endured not only his sulking but had undertaken most of Georgina's care these last few weeks as well. And neither Wright sibling had necessarily made it easy on her. They were both grieving Victoria's absence in their own ways. He, brooding and irritable, and Georgina, withdrawn and often near tears.

The kitten had been an additional balm to Georgina's soul, despite, or maybe because of, the kitten's mischievousness. Even now, the black and white feline was sending Harrison's desk contents into upheaval, scattering the papers and sending a pen off the desk's edge.

"Is Mrs. Victoria still gone?"

Though Georgina had asked the question every day since Victoria had left, his heart rent anew each time it passed her lips.

"Yes. Sorry, sweetheart."

Every other night, Georgina had ended their habitual dialogue here. However, tonight, over a big yawn, which had him stifling one himself, she said, "Tell her you want her to come back."

"I did," he said. "Aunt Isabella is taking a letter saying just that to England right now."

"But *you* should tell her. Not a silly letter."

He chuckled and tapped Georgina's nose gently with his forefinger. "Well, aren't you a wise one, my dear sister?"

Georgina nodded sagely in agreement, and he laughed at how his baby sister had suddenly transformed into the mature and insightful creature before him. "Come, let's get you off to bed and Wiley off my desk before he muddles my important business."

Georgina hopped down and scooped up Wiley, sending a few papers to the floor in the process. "For your fil-ant-ropey?"

And just like that, Georgina was back to a young girl again, trying her hardest to pronounce a rather intimidating word.

"Yes, my philanthropy."

"For kids who don't have mothers. Like me."

"Yes, dear. But you have me," he smiled over the pang in his heart at her astute observations. Georgina was so used to not seeing Richard—hopefully their father's permanent absence would be an easier adjustment than their mother's death had been.

"And Wiley."

Harrison scratched the kitten on the head. "Yes, and Wiley."

Georgina yawned again and made for the door. "And hopefully, Mrs. Victoria."

"We shall see, sweetheart." It was all he could say as she left the room.

When Georgina had gone, Harrison retrieved the papers from the floor and righted the remainder of his desk, intent on truly reading the documents this time.

Except he couldn't stop dwelling on what Georgina had said.

It was a wild thought, really. Not to mention one uttered rather offhandedly by a child who was often lost in her own imaginings. Even so, he couldn't dismiss it. *Silly letter.* What if his three-year-old sister had the right of it all along?

"Victoria, do pay attention when I'm speaking to you."

Victoria had quickly grown re-accustomed to her sister's piercing whine of a voice. And to her place as a mere hired hand among her family members. It'd been almost a month since she'd left America, but it might as well have been a lifetime. The days passed interminably slowly, and the nights even slower.

As if exasperated by Victoria's lack of a response, Arabella turned in her dressing room chair to face Victoria and snapped her fingers. "You're too often in your own head, sister. It's vexing." Arabella turned to face the mirror again and analyzed the scar-free features of her face. "Now, as I was saying, Percival and I shall be back by midnight. One o'clock in the morning at the latest. Benjamin and Daniel will need their supper. No dessert tonight, understand?"

Arabella chose a ruby pendant necklace from the lacquered wooden box on the dressing table and held it out to Victoria. Silently, Victoria crossed from the door and stood behind Arabella, working the necklace's clasp open to accept the tiny ring on the other end.

Arabella continued with her instructions, as if Victoria hadn't been serving as her nephews' unpaid governess for the past three weeks. "And bedtime is no later than eight o'clock please. Last time you kept little Daniel up until near ten o'clock, and he was a mess for nearly a week."

Arabella always exaggerated. Daniel *had* fallen asleep at

eight on the night Arabella was referencing. But he'd awoken to a large clap of thunder, and despite Victoria's attempts to comfort him, he had steadfastly remained awake until his parents had returned at ten. The boy certainly had his mother's obstinacy.

But Victoria held her tongue. She'd lived twenty-eight years as Arabella's younger sibling. Arguing with her was a fruitless endeavor. Arabella next proffered a brush, and Victoria pinned Arabella's onyx locks—the ever-present visual reminder they were related—into a coiffure.

A movement outside on the drive below snagged her attention, causing her hands to slip.

"Ouch! Watch the pins, Victoria," Arabella cried.

The brisk, determined gait of the petite frame making its way up the drive could only belong to one person. *Was that Isabella?* Victoria's heart soared, and she thrust the brush and pins at Arabella, taking off down the hallway and stairs at a near run.

"Where are you going?" Arabella protested from the upstairs bedroom. "Come back here, Victoria!"

Victoria ignored her and flung open the door to Isabella, who still held her hand aloft, ready to knock. Her features quickly changed from surprise to euphoria, and she enveloped Victoria in a hug.

"Oh, dear, it's so wonderful to see you again."

"You, too, Isabella," she said, giving her friend one final squeeze. "Come in, before November's chill gets into the house."

Isabella followed her, and Victoria shut the door on the stiff breeze trying to worm its way in.

"Isabella," Arabella said in a clipped tone from the stairs, dampening the happy reunion.

"Arabella." Isabella delivered her response just as crisply.

The two had never held each other in high regard. Perhaps Arabella's disdain was rooted in the fact that Isabella was more sister to Victoria than Arabella herself was. But that would mean Arabella cared about her feelings, something she had a hard time believing Arabella would deign to do.

"Thirty minutes, Arabella," Victoria said with as much authority as she could muster.

Arabella pursed her lips. Seconds passed. Would she deny the request altogether? Isabella, mercifully, remained silent. She, too, knew what worked—and didn't—when it came to Arabella.

Finally, Arabella spoke. "Twenty. Otherwise, Percy and I will be late." Arabella didn't wait for any further argument. She gathered the trailing hem of her gauzy white silk dressing gown and ascended the stairs again.

"She's still her usual pleasant self, I see," Isabella muttered.

Victoria stifled a laugh, which came out as a small snort. "Shh. She has excellent hearing."

"Most vermin do."

Victoria gave Isabella another half-hearted hush and whispered, "Come, we'll go to my bedroom where she's least likely to hear." She led Isabella to the back of the house, where she had taken residence in a small room once meant for hired kitchen staff.

Closing the door behind them, she tried not to squirm as Isabella's gaze swept over the hovel. Arabella had made it sound as though granting Victoria the room was an extreme favor, explaining Daniel needed his room—Victoria's former one—now that he was growing up. It was a demotion from the upstairs bedroom, but what other option did she have?

"How was the rest of your trip in Canada?" Victoria tried to keep her tone breezy as she cleared the corner chair of its flotsam so Isabella could sit.

But Isabella waved off her question and remained standing. "An entirely unimportant topic at this very moment. I need you to read this. Now." Isabella withdrew an envelope from her reticule and proffered it to her. "You may want to sit when you do so."

Victoria did as Isabella instructed. She took the envelope—on which her name was scrawled in a masculine hand—and backed into a seated position on the foot of her bed, trying to still her trembling hands.

She turned the envelope over, ready to glide her finger under the flap to ease it open. Only, the flap was already free. "The glue appears to have lost its grip."

"It's been on two continents and across an ocean, dear. This sort of thing shouldn't be unexpected. Now, just open it." Isabella took a seat in the chair, taking an inordinate interest in the floor below her feet.

Though Isabella had likely already peeked at the envelope's contents, Victoria lifted the flap and eased the missive out. Her impatient eyes skipped ahead to the letter's signature, its eight letters doing far more to her heart than they should be capable of.

Harrison's script, though neat, wound along the page in great loops. Deep furrows where his pen pressed especially hard to punctuate his meaning left an almost-braille like texture on the notepaper.

Isabella impatiently tapped her foot, but Victoria's heart pounded faster. Her eyes jumped back to the letter's top to read it in its intended order—from the beginning.

> *My darling Victoria,*
> *For one who is supposedly so good with words, both in my professional and personal pursuits, I find I am quite with*

nothing sufficient to convey my heart's contents. And its desires.

These weeks without you have been pure torture. I've regressed back to the sullen, miserable shell of a man I was when I met you. You should feel most sorry for Georgina and Mrs. Jones, though, who have borne the brunt of my heartbreak with commendable long-suffering.

I found myself often alone with my thoughts—for too much time, some might claim. Conflicting feelings and desires warred within me, all vying for the supreme position in my heart. But that spot had already been claimed. By you. You are my happiness. You are my joy. You are my future. If you will still have me, that is. I'm only sorry it took so long for me to sort it all out. (Isabella did forewarn you about me taxing your patience.)

I love you. And I promise to love you always, no matter what our future together holds. I fully accept our legacy will not follow the normal course of a married man and woman, but that doesn't mean it won't be as fulfilling, as joyous.

In my thoughts, I tried to separate sacrifice from joy and love and happiness, tried to tell myself the latter feelings couldn't exist with the surrender of something else good and desirable. I came to realize, though, that true happiness often comes through the very act of giving up something for someone you love. They are like grains of sand, impossible to separate out individually, needed by one another to bind together to support the weight of a life—two lives, I would argue.

There is some give, though. After all, the sand forms footprints when it bears weight. But, as we both know from Longfellow's wisdom, those footprints can bring hope to others who are also forlorn and lost in life's tumult. Our path, our life together—which won't be free of hardship yet will still be full of love—has the power to transcend our own two lives and inspire others.

Though she wouldn't be your own flesh and blood, Georgina would blossom under the maternal care of the most resilient, loving woman I know. And Wiley could use your patience and affection too. I'm afraid he'll turn rather scampish without you to keep him in line. It is I, though, who needs you most of all. Without you, there is nothing, I am nothing. Please, Victoria, say you'll accept me as your husband. Again. Forever, this time.

All my love, Harrison

Victoria didn't even try to stop the flowing tears. Unchecked, they ran in rivulets down each cheek and dripped onto the notepaper in big, fat, sodden circles.

"Good news, I take it?" Isabella asked, offering her a handkerchief.

Victoria swiped at her eyes and nose with the square piece of cloth, then met Isabella's all-too-innocent expression with a smile. "As if you don't already know."

Isabella dropped all pretense with a wave of her hand. "You know the limits of my patience, dear. Only so much entertainment can be had on a ten-day steamship journey." Isabella clapped her hands together. "Now, the real question is, what is your answer?"

Victoria balled the handkerchief in her hand and considered the letter in her lap again. "I—I don't know." She'd only come to know Harrison's true feelings mere moments ago. It was natural to need time to make sense of it all, wasn't it?

Isabella emitted a sigh and rose from her seat. She clasped her hands behind her back and paced the room's diminutive width. "Do you love him?"

"Yes—yes, of course I do."

"And his letter unequivocally states he loves you, no?"

"Yes, it does. However, I—" She swallowed around the thickness in her throat. "I—I can't give him what he wants."

"*Au contraire*, dear. His letter says he wants *you*, regardless of whether you can bear children of your own."

The tears broke free again, and, swiping them away, she shook her head. "No, Isabella. I can't let him decide now to deny himself something in the future—something he said he wanted."

"So, you think you know his mind better than he does?" Isabella was never one to mince words, but the question was one of concern, not rebuke.

"No, it's not that. I just—I'm afraid he will regret—will regret marrying me." She uttered the final words in a whisper, her emotions perching on a precarious brink again.

"I see, dear." Having stopped her pacing, Isabella pulled the chair closer to the bed and sat knee-to-knee with her. "Look at me, Victoria."

She did as Isabella bade, certain her eyes were swollen and red-rimmed by now.

Isabella placed a reassuring hand on her knee. "You, my dear, are worthy. Worthy of true happiness. And worthy of true love. Harrison's love."

Victoria opened her mouth, armed and ready with a myriad of reasons in contradiction of Isabella's statements, namely the physical marring of her body no one—especially Harrison—should want or desire.

"Please, dear, let me finish," Isabella cut in, fending off the interruption. "I don't know how else to say it, so I'll come right out with it. You have been sorely mistreated by others. I cannot expect to understand the impact that has had on you, but those who did so—and are still doing so"—Isabella cast a pointed eyebrow to the ceiling above—"are entirely unworthy of you. They see only skin-deep, at most, and seek to elevate themselves by using you as a footstool. You, who are the most kind, gracious, patient, selfless person I know. I see that. Harrison sees that. And even a somewhat devious, three-going-on-four-year-old girl sees that. Please see yourself as we see you. Please allow us to love you like you so deserve."

Victoria's head swam and chest constricted. Isabella had pierced straight to her core, skillfully bypassing the bulwarks she had carefully erected over the last few years. Bulwarks she thought protected her heart, when in fact, the opposite might have been true all along.

"I know I've given you a lot to sort through, dear," Isabella said. "So, I'll take my leave. Especially since Arabella will pound on your door here shortly. But please take what I said to heart. I promise not to rush you. I've had practice with this sort of thing, having waited out Harrison's introspections for a few weeks. Then again, I was in Canada for most of the time, but that's neither here nor there."

Victoria's mind snagged on one particular part of Isabella's soliloquy. "He's—he's thought it all through then? All the ramifications?"

"Quite. And you have his words," Isabella gestured to the letter in Victoria's lap, "as further confirmation. And you would've had them much sooner if that transatlantic telegraph was finished. But then again, I doubt he would've trusted such sentiments of the heart to an undersea line of wire. Better such declarations of the heart be delivered in person, no?"

Isabella squeezed Victoria's knee once more before rising. She reached the door only to turn around again, throwing her arms up in the air. "Silly me. I almost forgot." She rooted around in her reticule and withdrew a small, round object. "Harrison insisted you have this, regardless of your decision."

Victoria stretched her hand out and accepted the glinting

blue and gold ring from Isabella. The ring's weight in her palm was steadfast and sure. *Just like the promises spoken by the one who gave it to me?*

A knock sounded on the door. "We're almost through, Arabella," Isabella huffed.

"Victoria?" But it wasn't Arabella's voice that answered. It was a decidedly male voice, and one Victoria knew all too well.

B efore Victoria could respond, her bedroom door flew open, and the amber eyes, slightly crooked nose, and angular jaw she'd just been thinking of appeared in the flesh at her doorway. Her heart soared. Slightly disheveled but still devilishly handsome, Harrison entered the already too-crowded room, catching, and holding, her gaze.

"You're here," she whispered.

Without breaking eye contact, he handed Isabella a bundle of what appeared to be coats. It squirmed, emitting a squeal of protest, and from the depths of its fabric emerged a bleary-eyed Georgina, clutching Cat the rabbit.

The occupants of Victoria's room had doubled in so short a time, and with those she loved most. Was she imagining things? She couldn't speak, afraid that if she did so they would disappear and she'd be all alone once again.

"I couldn't leave Georgina behind." Harrison closed the distance between them in one large stride. His hand cupped Victoria's left cheek—the physical touch confirming this wasn't her imagination—and his thumb lightly skimmed over her scars, wiping away a tear she hadn't even known had fallen.

He darted his gaze to the piece of paper still clutched in her hands, then back to her.

"You read my letter?"

She could only nod as more traitorous tears stole down her cheeks.

"Every word is true." He thumbed the moisture away. "You must believe me."

Another nod, as if she were a puppet on strings, only capable of that one movement.

Something akin to regret crossed his features. "It was foolish of me to have conveyed my sentiments in a letter, rather than telling you in person."

This time, she shook her head. "You're here now," she managed.

"That I am." Harrison smiled briefly before his face grew serious once more. "I won't impose a time frame on a response. I simply needed to correct my blunder in that letter."

"Silly letter," Georgina piped up from Isabella's arms. Laughter rippled through the room's occupants.

Victoria rose to Harrison's defense. "I quite like the letter."

"Any part in particular?" He flashed a devastatingly handsome grin.

Mercy, how had he grown even more striking since she'd last seen him?

"The part about Wiley needing me was especially nice," she said, her impish side taking over.

Harrison flung his head back and laughed a full, unrestrained laugh. "Oh, how I love you, darling."

Victoria licked her suddenly dry lips. "I—I love you, too, Harrison."

He took her hands in his, and she relished the peace and

warmth of his touch. His fingers closed around the ring—his ring—still in her palm, and his eyes rose to hers, an unspoken question lurking there.

She swallowed another wave of rising tears and nodded, whispering, "If you'll still have me." Could he even hear her over the erratic thumping of her heart?

He slid the ring on her fourth finger then claimed her lips, erasing all her fears in an all-consuming declaration of enduring love. She would never tire of drawing strength from his wellspring of steadfastness.

She encircled her arms around his neck in her answering commitment to him. Nevertheless, she broke the kiss a few moments later for the benefit of their surely scandalized audience.

Isabella and Georgina cheered, and Victoria ducked her head into Harrison's chest in embarrassment. Her small frame tucked perfectly within his larger, stronger one, and with one small inhale of his familiar, intoxicating scent, her insides tangled. Would he always have this effect on her? She couldn't imagine ever growing tired of him.

"Well done, you two," Isabella said. Her piercing gaze lifted to Harrison's. "But how did you get here so soon? You couldn't have left long after I did to have arrived by now."

"The very next morning," he confirmed, gliding his thumb across the ring on Victoria's finger. "I couldn't wait another moment to fetch my betrothed from England."

"What is going on in here?"

Everyone turned toward the room's latest interloper. Fully bedecked and bejeweled now, with her chin raised, Arabella surveyed the room down her nose. "Victoria, who is this man?"

"You must be Arabella." He turned a knowing look on Victoria, likely recalling all she'd told him of her older sister.

But ever the gentleman, he sketched a small bow to her. "I'm Victoria's future husband, Harrison Wright."

"Preposterous." Arabella eyed Harrison up and down, appreciation gleaming in her eyes. "Someone like *you* couldn't possibly want *her*."

Arabella's words struck Victoria's newfound confidence, giving credence to the contrary thoughts—the ones that said she wasn't good enough or beautiful enough—that she'd worked so hard and for so long to drown out.

Harrison squeezed her hand in reassurance. "I stand before you in direct contradiction to that statement."

Arabella sputtered. "Well, you can't just barge into other people's houses uninvited. It's highly irregular."

"I believe it was the man of the house himself who approved my entrance. A Percival?"

Arabella drew in a sharp gasp, pursed her lips, then spun on her heel and stalked from the room. Her increasingly loud cries of "Percy" echoed through the house.

Victoria thanked Harrison for his defense of her with a return squeeze of his hand. She couldn't remain here for a moment longer. "Isabella, might I stay with you? At least until the wedding?"

Detecting the direction of her thoughts, Isabella smiled, nodded, and released Georgina to the ground. "A wedding!"

"And would your father perform the ceremony?"

"Yes, yes, no trouble on that score, dear." With a flourish of movements, Isabella sprang into action, packing what remained in the tiny room of Victoria's meager possessions.

Georgina crossed to Victoria, and taking the little girl into her arms, Victoria turned to Harrison and said, "Contingent on this arrangement being acceptable to you, of course."

He beamed and stepped closer, pressing a lingering kiss to her cheek. "It can't come soon enough. My carriage awaits just outside. Mrs. Jones is inside and will be overjoyed at this turn of events."

"And Wiley," Georgina interjected from Victoria's right.

"Yes, and the kitten. The carriage is growing quite full," Harrison said wryly.

"Room enough for me still?" she asked.

"Always." He smiled.

Laughing, she lifted to her tiptoes and stole a quick peck from his grinning lips.

His amber eyes bore deep into hers. "And then after the wedding, can I take you home?"

Victoria nodded.

Home.

Four letters had never sounded so wonderful.

So right.

Epilogue

19 years later—January 1873

Harrison beheld the expectant expression on Georgina's all-too-eager face, and everything within him warned that this would be a bad idea.

"Please, Harrison. Aunt Isabella's letter assures I will be completely safe the entire time."

Georgina proffered the missive, and as he read the contents, his doubts only gained strength. Of course, Isabella's eternal optimism would overlook the myriad of disasters a journey of nearly five thousand miles one-way could encounter. Georgina had only left New York City once in her twenty-two years of existence, and that had been the trans-Atlantic voyage to Victoria with him nineteen years ago. But a distance nearly twice as far? And without him or Victoria to accompany her? It was ludicrous.

From her position next to him on the settee, Victoria touched his forearm. From all their years of marriage, he intuited the meaning of her silent communication and surrendered the letter to her.

Georgina resumed her petition from her standing position before them. "The Hawaiian Islands, Harrison. Can you imagine? The eternal summer weather, the exotic plants, and new and unusual animals. It's Earth's veritable Garden of Eden."

Her carefully chosen words and accentuating gestures combined to form an admittedly persuasive campaign. She'd make a good lawyer, a profession that had finally opened up —albeit rather belatedly—to women within the past few years. But a profession he'd thankfully left behind, nonetheless.

"Understand our concerns, Georgina."

"You remarked just last week I should expand my horizons."

She'd caught him there.

He'd intended to encourage her to join him and Victoria on a train ride departing from the newly opened Grand Central Depot, not an almost solo trip across the entire continent and half of the Pacific Ocean.

Harrison raked his hands through his hair and sighed. He looked to Victoria, to her enduring strength he'd had to rely upon countless times during the last nineteen years. She was still breathtakingly beautiful. The laugh lines creasing the corners of her eyes and the gray streaking her hair were testaments that their love was withstanding the test of time.

As expected, no biological children had come of their union. But Victoria had been a devoted mother to Georgina, not to mention the countless orphans their philanthropic work assisted within the city.

How had providence—and some shameless scheming from Isabella—managed to bring her into his life all those years ago? Surely Isabella wasn't matchmaking Georgina with this trip?

Georgina had blossomed into a beautiful young woman, with a deceptively innocent face framed by a chestnut cascade of soft curls. Her wide, amber eyes above an all-too-often pout of rosebud lips had attracted the attention of a host of young men within the last few years. But Georgina's determination and will—the qualities she was now exhibiting with such conviction—had eventually frightened them all away. A rather serendipitous outcome for him.

Not that he didn't want Georgina to have the type of love he had with Victoria. Quite the opposite, in fact. But Georgina was still so young at only twenty-two, and, if he were being honest with himself, had quite a bit more maturing to do before matrimony could even be considered. And Georgina's actions testified to that fact. She'd always been more consumed with her menagerie of animals than any potential suitors of late.

Having addressed one doubt in his mind, he voiced another aloud. "Your health also plays a constraint, Georgina."

A scowl crossed her face before she schooled it into composure again. She never enjoyed speaking about the physical limitations her fainting spells imposed. But with such a taxing trek proposed, he had to address the issue.

"It's been months since I've had an episode," she petitioned. "I've all but outgrown them. I'll take the salts and oils. And I've learned much from shadowing Victoria during her ministrations with the orphans."

While the latter statements were true, the former weren't entirely accurate. The fainting spells still occurred, and it was their irregularity that worried Harrison the most.

Victoria's hand touched his forearm again, and he happily relinquished the conversation to her. "What if ..." she began, the calm cadence and tone of her voice soothing his frayed nerves. Hopefully, it was having an equal effect on Georgina's fervor. "A doctor accompanies Georgina? Dr. Livingston is well versed in Georgina's condition, and we'd pay for all the expenses of his passage."

Victoria's idea had merit. But could Dr. Livingston endure a ten-thousand-mile round-trip journey at his age? The old chap was getting on in age and had been preparing his son to take over the practice soon. Still, if Harrison had learned anything from the last twenty-two years of serving as Georgina's brother and caregiver, she would find a way to achieve her objective regardless of his decision. It was far better for him to dictate and orchestrate things than for Georgina to strategize with his back turned.

He met Georgina's unrelenting gaze. Her features twitched with barely contained anticipation at his response. He heaved a sigh, the last vestiges of his resolve crumbling. "I suppose I can inquire of him."

Georgina squealed and pulled him and Victoria into a hug. "Thank you, thank you, thank you! You will not regret this. I promise."

Somehow, he already had, but he couldn't very well retract his acquiescence now.

As if sensing his inner turmoil, Victoria gave his hand a reassuring squeeze.

Georgina made for the door, her petite form a bustle of retreating pink silk. "I'm off to pack. There is much to do. Isabella's letter says that since she's coming from Australia, she'll meet me in the Hawaiian Islands at the end of the month."

Harrison's heart heaved. Georgina would be so far away and for so long. "One more thing." His voice halted her in the doorway. "Under no circumstances are you to fall in love with a man on this journey. Agreed?"

She waved him off, the ruffles of her skirt flouncing with the movement. "That, my dear brother, is something I can most assuredly promise you."

And then she was gone.

He sighed. "She will be all right, won't she?" He was already unable to fathom the house without Georgina in it, and she was only just down the hall now. Imagine how it'd be when she was across the world.

Victoria leaned into his shoulder, right where she fit best. "Yes, she will most definitely be fine. As will we in her absence."

Though he had his doubts, as usual, he'd try his very best to follow his wife's counsel. It had yet to steer him wrong. "At least I still have you." He pressed a kiss to the crown of her head.

She snuggled in closer to him. "And I you."

The End.

Author's Note

When I first heard about Isabella Bird more than a decade ago, I knew I wanted to bring to light what this fascinating woman did and saw in a time when it wasn't common for a woman, and an unmarried one at that, to gallivant around the world by herself. It's an intimidating prospect to bring a real person from history into a fictional novel, and I wanted to ensure I did justice to her character while at the same time creating a compelling love story in a cast of characters that were my own creation.

In *The Wayfaring Widow*, I have tried to remain as true to Isabella Bird's actual travels in America in 1854 as possible. Isabella's first-hand account in *The Englishwoman in America* served as the basis for most of what you see within these pages. While some of the side characters are based on actual people Isabella interacted with on her journey, Victoria, Harrison, and Georgina are fictitious, though they feel very real in my mind.

Isabella really did dine at Longfellow's house in Boston, visit P. T. Barnum's tent at the Michigan State Fair, descend the

Biddle Staircase and reach Termination Rock at Niagara Falls, and visit the palatial Stewart's Dry Goods Store in New York City. The dueler dined at her table in Chicago, her train plunged through a prairie fire, and the Lake Erie crossing aboard the *Mayflower* was as treacherous as depicted here. Oh, and she really brought a walking stick back for a friend in England.

I took a few creative liberties, but only those that I believe enhanced the story. While Isabella visited several other cities and even Canada on her 1854 journey, I handpicked the cities that had the most draw and created the most convenient travel schedule for the characters in *The Wayfaring Widow* to visit.

I also could not confirm that the *Maid of the Mist* traveled between Biddle Staircase and Top of the Rock in 1854, so that exact route was my own invention, but one that I think was more exciting for you to read versus following Isabella's actual logistics of going all the way back over the suspension bridge in a carriage to Table Rock House.

Turtle Bay did exist in New York in 1854, though to my knowledge, Isabella did not personally visit it. It was the one bit of sand I could find in New York City at that time for Victoria and Harrison to make footprints in. Sadly, Turtle Bay, as well as a host of other New York City rivers and waterways, no longer exist, forever buried beneath the city's buildings and roads.

I encourage you to learn more about Isabella Bird, especially by reading her own travel accounts. I have only grazed the surface of her experiences in my novels. After all, as Isabella has said herself in *A Lady's Life in the Rocky Mountains*, "Everything suggests a beyond."

Discussion Questions

1. Had you heard about Isabella Bird before reading *The Wayfaring Widow*? What was the most surprising detail you learned about Isabella in the novel?

2. What historical places, events, or cultural details in the book stood out to you the most? What place in the book would you most like to have visited with Isabella in 1854?

3. Though women in the 19th century experienced greater freedoms than their predecessors, they were still subject to societal strictures and norms. How did these limitations impact Victoria and Harrison's romance?

4. What are your thoughts about Victoria and Harrison's first meeting and how it set the stage for their "enemies-to-lovers" romance?

5. How has Victoria's past impacted how she feels about herself and what she deserves in life? How does this trip help her discover her true worth?

6. How did Harrison overcome his own internal battles so he could pursue what he really wanted in his life?

7. How did Isabella help encourage Victoria and Harrison along the journey?

8. How did Henry Wadsworth Longfellow's "A Psalm of Life" poem deepen the romance between Harrison and Victoria?

9. Who would you cast in a movie to play Victoria, Harrison, and Isabella?

10. What do you predict will happen with Georgina on her 1873 journey to the Hawaiian Islands with Isabella?

Acknowledgments

The most important thing I've learned these last few years as a fledgling author is that publishing a book most assuredly is not a solitary effort. This book wouldn't be in your hands right now without the support and dedication of a host of others.

First, my family. Vince, you've always supported my "I have an idea" moments, and embracing my idea to pursue my decade-long dream of becoming a published author was no different. I'm so glad you are the one I get to share life's adventures and make "footprints on the sand" with. Leena and Cora, I see the same drive to create in you, and I hope you will relentlessly pursue your life's dreams and desires.

Mom and Dad, you've instilled in me the values of hard work, dedication, and never giving up—traits which have been absolutely crucial in this writing journey. Mom, thank you too for your countless hours reviewing this manuscript and providing your thoughts and impressions. Steph and Alex and all the rest of my family and friends, thank you for always being willing to shore me up in the difficult times and rejoice with me during the celebratory times.

Thank you to Linda Fulkerson, Jennifer Burrows, and all the other staff at Scrivenings Press for seeing the potential in me and my stories. The innumerable hours you've spent in bringing this book to fruition, from the editing to the cover design to the marketing promotions, haven't gone unnoticed or unappreciated. It's been eye-opening to experience what all goes into creating a book, and I'm so grateful to have the chance to partner with you on this.

Mimi Matthews and Heather B. Moore—thank you for taking the time out of your own busy author schedules to read and endorse my little book. I can never repay such kindness. You've been an inspiration to this author and I'm sure countless others as well.

Naturally, a book wouldn't be a book without readers to read it, so thank you to all of you for joining me on this journey. With the wealth of available tomes out there, thank you for choosing mine.

Finally, thank you to a gracious Heavenly Father, who has planted within me the ability to be a creator as He is. Though the work may be mine, the glory is all His.

About the Author

Casey Cline is a life-long bibliophile and lover of learning. Whether it's through formal learning, as with earning her degrees and licenses in business, law, and real estate, or through learning via other means, such as learning to quilt via YouTube video tutorials or schooling her awkward limbs in martial arts classes, she's tried to embrace a growth mindset, reminding herself that struggle and setbacks are part of the process.

Outside of work and time with family, she reads (historical romance is, no surprise, her favorite genre), quilts (while listening to audiobooks), bakes (especially pies with the crust from scratch), does jiu-jitsu (it's quite the adrenaline rush), shoots guns (her gun's name is Constance), and rides horses (her fourth-grade obsession is still going strong). Sometimes, she even does the last two at the same time in a sport called mounted shooting.

For more than a decade, she's wanted to be a published author. She's even had the idea for her book series for that long too, and is excited for this dream to become a reality. Casey lives in Nebraska with her husband, two daughters, and three cats.

You can connect with Casey at www.caseycline.com, www.facebook.com/authorcaseycline, and

www.instagram.com/authorcaseycline

A Troubling Suggestion

by Betty Woods

Clarisse Matthews still grieves the tragic loss of her fiancé and doubts she'll ever love anyone again. Particularly if she has to divulge the secret abolitionist ideas she keeps hidden deep inside that only her beloved knew.

After the lady Luke Williams loved spurned him and married another man, he will never risk giving his heart to another woman. Especially not to Clarisse who had to have known about her best friend's ruse and helped the woman to conceal it from Luke. He doesn't need a lady by his side to manage his family's plantation or forge a path to become an attorney.

But when Luke's cousin is deceived by a rogue, who only Luke and Clarisse know the whole truth about, they form a reluctant alliance to protect his cousin. Their feigned attraction grows into genuine love.

But will the differences between them become a wall too tall to climb or can they find a way to go around?

Get your copy here:

https://scrivenings.link/atroublingsuggestion

~

No Leaves in Autumn

by Terri Wangard

Marie Foubert grew up in an orphanage and struggles with feelings of rejection. As a Red Cross recreation worker, she interacts with the American men based in Iceland during World War II. Her growing attraction to seaplane pilot Stefan Dabrowski excites and concerns her. Won't he disappear from her life like everyone else?

Stefan hears his commanding officer describe him as exciting as last night's bathwater. One of his colleagues constantly berates him because of his Polish heritage and his superior flying skill. Despite being the squadron's most productive pilot, he is threatened with court martial. A showdown approaches to prove who's the better pilot and the better man.

Marie's cousin, passing through Iceland, tries to see her after spotting her photo in *Life* magazine. She declines to meet him, but Stefan encourages her to do so and learn why no one wanted her. She may gain a family after all.

Get your copy here:

https://scrivenings.link/noleavesinautumn

What Brings Us Joy

by Teresa Wells

1895: After losing their Georgia home, eighteen-year-old Delia Truitt and her family move to Blooming Grove, Texas, to work for a relative on a ramshackle farm. Set on helping her family dig out of their impoverished circumstances, she plans to open a dressmaker's shop, combining her sewing skills and her keen fashion sense. But owning a business takes money she doesn't have.

Unless she can finish her quilt in time to enter the county fair. The prize money would be just enough to open her shop. Determined and resourceful, Delia sets her sights on success—until her heart takes an unexpected detour when she meets handsome Clarence Parker.

Bent on respectability, Clarence refuses to let his past get in the way of his future happiness, especially after falling for spirited Delia Truitt. But his hopes shatter when headlines declare members of his former gang have broken out of jail and are heading his way, set on revenge. Though Clarence doesn't regret testifying against the outlaws, he fears his future with Delia is in jeopardy. Clarence will protect her from the killers, even if it means risking their future together.

Can Clarence keep her safe? And will Delia love him after she finds out about his past?

Get your copy here:

https://scrivenings.link/whatbringsusjoy

Stay up-to-date on your favorite books and authors with our free e-newsletters.

ScriveningsPress.com

www.ingramcontent.com/pod-product-compliance
Lightning Source LLC
Chambersburg PA
CBHW071553110726
47908CB00007B/2089